COOLER
THAN
BLOOD

Also by Robert Lane

The Second Letter

COOLER
THAN
BLOOD

ROBERT LANE

ISBN: 0692223932
ISBN 13: 9780692223932
Library of Congress Control Number: 2014909532
Mason Alley Publishing, St. Pete Beach, Fl

This is a work of fiction. Names, characters, places, and incidents either are the product of the author's imagination or used fictitiously. Any resemblance to actual persons, living or dead, localities, businesses, companies, organizations and events is entirely coincidental.

For my parents.

No two finer people ever walked together.

"The main trouble with being an honest man was that it lost you all your illusions."

—James Jones, *From Here to Eternity*

COOLER
THAN
BLOOD

CHAPTER 1

B illy Ray Coleman had never fucked a girl in Florida, and that was going to end tonight.

In Kentucky, he had lured one behind a Stuckey's, and things had gotten a little dicey, the little Asian bitch clawing like a feral cat until he finally shut her down. In Tennessee, he pulled off at Jellico just over the state line and befriended the redhead at the Arby's not more than a few blocks from the interstate. It was okay, but it wasn't the rush he'd gotten from his final act on Sally Wong, as he affectionately called the Stuckey's girl.

In Georgia, he started to panic when he was running out of boiled peanut signs without having met his objective. *What a long-ass state*, he thought. *Didn't some bumfuck burn it during that war? What was his name? Whatever. Didn't do a very good job, did he?* He pulled his 2000 two-door Honda Accord with $284,000 stuffed in the trunk off at the West Hill Avenue exit in Valdosta. He knew that if he went any farther, he'd have to do a U-turn and suffer the whole damn state again. He sure as hell wasn't going to do that. He found her at a fast-food joint less than a mile from the interchange. She said no. He dragged her behind some self-storage units, although he had to work hard to find an area that wasn't covered by security lights. When he pulled out, a pothole the size of a West Virginia strip mine nearly claimed the front end of the Honda.

Billy Ray figured that his brothers, once they saw that Junior and the cash were gone, would hightail it after him. He also knew he'd head for Fort Myers Beach, same haunt they'd always gone to. No big deal. By the time they arrived, his grand slam would be over, and he planned to floor it out of the state. Might even take a Florida girl with him. *There's a thought. I'll get me a Florida girl. Like you see in those magazines.* Billy Ray was torqued. *Nail me a magazine girl.*

His right hand came up and rubbed his temple, and he shook his head as if he were trying to get water out of his ears. Billy Ray's head was like a radio station in which the DJ had taken a long piss break, and two car ads were running over a song.

Just north of Sarasota, he pulled in for gas. He spotted a blonde with wide white sunglasses. Her breasts, like horizontal tent poles, pushed her thin tank top out so far that the bottom of it hung around her waist without touching her stomach. Billy Ray swore he saw the fabric move in the breeze that lifted off the hot blacktop, as if a stovetop burner had been left on. He hesitated. He rubbed his head. His hand came away covered with sweat. *No way, José. I'm hittin' the beach. Get a plan— work the plan. Yes, sirree. Pity. Sunglasses will never know what she missed—a real national tragedy.*

Ninety minutes later, he crested the Matanzas Bridge to Fort Myers Beach and took a hard right. Billy Ray checked into the same motel he and his brothers had always used, but he didn't go to his room. He tossed his shirt into the Honda and set out to hike the seven-mile beach. The sun fried his Irish-white skin as if he were a solitary egg in a black iron skillet suspended over a bonfire.

He spotted the girl from a good hundred feet away. She had straight brown hair and a brilliant blue bathing suit with sparkles. She looked better with every step. The woman by her side, in a white two-piece, was up for consideration as well but was probably knocking on forty. Billy Ray stopped and chatted with them. Introduced himself—super proud about that. It wasn't easy with Tom Petty beating the living shit out of his head. "Jenny Spencer," Sparkles replied. The older one didn't give her name, just gave him that look he was accustomed to receiving. Screw that. He moved on.

Jenny Spencer, Billy Ray thought. *Now there's a fine name for my first Florida fling. And that smile. That's magazine material. Oh, my head. My goddamned screaming head.* He slapped his head. He downed a couple of beers at a beach bar, where the bartender gave him some lotion and advised him to stay clear of the sun. He emptied the remains of the bottle into both hands and slopped it over his body. He kept his eyes on the girls on the beach. When they got up to leave, he stayed well behind.

They walked a few blocks, and Billy Ray noted the house they entered. He knew he had a few hours until dark, so he trudged back up the beach. At sunset, he drove his Honda down Estero Boulevard and parked in a public lot large enough to accommodate only a few cars. He watched the house. Billy Ray planned to wait until total darkness to yank magazine girl out. He wasn't sure what his plans were for the older girl, nor did it matter, for Jenny emerged on her own. She headed toward the beach. Billy Ray followed.

They met at an edge of mangroves just beyond where an inlet forced walkers to forgo the coastline and track on higher land. She wasn't difficult to follow, as she carried a small flashlight.

Jenny stepped hesitantly onto the sand. She picked her way through the mangrove roots that poked through the mashed-potato surface and threatened to impale her feet. Stray sticks

3

littered the ground. She came upon a deserted orange towel and figured someone had either forgotten it or had discarded it for a nighttime stroll. She reached a clearing and spotted Billy Ray as he waded out of a tidal puddle.

"Hey, there. Remember me?" he said.

"No, I'm new...Oh, yeah, sure, from this afternoon. Billy... Billy..."

"Ray."

"That's right."

"Nice out here at night, isn't it, Jenny?" They stood within four feet of each other.

"Can you believe how warm it still is? Is it like this in Georgia?" She felt an odd twinge, like low volts going through her, over his casual mention of her name.

"Georgia?"

"Isn't that where you said you were from?"

"Oh, yeah. It can be hot up there. Sherman! Yeah, that's his name."

"Who?"

"Nothin'. What are you doing?"

"Looking for turtles. My aunt says they come up this far." Jenny shone the light around the sand.

"That was your aunt? Whoa, she's hot too." Billy Ray slapped his head.

She's hot too? Jenny thought. *Did he just slap his head?* Her body stiffened. She flashed her light into his face and took a step back. His red hair was dull compared to his blazed skin. Lotion smeared his face. And his eyes—they looked like he had no idea where he was.

"Ooooh, girl. Get that light out of my eyes."

"My aunt's a little behind me," Jenny said, but it came out in a different voice.

"No, she ain't, magazine girl. I saw her drive away earlier."

Jenny hesitated. *He watched us? Should I run?* But what she would have eventually decided to do was of no consequence, as he was upon her and tugging at her cheer shirt.

Jenny screamed. Billy Ray threw a roundhouse that deadened her. He stripped off his shirt and shorts and shredded her shorts and panties. His hands groped her left breast, and his mouth found her right breast. He bit hard. She shrieked.

"Don't make a ruckus, or I'll do it again. You understand? We're going to have us a good time. I got enough cash in my car to last us years. Just a block away is two hundred eighty-four thousand big ones, baby. Ain't nothing wrong with us doing a little traveling, is there? Ooooh...what a fine trophy. They never going to believe I got me something like this."

Jenny frantically tried to fight back into the game. She attempted to roll over, but Billy Ray's left fist found her forehead and knocked her mind half out of her head. Jenny felt herself shut down and ignored her body like a rock ignores a crashing wave. *He can't hurt me.*

Billy Ray pushed himself up with his hands, his knees digging into the sand between Jenny's parted legs. "Hell-ooo, Flor-ee-da. Uncle Billy finally enters the Sunshine—"

Jenny reached out. Her hand found a stick.

CHAPTER 2

I was flat on my back on the deck of my boat, *Impulse,* when my phone, as if it were in the final scene of *Don Giovanni,* rang and vibrated. I was replacing a boat speaker and realized the guys who do it for a living are underpaid. The previous speaker had taken a bullet. Better it than me.

"Piece of shit," I muttered for the forty-second time that morning as I stretched in vain to find the wire coming from the radio box. And I'd been doing so well. My New Year's resolution was to drink expensive wine, eat more fatty foods—they really do taste better—and reduce my profanity. Six months into the year, and I was slipping. But what the hey? Two out of three ain't bad.

The phone stopped its obnoxious buzz on the fiberglass deck. I leaned back, relaxed, and took in a gulp of air so humid that it counted as a drink. Enough for one day. Tomorrow I'd let my neighbor Morgan give it a go; his arms make fish lines look like telephone poles.

"Jake, you look like you sweated away the Gulf." Kathleen stood on the dock and peered down at me. She, being the smart girl she is, had sat under the shade of the canvas while she sipped her morning coffee, spotted dolphins, and read a book. Why can't I do that? Kathleen ran in the mornings, but only in October through April. In the summer, she switched to beach yoga. She claimed the rotation gave her balance. I find that obsessions leave no room for balance.

"Speaker's been out a year, and I could have done this in January, but no, not me." I started to rise up but bonked my head hard on the aluminum underside of the center seat and went down for the count.

"Golly gee willikers," I said.

"See, you *can* do it. 'Oopsy daisies' is another one that's vastly underutilized. But if I were keeping track, I'm afraid you'd be failing miserably."

"No. I'm failing gloriously. There's a difference."

"Not everybody needs to dig bullets out of boat speakers."

"Pity them. Most men *do* lead lives of quiet desperation."

"And go to the grave with the song still in them, or something like that."

I cautiously rose, and my phone started to do the floor jig again. I grabbed the bottom of my T-shirt and wiped it over my forehead, but it was a wasted effort. I hoisted myself over the side and landed on my composite dock. Kathleen took a step back. I got it; I was a sweaty mess.

"That's exactly it," I said. "How's the book?"

"You going to answer it?"

"It's not you."

"Not bad."

"Worth the dough?"

That didn't warrant a verbal reply but a right jab to my shoulder. Kathleen favored hardback books, and a first edition of Somerset Maugham's *The Razor's Edge* rested on my bench. A "Hooked on Books" bookmark protruded out of the first third. It cost her a factor of a hundred compared to an e-book. She also favored physical replies over verbal.

"Well worth the dough. And it's wonderful reading it out here—where you read and the conditions that surround you affect your experience. Why *don't* you answer your phone?"

"I don't recognize the number." I lied; it was Susan Blake's number. She had called earlier while I was running and had left a voice mail. No way was I going to explain to Kathleen my relationship with Susan. I wasn't too sure of it myself.

The phone, like a dead moth, finally surrendered. Ziggy Marley came through the good speakers. The osprey that likes to crap on my boat's hardtop watched from atop Morgan's lift piling. It let out its distinctive series of screeches in the event that I'd forgotten about him. Feathery little prick.

"I think I'll use that in my class this fall." Kathleen taught English literature at the local college.

"My phone?"

"No, silly."

"Maugham?"

She sucked in her left cheek between her teeth, a primitive sign of deep thinking. She favored that side. Chewed on that side. Stuck her tongue into her port cheek when she thought no one saw her. "No." She strung the word out. "The reading experience. Where one reads being instrumental in forming one's opinion of the work. I'll divide the class into two groups, have them read the same book but in controlled environments, and then have them rate the work. Are you listening?"

I looked up from my toolbox, where I'd unsuccessfully fumbled around for needle-nose pliers. Morgan. I think he borrowed them. "Not in the least. But I was pretending to. Any points for that?"

"Half the class will read the book under Spanish moss in the shade of a tree. Maybe in Straub Park in downtown St. Pete. The other half will read the same work in short intervals, several times a day, in windowless air-conditioned rooms, and in different locations."

"Have we ever done it with Spanish moss waving above us?"

She tossed me a quick smile. Kathleen smiled every day, every hour, every few moments. She smiled like other people breathed. She ignored my Spanish moss inquiry and instead said, "I'm leaving. My best to Morgan."

She stayed a safe distance, landed a kiss on my cheek, and took off down my dock with a mug in one hand and Maugham in the other. I gathered my tools and went into my 1957 blockhouse on the bay. I was famished. I'd run five miles in the Florida sauna before I'd sweated away in the boat—the heck was I thinking? I took some of last night's trout Morgan and I had caught off my dock, cut it into pieces, and sautéed it in olive oil with chopped chives. I whipped up three eggs and scrambled them in a separate skillet. At the last moment, I added chunks of sharp cheddar cheese. *Eat more fatty foods.*

I always operate best when I possess clear goals.

I took my breakfast out to the screen porch and lowered the sunshade. I lived on an island, off another island, and my bungalow faced the morning sun. The beach was a half-mile from my front door, and the pink hotel, built on the sands of the Gulf of Mexico, was another half mile beyond that. I was especially fond of the hotel and, in particular, its beachside bar, where several bartenders depended on me for their livelihood. It was my contribution to trickle-down economics. We do what we can.

I finished breakfast and was stymied in my effort to get cold water out of the outdoor shower at the side of the house. I put on a clean-dirty T-shirt; it was pockmarked with permanent olive oil stains, fish residue, and every chemical I'd ever rubbed on *Impulse* in vain attempts to combat the sun and salt air. I remembered I'd left my phone recovering from a seizure on the deck of my boat, and that I had lied—it sounds worse than it was—to Kathleen about not recognizing the number.

Susan Blake.

I'd spent a single two-hour dinner with Susan, yet every minute, every look, and every touch of that evening lingered with me. I tried to wash her away, but like a well-waxed surface of a car, my feelings for her were protected and harbored from any attempt to erase, alter, or expunge. That was more than a year ago. I drove away that night vowing to never cross her path again. I was just starting to wonder if Kathleen was the mythical one for me, and Susan Blake, in many ways the opposite of Kathleen, was kick-ass competition. I didn't need or want that.

Susan had put herself through college then realized her brain wasn't wired for her ass to be in a chair all day. She took a job pouring liquid dreams, enlightened the bars' absentee owners on how to run a profitable operation, and subsequently became part owner of three watering holes in Fort Myers Beach. I couldn't imagine why she was calling me.

Nor could I imagine why she was now sitting at the end of my dock.

CHAPTER 3

She must have arrived when I was showering. That would have been a close brush—too close—with Kathleen. I headed down my hundred-foot dock and broke back into a sweat halfway there. I picked up the pace. I'd forgotten to put shoes on. Walking on coals would have been cooler. I sat next to her—not too close, not too far.

"Hey, Susan. How are you?"

"Hey, Susan. How are you?" Good grief, man—that's the sum of your parts? I whip off The New York Times—

"Didn't you get my messages?" she demanded.

"No. I didn't recog—"

"I need your help." Her interruption saved me from a second lie in one day over the same phone number. She turned to me, her dark eyes trapped under her bangs. The one evening we'd spent together flooded over me like a tsunami.

By the end of our leisurely dinner, my schoolboy heart had been radioactive, and no, it wasn't just the grapes. We had faced each other in the parking lot on a Florida night so thick you needed a snowplow to walk down the street. Susan was close to a foot shorter than me, but in no manner did that diminish her stature. I had just rejected her invitation to stroll on the beach and look for sea turtles.

"Has the bar business robbed me of my vanishing youth?" she'd asked.

"You haven't been robbed of a thing. Her name is Kathleen, and she makes me the luckiest guy in the world, but it's a close call with the runner-up."

"I'll take it. Who is he?"

"Whoever takes that walk on the beach with you."

That was after two glasses of wine and a beer. Impressive, right? Call me Mr. Monogamy, but if you don't know what the hell an anchor is for, you'd better get your ass off the water.

When I took her home, she'd given me a light kiss on the cheek then left the truck without a word. I had not walked her to the door. Susan Blake wasn't the type of woman to ask just any guy to take a walk on the beach unless both sides felt that once-in-a-lifetime tug. But there can only be one once-in-a-lifetime tug.

Sometimes I say that three times in row.

"Tell me…" I shook off the memory and pivoted on the bench so I could face her. I tensed up, which I thought was totally ridiculous. "What brings you north?"

She fidgeted with her fingers. "Nice place." She gave me a quick glance then dropped her eyes. Maybe she felt she was coming on a little strong.

"It'll do," I said.

She paused as if summoning her strength. "I…I need your help." She looked right into me. "She's missing." It came out fast, like water tumbling over falls.

"Who's—"

"She's been gone two days. There's no way she wouldn't tell me."

"Slow down. Take it from the top."

Susan blew out her breath and folded her hands tightly on her lap. "My niece. Came down to live with me, and I haven't seen her since Wednesday. That was a day after the police said she killed some guy on the—"

"The police think she killed someone?"

"She did kill him, practically gutted him like a deer...Oh, I shouldn't say that." Her speech started to gear down as she apparently realized there was nothing I could do in the next few seconds.

"Can they prove—?"

"I just told you. She killed him. Told me. Told the police. That's not the problem." She uncrossed her hands and ran her left hand down the top of her thigh then back up again.

"They got new beach laws down there?" I asked her.

"Self-defense, and they think she did the world a favor. The guy might have killed a girl up in Georgia and maybe another they're still investigating." She placed one hand on each side and nudged herself up. She crossed her legs. I looked away. I didn't want to look at those legs, those eyes, that body. I felt guilty having her there, but what choice did I have? A yellow cruiser with a tuna tower plowed by, and a dolphin jumped its massive wake. We watched as it passed, and then rows of its swelling wake were soon beneath us. They crashed into the seawall like liquid thunder and rolled down the wall.

"How well do you know her?" I said, but I was thinking, *How well do I know you?* Sounded like her niece had hit the road and was on the lam. Maybe Susan was blind to the obvious, but I didn't want to ride her too hard.

"She came to live with me less than a week ago. Just graduated from high school."

I turned back to her. "She from close by?"

"Ohio."

"How well do you know her?" I asked again.

"Listen, we've spent some time together over the years, but that's not the point. I know her. I know her very well. She wouldn't run."

"We all misjudge. It's hard to know people, especially—"

"How much time did we spend together, Jake?"

Women.

They can sucker-punch you with the flutter of their eyes. Do they even know that? Susan and I had dinner and nothing else. But she was right. We connected so fast that it threw the tides. If it's ever happened to you, you know what I'm talking about. If not, welcome to Thoreau's desperation club and take your song to your grave.

"Fair enough," I said in response to her question.

"You told me you located stolen boats, right? And when we met, you were looking for a couple of guys."

"Correct." I saw where this was going and thought of how to extract myself.

"She's in danger, and I know it. You need to find her. The police say since she's eighteen, she can go as she pleases."

"You tried her cell, her—"

"She left her cell behind. You *know* that's not right. I covered everything. Called my sister…She had to hear from a friend that her daughter had moved in with me. Her friends, her…She didn't have anybody."

"When was the last time—?"

"Are you going to get into that black beast and come help me or not?"

What was on my calendar for the next few days? Work out in the mornings until I nearly collapsed—I just loved that part of the day—fish, read, and after my Tinker Bell alarm clock went off at five, drink. The days I puttered around the house, Tinker Bell—I picked her up at a garage sale—kept me honest in the event I felt like opening something too early. I'd follow all that with a simple gourmet meal I'd prepare for Kathleen and whoever else dropped by. Sleep. Repeat.

My schedule was packed. Might even need to take one of those time management courses.

"Jake?" Softer now. Pleading, as much as someone like Susan would ever plead, as she sensed my hesitation. What kind of person says no?

"I'll leave as—"

She uncrossed her legs. "I'll have pictures and arrange for the detective to bring you up to speed." No gushing thank-you, just straight to the next item. "I need to go." She stood up. "You remember where I live?"

"I do. One more thing."

"What?"

"Her name?"

"Jenny Spencer."

CHAPTER 4

Morgan pulled his scooter into my driveway. He owned a scooter, a Harley, and a forty-two-foot Beneteau sailboat, *Moonchild*. Most people travel to find the elusive port of peace of mind. For Morgan, travel *is* the port.

"Hitting the road?" he asked. I assumed he was returning from the beach. Even though our homes have a two-mile bay view, he sojourned twice a day, late morning and sunset, to the Gulf. I checked my pocket for my phone for the umpteenth time. I had forgotten it a second time after Susan had left, and had just scorched my feet again in retrieving it.

"Fort Myers Beach for a day or two." I tossed my army duffel bag into the back of my black beast and hit the "close" button. It chimed. I wondered if I could program the close sound on a vehicle's tailgate like you can program ringtones. "Care to join me?"

"Let's roll."

"Need ten?"

"I'm good."

He parked his bike in my garage, hustled over to the passenger-side door, and hopped in. *Guess I'd better scramble.* I grabbed a couple of waters from the garage refrigerator and climbed behind the wheel.

"Clothes?" I said.

"I'll pick up whatever I need."

"House?"

"Alondra's cleaning today. She'll lock up."

"Hold on a sec. I forgot to leave food for Hadley."

"Hadley the Third."

"Right."

Hadley III's my cat. I'm temporarily watching her for a friend who permanently relocated to another island. I'm not fond of cats, and I'm highly suspicious that Hadley III is equally unfond of me. We'd developed a truce. She pounced on my chest our first night just as I had fallen asleep. I was surprised she had survived the impact with the wall. Tough girl. She now stays clear of my bedroom, and in return I feed her and leave water out so she doesn't have to lean into the toilet. I left her enough food for a year, got into the truck, and twisted the key.

The engine responded with a throaty growl, and Morgan spat out, "Wait." He jumped out of the seat—the man had the dexterity and movements of a monkey—and dashed through the door I'd just emerged from.

Morgan grew up on a sailboat and doesn't know his age, other than he's older than his sister, who operates the family charter business in the Caribbean. His parents believed that tracking one's journeys around the sun only creates unintended expectations and limitations. He meditates every morning at the end of his dock, as he'd been doing earlier when I'd departed for my run. He claims it fills his spiritual tank. My tank has a Florida sinkhole in it. A few minutes later, he emerged from my house with a wine box. He opened the passenger door, placed the box on the floor, and reclaimed his shotgun seat.

"Ready," he announced.

"Supplies?"

"Essentials."

He brought his legs up Indian style, pulled his sandy hair into a ponytail, and stuck in earplugs before I cleared the bridge that led off the island. Ten minutes later, he snatched his plugs from his ears and with the voice of someone who, having music directly injected into his head, assumes the world is much louder than it really is, blurted out, "I forgot shoes. You got some, right?"

"In the back." I rarely wear shoes around the house and have a habit of jumping into the truck without them. I keep several pairs of old Sebago boat shoes in the truck.

"Thought so." The plugs went back into home position.

We hit the Sunshine Skyway Bridge, which spanned the entrance to Tampa Bay. The vertical clearance was around 193 feet, and from that view, the water flattened out, and the sky started to drop down on you. It was just high enough that you started to get a sense of your inconsequentiality before you eased back down to earth.

I put the truck on cruise control at seventy-eight, and she fought the harness. Ninety was her sweet spot, and she didn't take kindly to others blowing fumes in her grille. We passed crosses along the side of the road that marked where someone's life had abruptly concluded. What's the interstate system going to resemble in a hundred years? Talladega cut through a graveyard? Here's something I know—if I knew where my cross would be, I'd never go there.

Two hours later, we crested the Matanzas Pass Bridge and descended into the public beach area of Fort Myers Beach. I'd spent a year living and drinking on the southern part of the beach after I left the army and before Colonel Janssen came knocking for my services. I'd needed some time to get in touch with my inner person. I found it as rewarding as rummaging around inside a half-empty garbage can. No need to do that again.

We pulled into the parking lot of the Point Carlos hotel-condominiums, less than a mile north of Lovers Key. Everything around there was "Carlos." Big Carlos Pass. Little Carlos Pass. San Carlos Boulevard. Carlos Surf and Suds—the only beachside bar I know that gives you a paddleboard for a half hour at no cost if you've had two or more drinks. (The owner, Kurt Lourdes, swears it was his best business decision. "Patrons love—I mean they flat out *dig*—watching other people fall off those boards.") All of it was named after Chief Carlos, a Calusa Indian and an enthusiastic practitioner of human sacrifices, as well as the possible killer of Ponce de Leon. Carlos's brother-in-law, Spaniard explorer Pedro Menéndez (Carlos, in happier times, had passed along his sister to be Menéndez's bride), had killed Carlos after Carlos himself took a few unsuccessful swipes at Menéndez. Evidently, being a major proponent of human sacrifice doesn't preclude one from eventually having naming rights to half the damn region.

I had booked a two-bedroom condo—all the condos have two bedrooms—for two nights, and now that Morgan was with me, I was glad I hadn't opted for a different location. The place was quiet. It was summer, and the western half of the Eastern Time Zone that swarmed the place in March had long departed. Fine with me. When the crowds leave paradise, paradise, not being fond of crowds, returns.

"Room for Travis, Jake," I said to the lady behind the counter. She had tousled rust-colored hair that splayed wildly out of an overmatched scrunchie. A *USA Today* was on the counter, and its colors already looked liked yesterday's news. To my right was a corner gift shop with resort towels, hats, T-shirts, and tin-soldier sentinel coffeepots waiting for the morning.

"I see you're staying for only two nights," Rusty said. "Gulf front, midlevel, or higher, south side?" I'm picky about the space I occupy. "If you'd like, we can book you for one more night, and the fourth night will be free." As she spoke, she stared into her computer screen.

"I'll pass. I only need—"

"We'll take it," Morgan chirped in.

I glanced at him. "I don't think we'll be here that long."

"Two keys for four nights will be fine," he said, keeping his eyes on Rusty.

"Certainly," she said and glanced up at Morgan. "And how will you be paying for this?"

Morgan said, "I won't be."

I placed my credit card on the counter then scrawled my name on a sheet of paper she'd slid in front of me. When I lifted my head, she was beaming at Morgan as if I wasn't even there. The man adored redheads and transmitted that five-bar signal with an uncommon clarity. I picked up my duffel and headed toward the elevator. Morgan followed with the box he'd brought out of my house. I double-punched the button while the elevator moseyed around on a higher floor. A woman who smelled like the beach joined us. She wore a floppy wide-brimmed hat, sunglasses, and a white cover-up. The last item was a real shame, considering what she appeared to be covering up.

"You forgot to grab shoes," I said as I stared at the floor. Morgan's second toe was longer than his big toe.

"Oops."

I looked up at him. "I assume you'll be in late tonight."

"If at all."

"What makes you think we need another two nights, even if it's just the price of one?"

"I'll walk to the grocery at midisland and pick up food. We'll need provisions for breakfast."

"That doesn't answer my question." I hit the elevator button for the third time. I'm sure that helped. "And how can you sit at peace in a truck for two hours without asking why we're coming here?" He'd done that before—hopped into my truck or boat without voicing curiosity as to the destination or the reason.

"Remember," he said, "I grew up on a sailboat. I need a reason to be stationary, not to travel. As for you, you're as nervous as I've ever seen you."

"The heck you talking about?"

"You. Your anxiety level is—"

"Skip it."

He paused a beat then changed tack. "It's an amazing beach. You do know James Jones pounded out some of his war memories a mile or so up the sand."

"King's Cottage, I believe." I hit the button again. "But what does that have to do with—"

"We could've driven from here to eternity, and your hands never would have left ten and two." Morgan rarely interrupted people but had done so twice in a few minutes. "You fought the wheel like I do at the helm of a fifty-footer battling a summer squall."

I started to serve up my retort but pulled up as I realized he had lapped me. Again. My aching left shoulder, courtesy of shrapnel from the Battle of Chora in Afghanistan, complemented with a bullet I'd taken to the same shoulder the night *Impulse* took one in a speaker, confirmed Morgan's observation. Hard to believe ten and two for two hours, but my mind had raced so far ahead of the truck that I barely remembered the drive. As for the Jones reference, it didn't surprise me. He'd told me the James Jones war trilogy was among his favorites. Mine as well. Kathleen had presented me with first editions for my birthday, and Morgan had borrowed them, as he planned to reread them.

"And"—guess he wasn't done—"whatever is eating you is unlikely to be resolved in a day or two, or else you would have told me why we're here."

"You had your plugs in." It was a weak defensive remark. I should have just taken the Fifth.

The elevator arrived—four stabs at the button, for future reference, is the magic number—and we stepped in after the lady. She exited two floors before us. The beach went with her. We both observed until the doors, like metal stage curtains, sliced our vision shut. When a woman leaves an elevator and a man is left behind, it's impossible for the man not to watch as she walks away. Above all, trust me on this.

"And you *never* would have left without the essentials," Morgan said.

I peered into the box he hugged against his chest: 1800 Reposado tequila, Grant Marnier, limes, a partially eaten block of Welsh cheddar, bread, wine, and tapenade. And speakers. The man is a connoisseur of what goes in his ears. He thinks Edison's gift—music from air—to be the greatest invention of all.

We entered our unit, and Morgan took the back room with double beds and left me the Gulf-front bedroom with the king. He announced he was going for a walk and would meet me at Fish Head. The door slammed shut, and I said, "Okay." I gazed down at the Gulf from nine floors up.

Jenny Spencer.

Susan had called when I was in the truck. She instructed me when to meet at her house and provided more details. The police considered Jenny's actions on the beach to be self-defense, yet she had run. Maybe she just needed some time alone. Maybe she was sitting in a dark booth, spilling it all to a priest. Maybe she'd do evolution a favor and go for the priest too. Hard to say. Dead bodies collect more than fleas. They collect interest, stories, guilt, and often revenge.

But those things had nothing to do with why my hands had been glued to ten and two.

I had called Kathleen before we'd left and informed her I was going to Fort Myers Beach for a day or so. I told her an old friend called and was worried because her niece had run away. I gave their names but omitted that the "old friend" was a hot woman I didn't trust myself to be around. Think that makes a difference? At worst, I'd get a ticket for being disingenuous.

"Teenage runaway?" Kathleen had asked.

I'd hesitated then said, "There's a body involved."

She came in late. "You're going back in, aren't you?"

When I left the army, Colonel Janssen had recruited me, along with my partner, Garrett Demarcus, for contract work. I'd been making a good living recovering stolen boats and could still take on an occasional misplaced vessel. Easy money. Guy buys a boat for half a mil and sells it to the Columbians for two fifty. He then reports it stolen and files an insurance claim for 500K. They acquiesce, and he makes 50 percent on his investment. It's not that simple, because it's burrowed funds, but that'll suffice. Scenario two: The insurance company hires me for 20 percent of the boat's retail value. I locate the boat and return it to the company. They pay me 100K and unload the boat. The same game occurs in the art world, but instead of turning the trick with a Donzi, they flip a Degas. It's not all tea and crumpets. Occasionally, I need to tango with men brandishing machine guns, but it beats the hell out of a daily commute and having some faceless corporation tell me I've got to change ten passwords every twenty days.

The most recent bullets, however, that had embedded themselves in both my boat's speaker and me, were the result of an assignment from the colonel. I had risked my life to retrieve a classified letter from the Cold War that was held by a man named Raydel Escobar. Kathleen had questioned why I put everything on the line every time. I had no answer but gave her a love letter from fifty years ago that had been in the same envelope as the classified letter. It contained an arrangement of words that expressed, beyond my capability, my feelings for Kathleen. That letter was now in her home. A man I never knew, from a time we didn't share, expressed what I could never say.

I had tried to assuage Kathleen's fear. "It won't be like last time. The police are involved. I'll just be there to help where I can."

"I'm fine," she'd said. But it came out too fast and with nothing behind it.

"I'll call you when I get a feel for how long I'll be there."

"Be careful."

"Always."

"Don't give me that crap."

"Okay."

My conversation with Kathleen faded in my mind and was replaced with my reflection in the glass. I turned away. It was time to return to Susan Blake's house. This time I'd have to get out of the truck.

CHAPTER 5

Susan lived on a street named after a bird. Other streets on the island were named after states. Not the most creative effort, but it sufficed, and at least they gave Carlos a break.

Her house, halfway down on the south side, was a golden stucco ranch with sculptured hedges and a shaved lawn. It backed up to a canal that led to Estero Bay, where at the moment, tailing reds lay in the shades of the mangroves, waiting for me to drop a live shrimp on them. Not today. A dark sedan rested in her driveway, so I pulled up behind a car the color and size of a large fresh lime. An osprey screeched, and monk parakeets chirped back. Crushed seashells littered the street. Fort Myers Beach, like the island I lived on and hundreds more throughout Florida, was nothing more than an inhabited sandbar.

I hit the doorbell before I had time to think. Susan opened it, and I followed her on a wood floor with varied-width planking through a great room to her back lanai, a spacious area that overlooked a small pool, her dock, and the canal. A twenty-foot Grady-White rested on its lift. *Impulse* is a twenty-seven-foot Grady. The back of Susan's home, like mine, faced south. Fate speaks a strange tongue. I tried to rein in my mind, which insisted there was a damn good reason she and I had connected that night. I avoided eye contact with her, which I thought was a totally gutless thing to do, but there you have it.

A man in tan slacks and a blue blazer stood and extended his hand. The sports coat appeared as if it hadn't seen a dry cleaner since he'd snatched it off the discount rack. His short-cropped hair matched his physique. His left shoulder was slightly lower than his right.

"Detective Patrick McGlashan, Lee County Sheriff's Office."

"Jake Travis."

A quick word about the fuzz and me: I avoid them at all cost. In my experience, there are two types of people with guns: those against me, who I want to put a bullet in, and a buddy in my foxhole, who I'd take a bullet for. I don't know where a man with a badge, or in this case, a man in a disheveled suit, fits into that world.

I shook McGlashan's hand. One finger sported a Super Bowl ring. I'm sure he was proud of that and was used to questions, but he wouldn't get any acknowledgment from me. We each claimed a wicker chair as if they had our names on them. He started right in.

"Ms. Blake wanted me to bring you up to speed. You work in the boat-recovery insurance-fraud business?" Translated: *you don't have a job, so why do I have to sit here and chat with you?*

"That's correct." My work for Colonel Janssen was strictly off the books.

McGlashan eyed me with a natural squint, as if he were looking right through me. I'd been verbose in my reply. I could have gone with "yes." Neither of us spoke until Susan broke the impasse.

"Detective, I'd like you to go over the crime scene with Mr. Travis. I know you've been over it with me, but I'd like him to hear it from you." Then she added, no doubt for both alpha males, "It would be most helpful."

McGlashan and I, while she spoke, held each other's eyes in a death duel. Like he was going to play ball with some beach bum. Like I gave a rat's ass about a Super Bowl ring.

"My pleasure," he said, but his eyes never left mine. I caught Susan out of my peripheral vision. *Help me out here.* Like a siren's song, her presence turned my head and consumed my full attention. I couldn't ignore her now like I had when I'd walked into her house and stared at her wood floor and then out toward her dock and the canal.

She wore a pink Blue Heaven T-shirt and white shorts. No shoes. Her dark chocolate-brown eyes, a perfect match of her hair, lay deep behind the edge of her thick bangs. Her pug nose and high cheekbones made her as attractive as I remembered. Her combination of strength and vulnerability, which I'd found so irresistible, was now tilted away from the former and toward the latter. She sat deep in her chair. Her arms were crossed tightly in front of her. Suddenly Mc-whatever-his-name wasn't even there anymore. I tried to push away my feelings, but Sisyphus would have had an easier time of it.

"What do you got?" I said, and switched my attention from Susan to McGlashan. I leaned forward with my elbows on my knees. A real team player.

"It's what I already informed Ms. Blake," he started in.

We got it, jock-o-boy. You don't want to be here, I thought, but said, "And what would that be?" I stared at McGlashan, but my mind took off on its own. I wondered if Morgan was at Fish Head yet, and if Melissa, the blue-eyed Aussie bartender who had informed me that she was gay—I must have been *totally* orbital that year—was still there. I thought of Susan in that tight black dress she'd worn out to dinner and wondered how many men had seen her in that. When I glanced back at her, she crossed her legs and uncrossed her arms. She had the thinnest, most muscular, feminine calves I'd ever had the pleasure of trying not to stare at. If the survival of the species depended on her calves and me—well, I'd find a way.

McGlashan cut Susan a look as if he wanted credit for cooperating. "Three nights ago," he started, "Ms. Blake received a phone call at ten thirty-five from Ms. Spencer requesting that she return home immediately."

I asked, "What phone did she call from?"

Susan took it. "Her cell."

"Where was she when she called?"

"Here, like I told you when we talked. She was at the beach and hadn't taken her phone with her."

Susan, to get the ball rolling, recapped for McGlashan what she and I had discussed during our phone conversation while I drove the truck and Morgan bounced his ponytail to whatever tune bounced in his head. She explained that when she had come home, she'd found Jenny recently showered and sitting calmly on the porch. Jenny told her a man they'd seen earlier that day had appeared on the beach and attempted to rape her, and she, in response, had picked up a stick, become a *matador de toros,* and gored him. Jenny, according to Susan, displayed alarmingly calm behavior.

I interrupted her. "She was in quiet repose when you found her?"

"Yes. As she told me the story, I thought she might be in shock, but she never showed any other signs."

"And what would those signs be?" My question came with an unintended tone of harshness, but I doubted Susan had ever seen anyone in shock, let alone known the difference between circulatory shock and emotional shock. McGlashan gave a smirk and settled back into his chair to enjoy the show. Susan gave me a look. We were all getting along just swell. Maybe before we parted, we'd draw names for Christmas.

"I know," she said in a tone that shut the door to further questions regarding her qualification to diagnose shock.

"We sat for hours that night, right here. We talked through the night. Around four thirty, I suggested we call the police. I hadn't wanted to do that before I felt she was composed." She knifed McGlashan a look. I surmised that he had already drilled Susan regarding the long wait to contact the authorities. "I wanted to make sure her initial calm was real and not masking anything."

I glanced at McGlashan and asked, "How did it play out?"

"When the call came in," he started in a tone that adequately conveyed his impatience with having to rehash the night to me, "it was assigned to me and another detective. Goes by the name of Eric Rutledge." He placed his elbows on the armrest of the chair and straightened himself up. "We arrived at the house, and Detective Rutledge did the interview. I went to the crime scene."

"Where exactly was that?"

"Are you familiar with the beach?"

"I am."

"South end, where the mangroves are. About a half mile from the end of the island. An inlet cuts in; evidently at high tide, the beach is gone, and there are paths and clearings in the mangroves. We found the victim in such a clearing."

"And the crime scene?"

McGlashan leaned in a bit. "You walk the beach? See the birds attack a French fry or a dead fish?"

"Ghoulish art."

"Mulched him over three square yards. We secured the crime scene, which at that point was a feast of the gulls."

I said, "Did you talk to Jenny?" But I was thinking, *Did she do that to a man on her own? With no help?*

"I stayed at the scene, and Detective Rutledge conducted a recorded interview with Ms. Spencer until six seventeen a.m.

29

His report indicates that Ms. Spencer did not know the assailant, Billy Ray Coleman. She'd seen him only once before the attack, and that was when he stopped earlier that afternoon to talk to Ms. Spencer and Ms. Blake while they were...sunbathing on the beach. Neither noticed anything unusual about the man other than he was about to forfeit a layer of skin to the sun."

"I said he hit his head," Susan cut in.

"That's correct," McGlashan said. "Ms. Blake does recall Coleman striking his own head, and Ms. Spencer did mention that in the interview."

I looked at Susan. "How was she during the interview?"

"I was here for only the first ten minutes or so. Then I had to get to one of my bars. I returned a little before six thirty, just as they were finishing. Jenny said it went fine, but she didn't really want to talk about it."

"You went to one of your bars?"

"Someone broke into Water's Edge and grabbed a case of liquor. Third time this year. The alarm went off."

"And you went?"

Susan brought her legs up underneath her. "Jenny said she was fine. I didn't plan to be gone as long as I was."

"Did Rutledge tell you anything about the conversation that took place in your absence?" I asked her.

"No." She gave a disgusted look and crossed her arms again. Half her chair held no purpose; she couldn't possibly occupy a smaller space. "He asked me to follow him to his car. But then he hit on me. He's one of those guys who won't shut up about himself. I thought it was inappropriate. Yakked about how after his sister—she had been sick and never married—had recently died, and he had to get a fresh start. Said he was new to the area but had a house on the island, not far from me." She shook her head. I shifted my gaze to McGlashan, but his face was stone. He made no attempt to defend his coworker.

"Did her statements to Detective Rutledge differ in any manner from what you and she discussed?"

"I haven't listened to the recording of the conversation she had that night with Detective Rutledge."

I shot McGlashan a glance. Certainly he would want to compare notes as to what Jenny had said immediately following the incident versus what she recited hours later.

"We planned to do a follow-up interview with Ms. Spencer," McGlashan said as if reading my mind, "and then have Ms. Blake listen. Ms. Blake had already indicated to us that she and Ms. Spencer discussed very little of the incident that evening."

I asked Susan, "What *did* you discuss?"

"Her life." It came out defiant, as if I'd attacked her and she'd victoriously countered. An osprey's call pierced the silence. I caught a glimpse of a Fountain speedboat slinking out of the canal. The name on the side was *Seaduction*.

McGlashan cleared his throat. "Detective Rutledge," he said, "stated that Ms. Spencer informed him that she and Ms. Blake reviewed the incident only briefly then talked for hours, without, apparently"—he cut Susan a look—"further discussion of the attempted rape and murder."

"Anything else that night?" My question went to McGlashan.

"Nothing." He shifted his gaze to me. "The following morning we received a lead on a deceased girl in Kentucky and a possible tie-in to a rape-murder in Georgia. Our break was the guy in the Peach State did it at a storage unit."

"Cameras?"

"Seven. Three busted, two with nothing, and one just fuzz."

I waited, but he was done. He wasn't under any obligation to pass the pipe with me. I asked, "And the seventh?"

He smiled. He knew he'd made me earn it.

"He slowed down going over a pothole. Good enough to put an alert out on the car. We found Coleman's Honda around ten the following morning, but there was little of interest inside it. The trunk had been jimmied with a crowbar and was open. Nothing but fast-food debris and fifty-three cents. Wiped clean around the trunk."

It was my turn to lean in and drill him. "Clean? As in no prints?"

"Not around the trunk."

"Why a crowbar? Why not break the glass and hit the trunk release lever?"

McGlashan seemed to consider that, or me, for a moment. "The lever was inoperable. We checked it. Busted on the floor of the driver's side. It had nothing to do with the damage caused by the break-in. A preexisting condition."

"Where was the car?"

"Few hundred feet from the scene. A little parking area that only holds a handful of cars."

I knew the area. Heavy oleander bushes draped the beach access lot like a vaudeville stage curtain. Except for a few units in an apartment complex directly across the street, the parking spot was barely visible.

Susan said, "Tell him about the...about her T-shirt."

McGlashan gave a slight shake of his head, as if he had no defense. "Ms. Spencer," he started in, "said her T-shirt was left on a branch. We found the rest of her clothing but not that. She insisted it wasn't ripped—she wasn't sure how he'd gotten it off her—but she was adamant that she'd left it hanging on a mangrove branch."

"And?" Susan asked, without letting air in between McGlashan's last word and her question.

"Her name was on the shirt."

"Someone beat you to it," I said. "Both the crime scene and the victim's car."

McGlashan leaned with his elbows on his knees, as if he were trying to restrain himself from vaulting out of his chair. A vein on the left side of his forehead came to attention, as if it also wanted to get in on the action. "We talked before you came. Ms. Blake said you served?" He asked it like a command.

I stayed with my back rested against the wicker chair but kept my eyes straight on his. "Five years. Rangers."

The vein backed down, but not McGlashan. "My son's there now. Final tour and due home in little over a week. Been working with the British SAS. Know anything about them?"

"He who dares wins."

There were a few ticks of silence that an osprey took advantage of. The right corner of McGlashan's mouth curled up. He gave a slight nod and settled back in his chair.

"Just like the gulls," he said. "Someone beat us to it. Beat us to everything. We have to consider that someone was hot on Billy Ray Coleman's trail that night."

Detective Patrick McGlashan had just climbed into my foxhole.

CHAPTER 6

Susan, like an embarrassed hostess who'd forgotten her duties, inquired whether either of us would like a drink. Without breaking eye contact, we both mumbled "no," although to be fair, he tagged his with "thanks."

"We ran the plates," McGlashan said. "A two thousand Accord, not worth the sand it was parked on. Windows were broken, seats torn. Someone scorched every inch."

It appeared that before we bonded, he planned on withholding the information that the insides had been searched. "Nothing but fast-food debris" was, at best, vague. At worst, if someone had shredded the interior, it was purposely misleading. I asked, "The crowbar?"

"Excuse me?"

"You said the trunk was jimmied with a crowbar. Did you find the crowbar?"

He shifted his weight. "I assume it was a crowbar, or some other blunt instrument that we didn't find. They didn't try, as far as we could ascertain, to steal the car—not that it had much value. Problem is they left behind an Alpine aftermarket navigation system and rear speakers that would blow out the Orange Bowl. Easy thing to fence."

"And your deduction?"

McGlashan must have tired of my staccato questions, or feared another unforced error like the crowbar, because he came back with, "What do you think?"

"There was something in that car worth far more than a grand and the simple time it would have taken to snatch the stereo."

McGlashan nodded. "Coleman had two brothers, Randall and Zach. The clan is suspected of running meth labs in Hocking County, Ohio. The sheriff up there thinks they're more than mom-and-pop; they probably export well beyond the county line. They live within an hour of Ms. Spencer's hometown, but we found no connection."

That garnered my attention. "Within an hour and no connection? Little tough to swallow, isn't it?"

"To date...no connection."

"Who's in charge?"

"Where?"

"The Coleman clan."

"According to the Hocking County sheriff, Randall, the older one, calls the shots. But they've got nothing to bring the boys in on."

Susan cut in. "What about Jenny?"

McGlashan and I both switched our attention to her, and I said, "What did you notice about Coleman when he talked to you?" I didn't think the question would move us forward, but I wanted Susan to be engaged.

"Not much. We'd never seen him before that afternoon. We were lying out, and he stopped by. Said a few words, introduced himself, said he was from Georgia, and moved on. He leered at Jenny."

"Leered?"

She shrugged. "Guys do it. Quick glance at me, then all over her, but he didn't stay."

"Sound like he was from Georgia?"

"No, now that I think about it."

"The head slap?"

"You know, like you do when a gnat bites you. But it was… different."

"Why?"

Susan considered that for a beat. "Because it was too…too violent, too hard for a bug."

"What else?"

"Nothing that I—"

"Think."

She shot me a glance, and I remembered I really didn't know this woman well, perhaps not at all.

"He was red."

"Red?" The word held so many possibilities: a Native American, the movie, the fish, losing money, a commie sympathizer, Morgan's latest flame.

"Serious sunburn. One step away from the emergency room."

McGlashan shifted in his seat. "If I may, let me recap what we know."

I ignored him and gave Susan a hard stare. "You're positive? Jenny had *ne*ver seen this guy before the encounter on the beach? A guy who may have grown up less than an hour away from her? She leveling with you? This girl you barely know, yet you know she's telling the truth?"

"We checked," McGlashan answered before Susan had a chance to leap out of her chair at me. "As I said, we found no connection. Even though Coleman's home isn't far from Jenny's home in Ohi—"

"That's not her home," Susan yelped at him.

McGlashan blew out his breath then caught himself. "From where she was living, every day for the first eighteen years of her life." My bet was that he and Susan had driven that around the lot a few times. He glanced at his watch.

"You have nothing to tie the Coleman boys to Jenny?" I pressed him again.

He paused, weary of my line of disbelief. "Nothing yet. The sheriff's office in Hocking County interviewed Ms. Spencer's stepfather—"

"He is shit," Susan blurted. "He wouldn't tell the truth on his mother's grave."

McGlashan let the moment defuse and addressed me. "The sheriff stated that neither Ms. Spencer's stepfather or mother knew Billy Ray Coleman or any of the Coleman boys. They weren't even privy to the fact that Ms. Spencer had decided to move in with Ms. Blake. She didn't even notify them of her decision to leave. Simply left without telling them." He leaned his good shoulder into the armrest of the chair. "Here's what we got on Ms. Spencer's disappearance. Ms. Blake came home from the grocery store two days ago, and Ms. Spencer was gone. No sign of forced entry, no prints. Her bag wasn't packed. Her phone was here. We interviewed the neighbors. One thinks she saw Jenny leave the house around ten in the evening, like she was taking a stroll, but with purpose, the neighbor said. No one saw any suspicious vehicles on the street. No one—"

"For God's sake," Susan said and leaned forward, arms on her knees. "She left without her shoes and her phone. *Her phone.* You really think an eighteen-year-old girl took off with fore-thought and purpose and left her phone?"

I glanced at McGlashan and raised my eyebrows.

"Rutledge examined the phone and saw nothing of inter-est," he said. "We're keeping it for the time being."

"And the chances of any girl bolting without her phone?" I asked him.

McGlashan placed his hands on the arms of the chair and maneuvered himself deeper into his seat. I didn't think he was the type to veer from company manuals and policies, but he wasn't a rookie. He addressed my question to Susan. I don't like it when I ask the question, and the answer is directed to someone else.

"Maybe she panicked. Maybe getting raped her opening night in Florida wasn't the scene she envisioned. Local sheriff's office in Ohio is questioning her friends. I think she'll show up. Hopefully she's not running from us. We made clear to her that our office sees no guilt in her actions. Maybe another guilt caught up with her. We...I...don't know." He shifted his gaze to me. "At this point she's just a missing eighteen-year-old who has run before." He paused and held my eyes for a few seconds. He was being asked to look for a girl with a history of fleeing. Literally bolted twice within one week. Jenny Spencer didn't make his top one hundred things to worry about.

He continued in my direction. "We've notified her mother, at her *old* home in Ohio, that if she shows to give us a jingle." He checked his watch again in a well-timed stage maneuver then stood. "I've got to go." He reached into his pocket and produced a business card for me. I stood and gave him mine. It had my name and cell number. "If you uncover anything, let me know." He tossed Susan a nod. "Ms. Blake, I'm sure she'll turn up. I can see myself out."

He went three steps, and I said, "Tell me about the follow-up interview."

McGlashan turned with an air of reluctance. "Standard procedure. Sometimes different things come out the second time around. Memories tend to travel their own path and at their own speed. We usually have a different person conduct the second interview, just to break it up. But I never got the chance." He turned back and strolled out the front door with a pace that challenged further questioning.

I asked Susan if I could see Jenny's room. I followed her down a hall and into a room with a cherry floor and closed white shutters. Jenny hadn't even unpacked. Her suitcase was open on the floor, and clothing spilled over its sides like it was trying to escape. Her bed was meticulously made, and a frayed stuffed yellow duck with a faded pink beak rested on the edge of the pillow. Above the bed hung a wooden sign: THERE IS A PLACE I BRING ALL OF ME, AND IT IS UNDOUBTEDLY THE SEA. I liked it. I entered the room and picked up a framed picture off her bed stand. A confident man beamed into the sun, half his face blocked by the shadow of his hat. He was on a boat. "Her father," Susan said from behind me, although her voice sounded far away. "She finds it difficult to speak of him."

"Tell me." I gently placed the picture back on the bedside table.

She went to the window and opened the shutters. She spoke with her back to me. "He died when she was twelve. Hunting accident in deer season." She spun around. "There's a word for that—*harvesting*, I believe. Anyway"—she took a step and smoothed out the bedspread—"that year they harvested four thousand one hundred twenty-nine deer and one man. She and her father were close. Her—my sister Angie—was never close to her only daughter. Angie's caught up in her own world and followed their son, Orry, on the motocross circuit. Jenny's dad, Larry"—she glanced up at me—"was a lot like you, spent years in the army. He bought an old boat, a Trojan, and he and Jenny used to go to Buckeye Lake on weekends. He was a wonderful man." She glanced away from me, but her eyes focused on nothing. "He could've done a lot better than my sister." She came back to me. "I'm sure he would've left her if it weren't for the two kids."

"She come down on her—"

"My sister remarried." She gave the bedspread a flippant shove, like the stupid thing didn't matter. "Guy named Boone, a part-time construction worker who wears sleeveless T-shirts and tinkers with an old Dodge Charger that hasn't turned over in years."

"How did Jenny feel—?"

"She spent only one day on the boat after her father died. Last summer with her brother, Orry, and two of his friends. She told me that Boone started calling her 'woman,' and it made her want to puke, and it was all she could do, being on her father's boat, to not just break down and cry." She took a step closer to me, as if words wouldn't suffice and were no longer capable of conveying the message.

"I take it that—"

"He came at her jaybird naked three days later when she was in the shower after cheer practice. Jenny said she screamed so loud she scared herself. He backed down but said he knew where she slept."

I stood quietly, an immensely difficult thing for me to do. But I'd learned my lesson. Susan had cut me off three times and had to get the story out.

"Jenny took off the day after she graduated. Didn't tell anyone. See that saying?" She nodded toward the wooden sign above the bed. "Said she saw it in a magazine while flying to Orlando for cheer competition. She told me she was five miles above the face of the earth when she decided to live by the sea… to come to me.

"I like that." She shifted her gaze to the sign. "Five miles above the earth when you decide to live by the sea. As if up there, the choices are so clear, so obvious." She turned back to me and picked up the cadence of her speech. "We had already bonded. We'd met several times over the years, and she spent a week here last summer. She texted me and said she wanted to come visit. Showed up a day later with a suitcase that I knew was packed for more than a visit."

"When did you learn of Boone?"

"Just the other night. She doesn't dwell on that. Her father"—she picked up the picture of a smiling Larry Spencer—"and his boat were the only two good things ever to cross her path." She gave a slight shake of her head. "She told me the old boat leaked, and her job was to sit in the cuddy and work the busted hand pump, but it was hard because she and her dad always rubbed the teak with oil, and it was difficult to pump with the oil on her hands. She said she tried"—she wiped her eyes with her free hand and put the picture back—"but it was so hard when it was slippery."

I glanced at the picture of Larry Spencer. Army man. Kept his teak well-oiled. I liked the guy. He'd fit in well in my world. "I'm sure—"

"She asked me if she had let her father down"—her eyes pleaded with mine—"when she was twelve and couldn't pump very well because of her oiled hands? She asked me if I thought her dad was disappointed in her. Said sometimes she dreamed of him, and in her dreams, he'd say, 'Pump, Jenny. Pump,' and then she'd wake up feeling he was disappointed that she couldn't pump very well, and she'd try to crawl back into the dream to talk to him. What do you say? What do you say to a girl who wants to crawl back into a dream to talk with her father?"

I blew my breath out. "Damned if I know." It came out disrespectful, although it wasn't my intent.

Susan landed a hard stare. "Someone took her," she said with a hard shift of her emotions. She faced me, her dark eyes streaked with tears.

"We don't know that. She was under—"

"Didn't you hear him? *Just* a missing eighteen-year-old. They don't care. Someone took her." She took a step toward me, but I didn't get it. My antenna wasn't high enough.

"You've got to understand McGlashan's position. She's eighteen. She already ran from one home without telling anyone, and after what she went through, he just can't—"

Another step. "She left her phone."

"She'll probably—"

"Didn't you *goddamn* hear me? I'm all she's got. Do you under*stand* that?"

I was oblivious to the charge of her words, the conviction of her mind, the strange brew of frustration, strength, and vulnerability that was coiled within.

"I'll ask around—"

Her right hand flew in fast. I started to move but decided I deserved it, and she needed to get it out. She slapped me hard across my left cheek.

"How can you stand there?" she shouted. "I'm all she's got. *Do you understand that?*" She struck me again, but this time with her left hand, as if all of her wanted to get in on the act.

I went to hold her, but she shoved me back with both hands and stumbled out of Jenny's room. I gave her a minute then found her sitting at the end of her dock, much like I'd found her sitting at the end of my dock. The late afternoon sun softened the weathered planks and cast an orange glow on the port side of her Grady-White. *What type of woman owns a Grady and wears a tight black dress?* Her shoulders moved up and down twice in slow motion. A great white heron, perched on the edge of her lawn, seemed to consider the scene and took a tentative step away. Good instincts.

"I'm sorry," she said but didn't look at me. "I shouldn't have done that. I don't even know you."

True, but instead I limped out, "I'll do my best." I wish I'd said something else. She turned to face me. Her voice was strong, which surprised me.

"I don't know…Maybe she did run. But everything I know says she didn't. She's me. She's me twenty years ago. I know her like I know myself. She's not out contemplating. Who the hell has time for that? She didn't run. She has nowhere *to* run. You heard Detective McGlashan—someone was after Coleman. Jenny's been abducted, Jake. Someone took her and—"

"And what?"

"No one gives a damn." She turned, but not before I saw the tears. "I'm all she's got."

Her closing statement came out like the last wisp of air from a birthday balloon long after the party was over.

CHAPTER 7

I left Susan on her dock and headed to Fish Head to meet Morgan.

The only semblance of outside walls were rolled-up crinkled plastic that in all likelihood hadn't been let down since the last northern blow in early March. Bright yellow-and-blue wooden booths ran against the side that faced the still waters of the marina. Leftover crayon drawings from the spring-break migration still littered the inside wall that separated the kitchen from the dining area. The humidity had curled the edges of the paper and dulled the once vibrant artwork of children. I grabbed a high stool next to Morgan and ordered a beer. No sign of Aussie. I drank a third of the longneck before I spoke.

"The detective is treating Jenny like a habitual runaway who's likely to show up. I don't—"

"Tossed her fifteen feet, believe that?" Morgan stared ahead at a dirty slushy machine that swirled green goo.

"Who?"

"Lady. Happened around three weeks ago. She and her husband were down visiting friends for a week. They went to view the sunset two blocks away while their hosts stayed behind and grilled fish. On their way back, a car hit them both. Tossed her into the struts of the bridge at Big Carlos Pass."

"You know them?" It came out in an accusatory tone. I shouldn't have asked, but he got me sometimes. The man was capable of mourning a farmer's natural death in China and often did. My phone vibrated in my pocket.

"We know them all," he replied. I wanted to reach for my phone but instead said, "Tell me."

"That's it. Took both of them to the hospital, where they realized she wasn't going to see sunrise. The staff wheeled their gurneys next to each other so they could hold hands one more time. They held hands at the sunset then held hands thirty minutes later on gurneys. Last sunset. Lights out." He turned and glanced at me for the first time since I'd arrived. "What did you learn about Jenny?" It wasn't unusual for him to recover quickly from his self-induced sympathetic state.

"You okay?"

"Jenny."

"She's gone and—"

"You need to find her."

"I'm aware of that," I said. "But—"

"Death is an opportunist who rides our collar every day. Get your phone. You're dying too."

"You're back that fast?" I reached into my pocket. I also decided I'd stick to T-shirts. No collars.

"Just took a moment."

It was a text from McGlashan. God bless him. I had texted him a question before I had even reached my truck after I'd left Susan's. I wanted to double back on a comment he'd made. I also wanted to see what type of team player he really was. If he ignored my text, as he had every right to, then my investigation would be that much more difficult. In response to my text, he provided an address on Susan's street. "I've got to go," I told Morgan. "I need to talk to someone who may have been the last known person to see Jenny. Catch you back at the condo." I drained my beer and walked out, leaving Morgan contemplating the green slushy machine. Marmalade's "Reflections of My Life," like a melodic omniscient observer to all below, flowed out of the pitted corner-ceiling speakers tucked behind the ends of the rolled-up plastic curtains.

The house was three down from Susan's. As I started my second series of raps on the sun-drenched door, it swung open. An advanced-middle-aged lady blocked my path, even though a light breeze would have swept her away. She had butch blond hair and silver earrings that dropped below the jagged ends of her strands. She gave me a glare and said, "My trees don't need trimming." An osprey screamed.

"I'm not here to—"

"Bushes are fine."

"I'm looking for the—"

"I already got me someone to do the yard. I appreciate your time." She started to close the door.

"—girl you told the police you saw walking with—"

"What did you say your name was?"

"I didn't."

"Why not? Your mother never teach you manners?"

"Jake Travis."

"See, you can do it. You law, Jake?"

"No, ma'am. Friend of the family."

"'Cause I told that man with the shoulder that looks likes it wants to fall right off everything I saw. I never spoke to her, just saw her skipping down the street that day. I was out with Happy—he's my dog. He's inside eating right now, or he'd be all over you, but you don't need to worry. I'll tell you, though...I gotta keep an eye on him. Got one osprey that tracks him every time he's out, and I'm afraid Happy might just go airborne one day. You see them birds flying with fish in their claws? Can you imagine seeing one with a dog? Lord, what a sight. Plus they screech all day and night. You can barely..."

A talker. God in heaven, I can't tolerate talkers. A year ago, I would have said I hate talkers, but Kathleen's been counseling me on how not to see everything in extremes. How not go through life like a sixteen-pound bowling ball smashing social gutter guards.

"My cat, Pamela—she's around here somewhere. Picked her up at the humane society. They got a day in and day out listed for all the animals." She dialed up her volume and leaned into me. "You believe that? Day out is when they euthanize them. I never thought of dying in those words. I was saying about those birds—"

Enough.

"I'm sorry. Your name?"

"I said, 'Those hawks give me a headache.' How do you think his shoulder got like that?"

"I didn't get your name."

"Never gave it to you. What is this, the first day for your new brain?"

I blew my breath out, took a step back, and put both my palms up. "Help me."

"What?"

"Help me find this girl."

She was quiet for a moment. Maybe there is a supreme power. "Sure. Sure, Jake Travis. I can do that. What are you standing outside for?" She extended her hand. "Patricia Wilkinson." I stepped over her threshold, and she led me in with a crushing handshake. "You go ahead and call me Patty. All my deceased husband's friends do. They're the only men in my life anymore. Besides, I never made a very good Patricia."

Two minutes, and a few thousand words later, I drained the last half of a beer Patty had popped on me. I sat on her lanai on a flowered vinyl couch that was under a picture of J. R. Ewing. She burned more calories talking than I did running, but I found myself strangely enjoying her company.

Don't think I'm softening down here; I wanted out of her house as soon as possible. I desired to see—and hear—as little of her as possible during my remaining days.

But I liked her.

I placed the bottle on a coaster next to a pink-porcelain crocodile ashtray that looked as if it had handled decades of smokes and said, "You noticed that Jenny walked with purpose."

"That's right." I waited, but no more words spilled forth. I think Patty had run the deck on the English branch of the Proto-Germanic languages.

"What exactly does that look like?"

Patty leaned in, and her earrings, like giant pendulums, followed a split second behind her head. "Like I said, I saw her leave the house and head down the street, toward the Laundromat. Told Funny Shoulder that she seemed in a hurry. No purse or nothing. I'd say that was with purpose."

"Anything else that convinced you she had purpose?"

"Yup."

"What?"

"Her feet."

Chatty Patty had suddenly gone underground on me. "What about her feet, Patty?"

"She didn't have on no shoes."

Patty Wilkinson took a sip of her bourbon on the rocks and shifted Happy from one knee to another. Happy's eyes fluttered open at the minor disruption then returned to dreamland.

"Did you tell that to Detective McGlashan?"

"No." She drained her glass and plopped it down on a side table but left her eyes and hand on it. She fondled the empty glass. "He, if you ask me—you know…" She brought her eyes up to mine. "You younger guys like your beer, but you'll come around to the real stuff one day. Trust me—we all take that road. Like I was saying, he didn't really seem all that interested. Know what I mean? Let me ask you something, Jake. What do you think the chances are of *any* woman walking barefoot on those damn shells that litter this street unless she thought it was just a quick trip or she was in a big-time hurry?"

I didn't bother to tell her I'd been down that road. "I imagine slim to—"

"Mr. Jake, there's nothing to imagine here. That girl was a scootin', and I'll tell you something else too."

I waited, but she was done. Patty Wilkinson displayed proficiency in both silence and noise. I kick-started her. "What might that be?"

"Wherever she is?"

"Yes?"

"She got nothin' on her feet."

CHAPTER 8

Jenny

*R*eally? *I wound up with Angie for a mom, and my dad—the only smile the Almighty ever threw my way—is corralled with 4,129 tick-infested deer and replaced with a pair of exposed armpits with a Hostess Twinkie for a brain. And then,* she thought, *I reach the promised land only to be attacked by a whacko with an aversion to sunscreen. And now I'm trapped in this horse shed with no shoes. All I wanted was to finally enjoy my youth, and now I've got to grow up fast. Warp speed, girl.*

She glanced around for the fifty-thousandth time, but nothing had changed. A single-car garage. Old. A solitary bulb hanging from the rafters by a black wire the thickness of a pencil. The doors hinged on the side and swung out. Green picnic bench seats, eight feet in length, were stacked one atop another. They'd been painted, by Jenny's estimate, at least three times. When she did sit, she sat on a white Adirondack chair with a broad armrest painted green to match the picnic table benches. Most of the time, she paced. It was five steps before she hit the grill with no propane tank and was forced to turn toward the door. She'd done five gazillion round trips.

Above her was a rowboat suspended by an old ski rope. Jenny had climbed on top of the green benches to peer inside the aluminum boat. Nothing but old life jackets that held a decade of dust, mouse turds, and a once-white life preserver cushion with a faded blue anchor design on one side and diagrams for tying nautical knots on the other. She didn't find any of it particularly disgusting. After Boone walked in on her when she was in the shower with his stiff prick that looked like a celery stalk with a swollen mushroom cap on top, then showed his grocery-bag ass on the way out, there wasn't much the world could serve up to gross Jenny out. A workout mat with two clean sheets abutted one wall and served as her bed. Three bamboo fishing poles that practically ran the length of the garage hung from hooks. Jenny tried not to look at them because when she did it made her miss her father. Not that he, as far as she knew, ever had a bamboo pole, but that didn't matter. He would know about them and tell her how to use them.

"Hey, bozo," she yelled. "I got to pee. You hear me?"

Bozo only came every four hours. Or was it three? No clue. He wore a green facemask, like the guys she went skiing with at Mad River Mountain, west of Columbus. But those guys were her age and dug the retro look. Her bozo never spoke, just led her to an outhouse with a Liberty Bell knocker on the outside, red shag carpet on the inside, and a black-and-white picture of the TV cast of *M*A*S*H* on a wall. There—in an outhouse in Florida—stood the final bastion of the seventies.

The only other structure on the property was a tin-roofed, colorless, single-story home with a front porch. One corner was a solid foot higher than the opposite end. A few trees with blankets of Spanish moss, a blue minivan on a gravel lot, and an entire landscape of nothing completed the canvas. Jenny didn't know Florida could be so empty. They certainly kept that out of the magazines, didn't they?

Not that she was supposed to see any of it.

"Keep that hood on at all times, girl," Green Mask had told her the first time he'd come to take her to the outhouse. He had placed a burlap sack over her head while they were still in the garage. It smelled like the chicken incubator in Mrs. Sobisky's first-grade class. That was when Jenny discovered she didn't like cute things if they smelled. He led her out of the garage and to the outhouse.

"You put it back on before you come out, or I'll kill you. Understand?" He closed the outhouse door.

"Sure," Jenny had replied. She dropped the sack down the hole and did her business. She stepped out of the outhouse and batted her eyes at the sun.

"Kill me."

He had not.

Instead, he had inflated the atmosphere with enough air to launch a hot air balloon, jerked her right arm, and yanked her back into the garage. After that, he never covered her head, but it didn't matter. Jenny never imagined a place so perfectly synchronized—flat and meaningless.

Her stomach rumbled. Bozo brought food three times a day, and the final time was approaching. He always served the same questions, and she always smacked back the same answers:

"Where's the money? What did he tell you?"

"I don't know. I already told you."

Jenny surveyed the garage. *There's got to be something*, she thought. *After all, I did Glow Boy with a stick.* But she'd already searched the garage and found nothing to use as a weapon. An ancient refrigerator with a pull-down handle and a monotone hum held a case of bottled water. She opened the refrigerator to get a water she didn't need. She contemplated the bottles for a moment then placed three of them in the freezer. She climbed up to the rowboat, tore the straps off the boat cushion, and put them in the pockets of her shorts.

She sat. She paced.

She sat again in the chair and fingered her light blue T-shirt. Still somewhat clean, but how many days would she have to wear it? She leaned back and closed her eyes. Her hands twitched. No phone. She hadn't gone a day without her iPhone since never.

She listened to Snow Patrol's "Run" in her head.

She performed her mental chants: *I'm going to watch a sunset on the beach. I'm going to blaze out of this place. I'm going to wring life until it begs me to stop.*

She did push-ups on the floor. Crunches on the exercise mat. She paced. She sat.

I can't believe, she thought, *that I walked out of Aunt Susan's house—oops, forgot she doesn't like that "aunt" stuff, probably reminds her that she's related to my mom—walked out of Susan's house without my phone or shoes. Ouch. But he said it was urgent, and what was he doing there in the first place?*

Jerk.

CHAPTER 9

I survived the Chatty Patty show and headed to the Laundromat at the end of her street. If Jenny had dashed out to meet someone, and that someone had abducted her in a car, he—or she—most likely would have pulled into the Laundromat parking lot. I decided to drop anchor, throw a line in, and see if I got any bites.

It was vacant, and a lone dryer hummed a dissonant tone. A corner-ceiling TV was turned off. A fan whipped at high speed and threatened to lift the roof off. I claimed a metal chair and took out the picture of Jenny that Susan had given me. Senior portrait. Confident. Hair the color of sea oats at sunset. The flawless, silky cream skin of the young. Hazel eyes that looked like she'd grown up fast. Kathleen had hazel eyes; on different days, even different times of the same day, they changed colors, as if to foil me so that I could not answer even the simplest of questions; what color are her eyes?

A guy in a Badgers T-shirt came in. I flashed him the picture, and he said he didn't recognize the girl and asked if she was my girlfriend or daughter. A lady with flabby arms who wore a Caribbean bluish-green sleeveless top was next. She went to the dryer, and no matter how I smiled or what I said, she was petrified of me. I felt bad for spoiling that special moment that was reserved for when she folded her clean, warm clothes.

I endured for an hour and talked to three other people. I received an offer for drinks, one to share a toke, and unsolicited advice. "Put her on the board," said the thin man, who put his wash in with one hand while he held his beer with the other. "You'd be surprised. Everyone who comes in here looks at that thing. Anyone saw her, they'll let you know. We're a..." He paused to drain the rest of his beer in one act. "...pretty tight group around here." He tossed the bottle into a green tin trash can, and it rattled off the inside.

I got Jenny's picture out of my shirt pocket and found a pen under a table. I removed from the board someone's faded notice that they did yard work, trimmed trees, and painted. References upon request. "Request" was spelled with a "g." I turned the soiled paper over and scribbled on the back, "If anyone has seen this girl, Jenny Spencer, please call me. She's missing and in possible danger."

I took a picture of the picture with my cell.

I tacked Jenny's picture onto the bulletin board next to a picture of "Sidney," a calico cat that was AWOL. "Call Avery. Fifty dollars to whoever finds her." Smiley faces in each corner. Heavy-stock paper. Strips of cut paper with a phone number hung at the bottom of the notice. A lot of pets in Florida are named Sidney; it's a variation of Disney.

I left Jenny hanging next to Sidney and walked out the door. I made a mental note that when I found her, I would get her picture off the board. I couldn't take the chance that she would ever go in that Laundromat and see herself like that.

And if I failed? Someone like me would eventually come along, turn my paper over to compose their own notice, see that it was used on both sides, and float Jenny Spencer into the green tin trash can.

At the condo, I ignored the indolent elevator and took nine fights of steps two at a time. Morgan sat cross-legged on a chair on the screened balcony. He faced a wall of black. At night, on the Gulf, there is nothing.

"Don't tell me that you and fire engine lady didn't ignite," I said as I dropped into a chair behind a round glass table. I gently pushed the table away to allow myself more room.

"Teresa had to leave for a couple days. Nothing she could do about it. I told her I'd be back. Teresa Vittjen. It's good karma when a woman matches her name. How's the Jenny hunt coming?"

"Fade into You," floated out of Morgan's portable speakers. It's a song that should never see the day; it belongs to the night and the water. I thought of Kathleen's theory that the experience one has reading a book may be enhanced by one's environment while reading. Music certainly affects us that way.

"No quick scores," I said. "I don't want to know the statistics for lost people who are eventually found alive if not located within the first twenty-four or forty-eight hours. Every tick of the clock, and her chances diminish."

"Every beat of the second hand, and she's closer to freedom."

"That's what I meant."

"What's next?" A cup of tea sat on the glass table, and the faint aroma of whiskey laced the air. The whiskey wasn't in the essentials box, so I assumed he'd hit the liquor store at Santini Plaza after Fish Head.

"I need more information on the Coleman clan, but I don't want to leave Jenny."

"What makes you think she's here?"

"She's here. At the twenty-four-hour Laundromat, next to Sidney, listening to the ospreys and parrots."

"Monk parakeets," Morgan said, "also known as Quaker parrots. They're not indigenous to the United States but were brought here as pets more than fifty years ago and released into the wild." He took a sip of his tea. "They're common in Florida but are hardy little creatures. Supposedly even Chicago has colonies of them. Who's Sidney?"

"A cat."

He let that go.

I went to the kitchen, poured a few shots of Maker's Mark into a tumbler, and dropped in two cubes. I usually add a little Coke, but we didn't have any. A pity. I returned to the patio, and we sat in silence. When Garrett and I are together, we fill the air with words. Morgan and I can—and often do—fill it with silence.

I'd never seen Jenny, never heard her voice, never touched her hand. I only knew her aunt, Susan, from a brief encounter at her bar and a dinner we shared afterward. Those brief moments held contempt for any dictum that stated time is a critical ingredient to friendship. Out of seven billion people, I—the only one who really knows what the hell is going on—had been the one to put Jenny on the bulletin board. In many ways, I wish I hadn't. I'd made her my responsibility. No matter the outcome, I'd be the one who took her down from that board. I would not let that be a tragic moment. It's not that I wanted to win; I have a strong aversion to failure.

I went inside and called Susan. After a brief conversation, I secured an airline ticket on my iPad. I went to tell Morgan, but he'd gone to bed. I sat on the porch until my thoughts dried up—an event that coincided with the last drop of bourbon in my tumbler. I left a note on the kitchen counter.

CHAPTER 10

The thump of the 737's tires jolted me from a dream in which Larry Hagman was frantically pacing and protesting, "Who shot me? Who shot me?" What was his problem? Even my alarm clock—*especially* my alarm clock—Tinker Bell, knows that Bing Crosby's daughter shot Peter Pan's little boy.

After listening to Susan describe Jenny's dysfunctional family, I doubted Jenny would ever again ford the Ohio River. But I wanted to learn more about the Colemans. Despite McGlashan's assertion, they were physically too close to Jenny not to have *some* connection.

I also had a score to settle.

Even though I had preferred customer checkout for a rental car, I still had to wait as a lady in front of me wearing a cropped jean jacket lobbied for a convertible. They were out. She finally surrendered when the equally frustrated employee started answering her whining pleas in Spanish. She huffed away dragging a clacking suitcase with a busted wheel. The luggage tag read, "I come with baggage." I snatched my keys to my rental, which was billed as full-size. My legs practically stuck through the front grille. An hour later, as the four-lane road sculptured down to two, I entered Wayne National Forest in Southeast Ohio. As I wound my way through the hills, every corner brought another picture. I also saw more highway patrol cars in a ten-mile stretch than I'd seen in Florida over the past year.

At the edge of Greenwood, a river snaked alongside the road, and a man with a pickup truck had pulled off by the bank and set up shop for the day. Hand-carved wooden bears and birds on stumps littered the ground around his pickup. I stopped. We chatted. I moved on. A half-mile closer to town a tall sign that read THE SANDWICH SHOP towered over barren pavement, weeds, and trash. Small towns don't regenerate. I passed a community swimming pool, forked left across from a gas station with a produce stand on its lot, and stopped at a red light that hadn't had a real job in years. Only one vehicle came from either side, and it went straight through. Snoopy hung from the rearview mirror, and the driver, in the middle of the intersection, spat a wad out his open window. Two more turns, and what passed as the town was well behind me.

A man was outside when my car crunched up the gravel driveway.

"What do you want?" he demanded before I shut my door.

He wore a sleeveless Browns T-shirt that, like the Browns, had peaked long ago. He was hunched over a Dodge Charger that was parked off to the side of a detached three-car garage. All three garage doors were open, and a dusty, blue, plastic canvas covered the top of a wooden boat. The trailer tongue was in the dirt. Whoever had backed it in was lazy. A gutter, with enough foliage in it that it needed a weed whacker, hung a foot below the roofline. No downspout. To my right was a house built into the side of a hill. The ground was a mixture of dirt and matted grass that rarely received the sun's direct rays. I was at the low end of the AM dial.

He backed off from the Charger as I approached.

I asked, "Boone?"

"What's it to you?"

"I'm looking for Jenny Spencer."

"Who the hell are you?"

Some people do patience. They do it well and use it as an effective tool to meet their objectives. They insist you get more bees with honey. Maybe so, but my circuit board isn't wired that way.

I marched straight into him and declared, "You walked in on her." He dropped his right arm to his side, his fist tightened around a wrench.

"You got no—"

While he focused on my arms and upper body, my right foot went through his stomach as the tail of his words came through his lips. He doubled over on his knee, and I was behind him. I placed my right arm around his neck, brought my left hand up, and put him in a rear naked chokehold. My mouth was inches from his left ear. He smelled. Tobacco. Sweat. Skin that hadn't been showered in a month of Sundays.

"I know you, Boone." I eased up on the pressure; I didn't want him to pass out. "Where is she?" He struggled to get oxygen into his lungs. "I'm waiting."

"My son...be home soon."

"He's not yours—he's Angie's. God won't let a man like you reproduce. It's not in the best interest of humanity. Do you know where Jenny is?" I let up on the pressure.

"No," he managed to grunt out. "She took off a week ago to Florida to live with Angie's sister. She never even told us. We haven't heard from her since. Cops called, said she ran south, did a number on some guy, and now she's missing again."

I squeezed.

"That's all I know."

"Where's Angie?"

"At work."

"While you dick around with a worthless set of wheels. You a man?"

"What?"

"Are you a man, Boone?"

"The hell you—"

"Say, no, Boone. Say, 'I am not a man.'" I pressed my mouth up against his right ear. "I'm going to leave your little soldier in the front seat of that Charger. That's what you get for parading it in front of her while she was in the shower. You want that?"

"I don't know what—"

"Boone, Boone, Boone." I shot whispers like miniature cannon shots in his ear. "You've got less than thirty seconds of manhood left unless you tell me the truth. Billy Ray Coleman."

"What about him?"

I squeezed. For all I knew, he was telling the truth. But I needed the exercise. I moved my mouth to his left ear. "I'm over here now, Boone. Tell me what you know."

"He came out of the oven too early. He's not right."

I squeezed harder. "You told the cops you didn't know him."

"Let me go, and I..." He kicked out his legs.

I slammed him onto the concrete dirt and fell on top of him, still gripping him in the chokehold. His face flopped so his right cheek was up. McGlashan had told me Boone and Angie had denied knowing the Colemans. My mouth was over his eye. "Tell me about him."

"Just heard of him—that's all."

"You're lying."

"Never met him."

I paused, and Boone picked up on my hesitation. "Let me up," he said. "I told you everything I know."

"Fine. Let's converse." I released my hold and stood. He rose and teetered away from me. When he did, my left foot sank into his stomach and punched his breath out of him. It was a light kick. I needed him to maintain cognitive conversational abilities. He reacquainted himself with the ground and shot me a look.

"What the hell?" he gasped.

"I changed my mind. I'd rather kick you senseless than hear your lies." I took a step so that I was directly over him. I squatted on my knees. "I'm your last friend in the world, Boone. Talk to me, and I'll let you go back to your asswipe life. But don't make me earn it piecemeal."

He got to his knees but rose no further. He glanced up at me as if seeing me for the first time. A ray of sun managed to split the trees and sear his eyes. He squinted and tilted his head to the side. I didn't know if he was holding back, but his admission of some knowledge of Billy Ray, coupled with his apparent denial of such knowledge to the local sheriff, reeked of dishonesty.

I asked, "She ever know him?"

"Who?"

"I won't ask again, Boone. I can*not* emphasize that enough."

He blew his breath out, brought his hand up, and rubbed his neck. I stood and took a step back. He cut a glance at his Dodge Charger then at me. Priority time. "Not Billy Ray," he said. He hesitated then started back up. "She spent a day with his brother Zach, but she never knew nothing 'bout Zach's family. Orry brought a friend on the old boat one day last summer, and that guy brought along Zach. I don't think they even saw much of each other again. Orry don't even know him. Don't run with him, really. But Zach told Orry—they was talking, you know—that he had one and a half brothers. Older brother,

Randall, and Billy Ray, who was never right. That's the one she did in on the beach."

"Jenny ever see any of the other Colemans?"

"No. Not that I know."

"She ever mention Zach?"

"I told you—"

"Tell me again."

"No. Far as I know, she never saw him or talked to him again. But she would know him from that day on the boat. They chatted, got along real fine. He was a good-lookin' kid. I'm gonna stand. You gonna kick me again?"

"Let's find out."

He eyed me and rose slowly, taking a step back as he did. I was getting closer to finding Jenny. Paranoids don't tolerate coincidences. There had to be some connections between Jenny's disappearance and the remaining Colemans. "You told the sheriff you didn't know any Colemans."

Boone nodded like we were good friends. "I was protecting my family."

I didn't trust myself to respond to that. "If I find out you've lied or are holding back, I'll return. Do you understand that, Boone?"

"I got friends, and—"

"You'll be on your back under your car one quiet morning listening to the birds chirp. You'll feel my hand on your ankle. Now is there anything else I should know?"

He cleared his throat and dropped his eyes. A squirrel with a nut the size of its head scurried behind him and rustled last fall's leaves that still lay on the ground.

I asked, "Yes?"

"I think..." He coughed. "I think they, the Coleman brothers, are into chemistry, big time, if you know what I mean. That's just what I heard."

"Keep talking."

"That's it, man. Really. You pick stuff up, listening in the bars around town. What happened to her? Sheriff said she killed Billy Ray in self-defense, and then the Florida law called and said she just plain vanished. You think them other Colemans went after her?"

I gave him my card. "I'm touched. You suspect anything, you give me a call."

"Why do you care?"

"You don't get questions. For your sake, I hope I find her fast. Otherwise, I will bury you in that shower stall in the name of common justice. I believe I get a tax deduction if I waste you."

He opened his mouth as if to speak then shut it.

I left Boone motionless by his Charger and stuffed myself into the rental car. I made one stop in town and decided that Greenwood was a fine place for what I was doing—leaving.

McGlashan had texted me the Colemans' home address in response to my text to him the previous night. He had also said the Hocking County Sheriff's office had paid the Colemans a visit yesterday, but no one was home. I wanted to take a look for myself. I'd just brought up directions on my phone when Kathleen called.

"Why aren't you in the seat next to me?" I answered and took a bite out of an apple. I had bought it from a man in a plaid shirt at the produce stand. It was a challenge eating the apple, placing her on speaker, and navigating back to the map app. At least I wasn't texting.

"Look hard—I'm there beside you," she said. "Where are we?"

"Ohio."

"Ohio?"

"Iroquois word. It's south of Canada."

"Not much isn't. You take a wrong turn going over the bridge?"

I took another bite of the Royal Gala. "I need to look for some people who were the last to see Jenny and make certain she didn't double back."

"Is it possible she's there—in Iroquois country?"

"Unlikely. I'm only giving it a day."

"And then?"

"Good-bye, Columbus."

"Think positive."

"Hello, Kathleen?"

"I like that better."

I lowered my window and tossed the core into the ditch. The roar of the road invaded the car and was sucked out just as quickly when I raised the glass.

"How's Maugham?"

"Sleepy, but good."

"That's my recollection as well."

"You've read it?"

"'The fact that a great many people believe something is no guarantee of its truth.' Book's worth it for that alone."

An SUV blowing smoke and doing ten was suddenly in front of me. My right turn onto the Colemans' driveway was a short distance ahead. I decided to settle behind the SUV instead of punching the pedal to pass on a two-lane road in a car that had less horsepower than Fred Flintstone's. "Tell me about you," I said.

"Sophia and I are painting my library."

"And Sophia?"

"She hasn't displayed any inclination to hunt you down with a butcher's knife, if that's what you're asking. I think she's relieved to be out of the marriage."

Sophia Escobar and Kathleen had become close friends two minutes after they'd met. That was about a week before I—FBI Special Agent Natalie Binelli did the official act—put Sophia's husband, Raydel, behind bars. He was in possession of the Cold War letter and was leveraging it as blackmail to reduce his IRS bill. He also was an unwilling participant in human trafficking. The "unwilling" part knocked a few years off his sentence.

I inquired, "Do you have any clothes on right now?"

"I thought we were discussing Sophia."

"Does *she* have any clothes on right now?"

"Dream on."

"Just curious."

"Are you interested in my life," she asked, "or just my body?"

"You think a man is capable of making that distinction? But if it makes you feel better, tell me about your life."

"Well, since you're so genuinely interested, we decided not to do an accent wall. I think that phase will pass and—"

"Kathleen?" I was at the Colemans' drive, and there was a problem.

"I was—"

"I got company. Time to punch the clock."

"You know, don't you, that *my* interest in *you* is purely physical?"

"I like where this is going, so keep that thought." I disconnected and pulled off to the side of the driveway. The Colemans' house was set back about a hundred yards.

I don't know how many sheriff's and police cars Hocking County, Ohio, fielded, but I'd bet Kathleen's first edition of *The Razor's Edge* that every one was parked on the Colemans' property. And if I was wrong?

Not my book.

CHAPTER 11

I continued up the dirt-gravel drive, and fifty feet from the house, a man with a gun stopped me. He had a badge as well, but a badge doesn't rattle my attention like a six-shooter does. I hit the button again, and my window obeyed. I like things like that.

"You a friend of the Colemans?" he demanded. He looked as if his clothes had been pressed while he was still in them. His hair wouldn't ripple in a typhoon; not a crease marred his uniform, and his sunglasses covered the top half of his head. He had enough communications gear on his left shoulder to coordinate a NASA launch. A tag on his uniform said, "Kevin Trimble."

"I'm being retained to look for a girl, Jenny Spencer, and—"

"May I see your driver's license, please?"

I handed it over to Kevin, along with my Florida PI license. He separated them like playing cards and studied them in his left hand. His right hand remained free and in the vicinity of his gun.

"What's your business here?"

"I've been retained by the family of Ms. Spencer to try to locate her. She was attacked a few nights ago by one of—"

"We're fully aware of what happened to Ms. Spencer." He handed back my PI license but not my driver's license. "Why are you here?"

67

"I wanted to take a look around and see if there's anything that would help me locate her. What brings the cavalry out? Just get a warrant?"

"You don't think we're competent in that area?"

"Pardon?"

"You don't think we're capable of searching the premises? I think we can do our job better without civilians, Jake."

"I'm not doubting your competence, Kevin. I would just—"

"That's Officer Trimble to you."

"And that's *Mis*ter Travis to you."

Trimble and I did a few rounds of staring, and then he said. "Stay here." He walked off with my driver's license. Like I was going to skip town without it.

I got out of the car and leaned against the side. I texted McGlashan that the cavalry was camped outside of the Colemans' and inquired if he could put in a good word. I pondered where to rest my head that night, as my flight was late tomorrow morning. I debated whether to return to the airport and grab one of the on-site hotels or take a cabin in the nearby woods. Southeast Ohio was where the final cube of ice during the last ice age, around twenty thousand years ago, had finally succumbed to the sun and deposited foliage from Canada. Global warming isn't a bad initiative around here—twenty thousand years on the global clock was three seconds ago. Maybe two. As far as an airport hotel room, it would have free chocolate chip cookies in the lobby and go downhill from there. I could already taste it. Smell it. That was close enough for me.

Fifteen minutes later, another man with a gun marched toward me. He halted about four feet away. "Mr. Travis?" He held my license, or what I assumed was mine, in his left hand.

"Yes."

My new visitor was the Pillsbury Doughboy with a badge. He looked as if he finished off a six-pack every night and thought covering his habit with a uniform would add credibility to his lifestyle. His reflective sunglasses mirrored the green hills and blue sky. His ears were beet red, as if he and Rudolph shared the same gene pool. No nametag.

"I'm the sheriff in charge here. I got a call from a sheriff's detective in Florida that you're an ex vet and that I'm to share with you what we got."

Ex vet? Isn't a veteran already an "ex?" But at least McGlashan had come through for me, and hopefully Glow Ears would let me play. "Thank you, sir." I said. "I'd be most appreciative of any information you have." You have no idea how physically painful it is for me to talk in that manner.

"I don't."

"Don't what?"

"Have any information I'm going to share with you." He handed back my license.

"You're not going to play any reindeer games with me?"

"What?"

"Help me out here? Do what's in the best interest of finding a missing girl?"

"You need to leave now, *Jake.* We're conducting an investigation on the property, and it's closed to intruders." He flashed me a fake smile and followed it with, "Have a nice day." His right hand rested on his service revolver.

"Will you reconsider having me assist you? After all, this will always be the first time we meet—our country song."

"Leave."

"Perhaps confer with Dasher and—"

"Get the hell out of my county, son." He fingered his gun.

"When the elves unionize, Sheriff," I said as I twisted into my car, "you'll feel the power of the little people." I threw Flintstone's car into reverse.

I know. Childish. Insipid. It didn't even make the grade as a sophomoric retort, but he got to me. My chain gets yanked when people dislike me before I realize I dislike them.

It was a little more than a half hour drive back into Greenwood. I should have asked Boone the name of the Orry's friend who'd brought Zach with him on the boat last summer, but I didn't think that would lead anywhere. No excuse, though. I stopped at an outdoor store that doubled as a munitions depot. It had a more extensive firearm and knife selection than anything I'd seen, *in aggregate*, during five years with the US Army. No foreign armed force (Kent State, 1970, was internal) had invaded Ohio since Morgan's raid in 1863. But by gum, these Buckeyes were ready for the next son of a bitch to set foot on their land. I selected what I needed for the night and received directions to a campground. I hit a grocery store and a liquor store and killed time at a bar, where I was instantly recognized as someone no one knew. I drove back out to the Colemans'.

Rudolph and the herd had pulled out. I approached the property from the back side and hiked through a few hundred yards of dying ash trees before I arrived at the house and the pole barn. A yellow police tape laced the barn as well as the house. A gray cat didn't seem to mind as it sulked around the partially open sliding door. I wondered how many dead geckos Hadley III would have for me when I returned.

The barn was clean. I assumed the sheriff had confiscated any equipment used in the clandestine chemistry trade. Stainless steel shelves and stained tables were all that remained from a lab that likely produced methamphetamine, commonly referred to as meth. Facemasks littered the floor. I strolled behind the barn but found nothing except dead grass in the circular pattern of barrel bottoms. The house was next. It was locked. I busted the window on the back door. I searched the rooms.

The only items I found of mild interest were several brochures in a kitchen drawer beneath the silverware tray. I stashed the brochures in my pocket. As for the silverware, no one had bothered to keep the forks, spoons, and knifes separate from one another.

Even though it was late, it was still light. I was a thousand miles north of home, and the curvature of the earth afforded me over an hour more of daylight, split evenly at both ends. I headed south on Route 33 and took a right at the Shell station, like the man with the lip ring at the munitions depot had instructed. I navigated cautiously, as he had warned, around the boulder that encroached upon the road and narrowed it to a nasty one-lane turn. A stoic crooked cross struggled to clear a clump of Queen Anne's lace that swayed in the breeze; someone hadn't paid attention. I pulled into a deserted campground. Lip Ring had said the owners of Camp Tecumseh didn't have the funding to operate the camp for a full summer, and it wouldn't be used until next week.

Moses had planted the pine trees. A small pond with one shoreline curved like a woman's hip centered the camp. Kayaks rested on its muddy bank. A dozen cabins circled the pond and battled the trees for airspace. A solitary male mallard paddled across the glassy water, and its wake followed without choice. My eyes are drawn to displaced water. I understand the physics, yet it retains a magical fascination to me. A dirt road disappeared higher into the wooded hills, where in the fading light I could still make out a lonely cabin peering between branches.

A truck in its third decade pulled up behind mine, and a man in his seventh got out and sauntered over to me. He wore a pair of jeans and a cream shirt, both twice the size they needed to be. He was a slight man and stood under the massive trees.

"Campground's closed," he said. The gentle float of his voice was incongruous with the implications of his words.

"I know," I said. "I'm only here for one night, and I heard this is a special place. Hoping I could just lay my mat in one of those cabins, if you don't mind."

"From around here?"

"Florida."

"Long way to camp for one night."

"It is."

"Where you off to in the morning?"

"Airport."

"Anybody joining you?"

"Just me."

"Take your pick. They're all empty."

"What about that one up there?" I pointed to the high cabin that overlooked the others.

"That's Wyandot. She's a good one. You can take your car up the road and park it there. Have a pleasant night." He started to turn toward his truck.

"Mind if I use a kayak in the morning?"

He turned around slowly. "Help yourself. But the pool's locked." He skipped a few beats then continued. "Careful if you jump the fence."

As he drove away, I made out the bumper sticker on his fender—EVERYTHING A MAN NEEDS: AN OLD PICKUP, A YOUNG WIFE, AND A MAP BACK TO KENTUCKY.

I navigated my car up the narrow path and parked by the cabin. As I sat on the deck, twilight softened night's arrival with the patience of a glider that took a mile to drop the last fifty feet. I poured some bourbon into a plastic cup. I unwrapped a cigar, smelled it, clipped the end, lit it, and took a deep drag. Those acts, coupled with the selection of the cigar, represented ninety percent of the enjoyment I receive from any cigar. The temperature went down with the sun, which rarely happens in Florida.

I swatted bugs all night.

At five thirty, a half hour before sunrise, seven million birds woke me.

I took a kayak out and did cartoon circles in the stagnant pond. I beached the kayak where I had found it, scaled the pool's fence, and stripped off my clothes. I dove in the unheated pool and nearly cryogenically froze my body. I did my forty-minute swim in thirty minutes.

I returned to the munitions depot and left Lip Ring the simple provisions: a mat, thin blanket, and pillow I had purchased for my one-night stay. He asked if I would like my money back. I said the gear was his. He told me to come back soon. I made two stops on my way out of town.

CHAPTER 12

I retrieved my truck at Southwest Florida International and headed to the Buccaneer Motel on the northern end of Fort Myers Beach. Several Buccaneer brochures in various stages of fading had been in the drawer—under the deranged silverware tray—in the Colemans' house. Perhaps they frequented the joint. It was worth a stop.

The one-story building was off the water and across from a closed oyster bar. The motel was likely built in the 1950s, but it was neat, clean, and recently painted. A few cars dotted the asphalt parking lot, where steam from a morning shower dissipated into the air. A pair of brightly painted metal chairs rested outside each room. The beach, bars, and restaurants were within a two-minute walk. The old gal had location going for her.

A woman's back was to me when I entered the sparse lobby and stepped onto the spotless linoleum. She turned as I approached the counter. "May I help you?" she asked.

She wore a soft white shirt. A loose string laced the top in lieu of buttons. Several layers of necklaces dropped low on her freckled chest and rested on the top of her breasts. I wanted to drop low on her freckled chest. Strawberry-blond hair sprouted freely on both sides of her face.

"Certainly." I already had my phone out. "I'm looking for a couple of guys I believe may have stayed here in the past."

Upon my request, McGlashan had texted me pictures of Randall and Zach Coleman that he had obtained from Rudolph. He also had shared with me that the Hocking County sheriff *had* just received a search warrant, and that was why I'd been blindsided by the posse at the Colemans'. I planned to flash the pictures around in hopes that someone would recognize them. McGlashan's degree of cooperation indicated to me that he had more pressing matters to pursue than chasing down a runaway teenager. If he were actively engaged in finding Jenny, he wouldn't be outsourcing his responsibilities.

"I'll pass," she replied. She hadn't even bothered to glance at a picture of a smiling Randall Coleman after he'd been arrested for DUI.

"You didn't even try."

"Nope." She shuffled some papers.

"How about if I give you a million dollars?"

She glanced up at me. She looked as if she belonged at a photo shoot for an album, back in the day. I wasn't of buying age when albums had their initial run, but I have a decent—high-triple-digit—vinyl collection. I like fondling my music and am especially desirous of back covers, or inside sleeves, on which a third party has written about the recording session. Such verbiage is referred to as "liner notes." The rear cover of Sinatra's *September of My Years* stirs the graves of English poets—*Of the bruising days. Of the roughed lips and bourbon times. Of chill winds, of forgotten ladies who ride in limousines.* I get rocked before the needle even scratches the record. I also prefer to hear the music the way it was originally heard. I play my swelling collection on a 250-pound 1961 floor-model maple Magnavox—*great voice* in Latin. The turntable has "Imperial Micromatic" written beside it and "Stereophonic High Fidelity" etched across the inside back. Kicks the living shit out of "iTunes."

She said, "Cash up front."

"A girl is missing, and I think this guy might be involved. I'd appreciate any help you could give me." I wondered what she would look like covered in whipped cream.

"What's your name?"

I extended my hand over the counter. "Jake Travis."

"Tuesday." Tuesday had soft hands.

I flashed her my phone again. "I have reason to believe this man might be involved in the abduction of a young girl, from this island, less than a week ago, and—"

"Does this have anything to do with Susan Blake's niece?"

"Do you know her?"

"Which one?"

"Either."

"Susan and I go way back. We served on the chamber committee for business owners for years."

"You're the owner?"

"This sick puppy is mine. Susan hire you?"

"More like a favor. We met a year ago, had dinner, got along, and now she needs help."

Tuesday leaned in across the counter. She smelled like warm vanilla, and my appetite surged. She held that pose for a few seconds then inquired, methodically, in half time, "Are you the guy who invited her to dinner, primed her for information, and then ditched her?"

"I don't know about 'ditched.' I left her standing—"

"Jake, right?" She tilted back away from me. What a sad world. "I don't know you, but I know one thing." She paused. I had no choice but to go in without armor.

"Go ahead."

"You walked away from Susan Blake. Congratulations. You're my new dumbest person in the world. And to think your vote counts as much as mine."

I wanted in the worst way to counterpunch, but sometimes you have to stand and take it.

Once the Susan connection was on the table, Tuesday called in the reserves. She allowed me to search the room that had been assigned to Billy Ray. It hadn't been booked to anyone else and was clean; the housekeeping log showed that it hadn't been serviced. Tuesday explained that meant the room, even though paid for, was never used. At my insistence, she summoned all her employees to stop by the Matanzas Bar and Grill so I could interview them. It was on the bay across from her sick puppy and just a long enough stroll to sweat my shirt. I knew the place well from my year on the beach.

I took a wooden stool at the mahogany bar that preserved old postcards of Florida under strata of shellac. That is where the past belongs—immobilized under transparent layers so we may see it but never touch it again. Black-and-white pictures of the damage from Hurricane Donna hung on the wall to my right. She was the last big one, a cat four in 1960, until Charley swung by in 2004. Grouper gave me a tuna salad on wheat toast and an iced tea. He wore a polo shirt with his restaurant's name and a spotless white apron folded down at the top and tied around his waist. His real name was Peter. But young Pete's first word had been cast from his lips while his father fished the piers of the canal behind their home. His mother's protests were never enough to overcome what the stars had ordained.

"What's the deal again?" he asked. He untied his apron, tossed it under the bar, and wrapped another clean one around his midsection. He picked up a glass and dried it with a towel.

"I'm camping out here while she calls her employees. They'll drop by within the hour. She wanted me to send a photo to their phones, but I insisted on a face-to-face. Only four, including Tuesday, rotate on the front desk." Grouper knew Tuesday and Susan as members of the local bar and restaurant association, and I had filled him in on Jenny's disappearance.

"She was okay with sending them here?"

"Why not?"

Grouper shrugged. "Nothing. I hope that girl surfaces. But she *is* eighteen. Maybe she just needs to hang with herself after what she went through."

"You know much about eighteen-year-old girls?"

"Nothing."

"Makes two of us. But as a breed, I don't think they're a solitary species." I changed tack. "What are you doing with Susan to the south and Tuesday to the north?"

He put down the glass and shrugged again. "Susan, underneath—she's got a bit of a nuclear streak. I just don't swing from that tree."

The man changed his apron five hundred times a day and operated one of the nicest waterfront places I'd ever been to. He sported two pierced ears and was president of Big Brothers Big Sisters of Southwest Florida. He reopened the organization after it had shuttered its doors and left five hundred children proof that no one gave a damn. He swung pretty effortlessly from tree to tree, but I didn't challenge him on that.

"And Tuesday?"

Grouper didn't have a chance to answer, as a girl blitzed me from my right like a heat-seeking missile. "Are you Mr. Travis? 'Cause I'm Allison, and Tuesday asked me to stop by, and it's my day off, so whatever it is, make it snappy." She popped her gum the split second her verbal attack ended. She took the stool next to me.

She wore a low-cut brown sundress and smelled of suntan oil and spearmint. Her thick jet-black hair was wrapped in cords that fell down the left side of her head and beyond her shoulders. Her clavicle looked like a hanger with skin and two balloons on it. She slid over onto the half of her stool that was next to me. She was the type who invades the space that separates strangers. I held my ground. Pleasure to do so. I gave her the background pitch and brought up the pictures on my phone. She hesitated at the picture of Zach.

"Curly's cute," Allison said, "but here's a flash for you: I've never seen those guys. I'm mostly part-time when someone calls in sick, like Daniel does about every day 'cause he can't handle a watered-down margarita on a full stomach, but Tuesday puts up with him 'cause he's been there, like, forever. I gotta go. Sorry I can't help you find…"

"Jenny."

"Right." She slid off her stool and touched me lightly on my right arm. "I was yanking your cord, not knowing her name and all. We're having a fire on the north beach tonight. Why don't you drop by?"

"You see them, or hear of them, I'd appreciate a call."

I gave Allison my card. She tilted her head and placed the card in the low front pocket of her sundress. Her bony right hip brushed against me on her way out the back door. Her essence hung around like humid air after a downpour.

An older lady with blue-and-green fingernails was next. "You can call me LeAnn," she said. She wore a force field of perfume. I scooted to the far edge of my stool in search of fresh air.

"I was at the flea market and don't take too kindly to having to drop by," she said, "but I'd do anything to help find Susan Blake's niece." The photo I showed her meant nothing to her. I checked her name off the list that Tuesday had scrawled on Buccaneer stationery.

"What's the deal with Tuesday?" I asked Grouper after LeAnn had left. "She's just across the street from you, and for my—"

"He's been waiting for you. Came in a second after your last one." He nodded down the bar, where a man sat with his feet on the bottom rung of his stool. His right knee bounced up and down, like he was drilling for oil. His sandals were on the floor under his stool, and his right hand caressed a half-full or half-empty—your choice—glass of amber liquid. I grabbed my iced tea, shifted four seats to my left, and settled next to the last name on the list. I'd been waiting for him. Tuesday told me he was the one who had checked in Billy Ray.

"Daniel?" I asked. His blue eyes looked younger than his face, which the sun already had started to tighten and crease.

"That's me."

"I understand you were at the front desk a few days ago when Billy Ray Coleman came around."

"Yup. Surprised he was here without his brothers."

"You know them?" I held up my phone with Zach Coleman's picture. He gave it a cursory glance.

"Yup." He took a sip of his beer.

"Tell me."

"Sure." His eyes seemed to bounce around, even though he was looking at me. He didn't speak.

"I was thinking *now*, Daniel."

"Oh, yeah, I got it. Well, that's Zach Coleman. Not a bad dude. If you're looking for someone, you know, who did something bad, and Tuesday said you were, I doubt it's him."

"Why do you say that?"

"'Cause he's a follower, know what I mean? Now his brother, Randall? That's the man. Know what I mean?"

"Enlighten me."

Daniel rolled for ten minutes, not that he had that much information, but the man couldn't talk in a straight line. The salient facts, however, finally surfaced. The Coleman boys had been in numerous times over the years for weeklong stays. Randall paid with cash. Always Randall. Always cash. Zach gawked at the girls, and the girls gawked back. Billy Ray spent time wandering the parking lot and beach when his brothers brought girls back to the room. They partied hard, but Randall always palmed Daniel a pair of twenties.

"Tuesday," he said, "wouldn't put up with rowdies, but they'd come down in March—what the hell did she expect? I know we ain't the Lani Kai, but we ain't Disneyland either, man. You gotta go north for that kiddie shit." I assumed he meant Walt Disney World, but I didn't make Daniel as one who'd squabble over geography or proper corporate names.

"Anything else you heard or might recall that would be beneficial to me?"

"Nope." He brought his right fist up to his chest and suppressed a beer belch. "They did say..." He paused as if he expected another burp, but it didn't come. "They did...that means I think heard Randall mention...no, it was Zach. Yeah, Zach said it. No way would Randall say it—he's too tight, you know? Randall runs like a river. All smooth like, but you never know what's around the bend, know what I mean? One moment you're enjoying the scenery, and the next you're in the fight of your life. You ever do any white water rafting?"

"What did Zach say?" A middle-aged woman with a pleasing figure in tight jeans strolled past us.

"God*damn*, you see that?"

"It's a wonderful world, Daniel. Stay with me. What did Zach say?"

"Zach? Oh, yeah. Not to me. But they came in one night, and Zach asked Randall if they were going to the farm."

"They got land up in Ohio."

"Yeah. I took copies of their driver's licenses. Had to, even though they was always cash. Tuesday wanted to be able to locate anyone in case they did damage. Anyways, Randall said yeah, something about going to see Wesley—said they'd be back for dinner. I thought, is he gonna fly up there and back, you know, Ohio, in one day just to see some guy? But then Randall asked Zach if he put gas in the car, and I wondered if Randall was talking about meeting this guy at some local place, you know?"

"Wesley. What did he say about Wesley?"

"I dunno. I just remember hearing the name. I had a friend once named Wesley, and I figure that's why I remember that. Wesley Varker. Sweet Lord, did he ever have one hot seventy-two Camaro."

I leaned closer into Daniel. "Tell me everything."

"White, with a mean blue streak down the middle of its hood and—"

"Wesley, Daniel. Not the wheels."

"Okay, throttle it down there, man. That's really it."

"Last name?"

"Naw. You spotted that broad just now, right? Damn, she has to be pushing fifty and to sport new high beams like that?

And those jeans? That's hot, man. These older babes, you know, are just starting to wake up to—"

"Look at me, Daniel." He refocused his eyes on mine, but I suspected it had been a long time since he hadn't had any sea fog in his vision. No matter how close anyone got to him, or where he sat on the stool, he'd always be far away. "Tell me about the farm."

"I just did."

"What else?"

"Like what?"

"They mention any roads?"

"Don't think so."

"How long it took to get there?"

"Not really. Like I—"

"Think, Daniel."

He backed away from me, reached for his drink, took a slow sip, and said, "That's it. Nothing. Got it? Randall said he'd be back and that—"

"When was he?"

"What?"

"Back, Daniel. When did Randall get back?"

"I dunno—"

"Think. You do know."

"Dude, whatcha do, chew through your leash this morning? I was off a few hours later. I don't know when he came back. You got it? I'm empty here, man. Bottom of the well. Zippo. Empty. Gonesville."

I was done with Daniel and wanted to run a search on any properties belonging to the Colemans in Florida. I thanked him for his time and started for the door.

"Hey," he said from behind me. I turned around. He held his mug in the air. "You good for this, right?"

"I got it."

I went outside to the side deck, which fronted a canal, and took a seat at a table under an umbrella with a vodka name on it. A snowy egret greeted me. "Sorry, buddy. Nothing for you." The bird showed no expression as it took a tentative step closer to me.

I called Mary Evelyn, Garrett's secretary. She knew that Garrett, who practiced law in Cleveland, and I did jobs for our former colonel. Colonel Janssen didn't know she knew, but that was his problem.

"Mr. Travis," she proclaimed, interrupting the second ring.

"I'm sorry. He's not here. Can I get Jake for you?" I asked.

Getting Mary Evelyn to address me by my first name represented a rare failure in my life. She knew this and relished the game. She was eastside Cleveland, never-married, last-generation Catholic. Current culture had all but extinguished her kind. Maybe the government will grant her people casinos one day. She had slipped once and uttered my first name, but it had been accompanied by weakness on my part, and we'd never mentioned it. Like a time-out during a children's game.

"Would you like to speak to Mr. Demarcus?"

She knew that if I didn't want to play with her, I would've called his cell.

"No," I replied. "It's just that I've been diagnosed with pancreatic cancer—not much time I'm afraid—and if I could just hear my name from your lips. The doctor said sometimes the strangest kind acts can cure us. I freed a butterfly, talked a stranger into recycling, and sold my possessions to support homeless cats. You're my last hope."

"My sister was recently diagnosed with pancreatic cancer."

I couldn't take the chance. "I'm sorry. I had no idea."

"No, wait just a minute. That might not be right. I think it was a pancake dinner she was inviting me to. Yes, I believe *that* was it. This Saturday at seven. St. Bartholomew's."

"That's below the belt."

"Mr. Travis, there are no rules in our battle. You, of all people, should know that. I'll get Garrett for you."

"Garrett. See? You do it for him."

"I do."

"Actually I called to ask a favor of you," I said, and explained what I wanted. I asked her to check on any Coleman property within a two-hundred-mile radius of Fort Myers and to use the titled property in Ohio as a base. I told her to check under other family names as well. She asked what other family names, and I replied that I had no idea.

"Maybe a 'Wesley,'" I said.

"Wesley? Anything to go along with that?"

"Wesley makes the very best?"

"Hmm...I could use some cocoa beans. That's all you got?"

"Bottom of the well," I replied, stealing Daniel's phrase.

She said she'd get right on it, and I doubt she hesitated a second before giving it her full attention. I called the Hoover Building and asked for Natalie Binelli, the FBI agent who had put the cuffs on Raydel Escobar. She had been engaged in undercover work while I'd sought to recover the stolen Cold War letter. We had met in Escobar's kitchen, and I shoved her into a wall and threatened to break her wrist unless she dropped her Glock and cooperated. I nearly *had* broken her wrist. I got her voice mail and left a message.

My next call was to Brian Applegate, an intelligence geek at special ops at MacDill Air Force Base. He said he'd get back to me. I had hesitated to call him, as I didn't want to put him in an uncomfortable position, but he could take care of himself.

On more than one occasion, he had refused to give me information. Other times he had proved invaluable. I doubted the Colemans would be on the national security radar, but I wanted to cover all bases and knew that US intelligence was the largest radar on the planet. Colonel Janssen wasn't an option. He'd made it clear that he wouldn't get involved in our extracurricular activities. He had intervened once. Never again.

I went back inside to say good-bye to Grouper. The lady in the Conch Republic baseball cap behind the bar told me he'd stepped out for a few minutes. Daniel was gone as well. I walked out and realized that Grouper hadn't answered my question about Tuesday. I'd have to catch up with him later; I didn't have the time now. Missing people are like drifting rafts on the ocean. Every second the chance of finding them blows farther into the hostile sea. I wondered whether Jenny was even still breathing. I tried to kill the thought, but it doesn't work that way. I didn't make it more than ten feet before I spun and went back into the restaurant.

I gave Baseball Cap a twenty and a ten to cover my—and Daniel's—tab.

CHAPTER 13

Jenny

I smell, but not like me, she thought, *or anything I thought I could ever smell like. Even after days without a shower—not that I would know what that's like. I smell like this place. Stale.*

No. Not stale.

Quiet. Can one even smell quiet?

Forgotten? That's it.

I smell forgotten. I didn't even know "forgotten" had an odor. Well, there you have it, children. My God, the stuff in this world that you've got to pick up on your own.

She couldn't figure out how they knew she'd been with Billy Ray. *Had to be my cheer T-shirt with my name on it*, she thought. *And I worked so hard for it. Were they watching that night? No way. Did they get there before the detectives? The one with the goofy shoulder said they never found my T-shirt. Maybe a bird took it. Who knows?* She'd grown weary of thinking about it. Grown weary of thinking about anything.

And what's with Zach? One day on a boat, and he remembers me? I told him I had visited my aunt—and he filed that? Well, after all, I remember him. He was cute. Still is. I don't think he'll hurt me, but I won't hesitate on him. She went over it all again in her head.

He had called a few nights ago—how he had her number she didn't know, but Cami had snuck it onto her Facebook page a couple of years ago when they'd gotten into that tiff over asking Sean McCann to the Valentine's Day Sadie Hawkins dance. Zach had told her to come down quick to the Laundromat. "I got something for you—can't leave. I'm at the corner, waiting for a ride." At first she didn't remember him, but then it kicked in. Seriously curly hair. "What are you even doing in Florida?" she had asked, but the line was dead. She darted out of the house and spotted him at the end of the street by a blue van. "Jen, over here," he'd said. *And like an idiot,* she thought, *I went straight to the van, thrilled to see a somewhat familiar face. Whoopee, girl, your Florida experience getting better by the minute.*

She never saw the other man approach behind her but felt a pair of hands on her back. Her face hit the gray cloth seat, and the stub of a stale French fry found her left eye. He scrambled in behind her and shut the door. He wore a green mask. He tied her hands behind her back and bound her ankles while Zach drove. She was too confused to feel fear. They questioned her about the money. "What did Billy Ray say? Where is it? We saw the car," Zach had said. "It was busted open." They questioned if she knew Billy Ray from back up in Ohio. "Did you run together? Plan this whole thing out?"

"Are you nuts?" she retorted. "Zach, what are you doing?" She thought they'd let her go once they realized she didn't know anything. After all, this was Zach, one of Orry's buds. Right? That's what she told herself, although she remembered asking Orry about Zach after the day on the boat. He said his other friend had invited Zach at the last moment, and Orry didn't really know Zach.

Then they had stopped, and the taller one with the mask said he was tired of wearing a mask and blindfolded Jenny. That's when fear came around fast—like that sucker was just waiting to club her over the head. They talked about their portion of the money, as if it weren't all theirs. After a while, Jenny had realized they were no longer discussing Billy Ray—as if she were Dorothy, and by melting Billy Ray, she had done them all a favor. *Hello*, she'd thought. *I took this guy out last night, and you obviously knew him pretty well. Anyone care?*

They didn't. But they cared—and cared deeply, Jenny realized—about the money.

And who had beat them to it.

She stood and walked to the refrigerator. She opened the bottom freezer drawer and pulled out one of the three bottles of water she had placed inside. Not yet frozen. Slush. She tied a strap from the boat cushion around the cap and swung it in the air. *Pathetic*, she thought. *Like a Neanderthal swinging a club. But at least Neanderthals had those spiked things.* She put it back.

She paced. She sat.

The Adirondack squeaked.

Jenny leapt off the chair and went to her knees. Exposed rusted nails, firm when Ike was president the first time around, bridged divorced pieces of wood. She grabbed the left arm of the chair and jerked it back and forth, up and down, side to side. Really? *Stupid thing acts like it can't support a fly, but you go to tear it apart, and the old warrior gets an attitude. Still*, she thought, *I've got nothing else to do.* She finally dislocated the arm from the rest of the chair and pounded the nails on the concrete floor.

She reached into the freezer and grabbed the bottle that was tied with a strap. *How to do this?* She notched two small holes into the topside of the bottle as it rested between her bare feet. She worked the head of a nail into each hole. She placed the bottle in the freezer against the side wall and pushed two other bottles up tightly so the bottle with the nails wouldn't roll. The nails limped off to the side. *Idiot. They need to be in deeper;*

otherwise, it'll have no strength. She repositioned the nails and the support bottles.

For the uncountable time, she thought, *What do they think I did or know? I told them Grease Boy said he had two hundred and whatever big ones. Is that it? They think I took the money? And what? Keeping me here will break me?* She played "Run" in her head to keep her thoughts from wandering down dark paths.

She did some push-ups and sit-ups. *Gotta keep in shape.* She checked her bottle in the freezer. *Calm down. Ice takes time.* She envisioned her weapon and wondered whether the strap would hold. Could she use it on Zach? *Hell, yeah. That slimeball tricked me.* But she hadn't seen him since that first night. It was always Green Mask who brought her food and escorted her to the out-house, which was seventeen steps away. She managed to stretch it to twenty-one steps; she figured the extra steps were good for her and prolonged her fresh-air time. *Another major bummer*, she thought. *My skin's going to turn plaster pale. I wanted to get one of those rich native tans, like Aunt Sus—just Susan, you dimwit.*

Is my life in danger?

Holy moly, girl. Where did that drop from?

Face it, she thought. *It's been there all the time.* She wondered what her father would say, for in Jenny's mind he had never lied to her. She could hear him now: *Be strong. Take it in with strength.*

They were approaching the marina just as a summer squall erupted and threatened to blow the water clean out of Buckeye Lake. Instead of his usual cautious, slow approach, her father took the Trojan in hard and fast. She was certain they would crash into the dock. Larry screamed the Trojan's engine in reverse at the last moment. "When things kick up," he'd told Jenny when she'd asked why he'd gone in with such speed, "you need to take it in with strength. The tougher the weather, the stronger you drive. Remember that, Jen. When it's nasty, be strong and take her in with strength. Be nasty right back." He had let her steer the boat several times, but Jenny couldn't imagine ever being good enough to race the boat into the dock. She didn't comprehend the reasoning.

She got it now.

Pretty boy or not, when my bottle's ready, the first guy through the door gets it. Besides, he's the worst enemy—someone who posed as a friend. Then what? Run? I'll worry about that later. Right now, she thought, *it's focus time.*

Nasty right back.

CHAPTER 14

After I left Grouper's place, I drove to Water's Edge, Susan's bar. It had no parking, so I pulled into a spot in front of a Wings store. I made certain my front bumper made contact with the CUSTOMERS ONLY; ALL OTHERS WILL BE TOWED sign and strolled across the street. I wanted to fill Susan in on my trip up north. She was a blur behind the bar.

She didn't slow down to address me. "Find Jenny," she commanded as she worked three glasses in a row on the counter.

"I'm doing what I—"

"Now."

She dropped two drinks in front of a couple, and the lady practically had hers at her lips before Susan's hand was off the stemware. She spun around to finish the third. From behind her, a man with his eyes glued to her ass instructed her to "go easy on the ice, babe." Her jaw clenched, and her hand tightened around the glass.

When I'd first met her, she'd told me the ones who come directly from the airport are the worst. Their senses quickly overdose on the blue sky, palm trees, endless Gulf, alcohol, and girls in thongs. Susan said the newbies are easy to spot; they chatter like chipmunks on weed into their phones. She spun around, placed the hurricane glass in front of the man, and worked her way down the bar, taking orders. It wasn't the time or place. I walked out and onto the public beach on the other side of the pier.

The sinking summer sun hadn't surrendered any of its intensity. I crouched in the shade of a deserted beach umbrella. On the Gulf, a listing sailboat came about, its spinnaker dancing in front of the sun like a ballerina flirting with a spotlight. A black skimmer approached me as if I were its long-lost buddy. Must've been my day for birds. I dialed McGlashan but got his voice mail. I was halfway through leaving a message when he called.

He asked me how I'd enjoyed my trip up north. I thanked him for greasing the rails with his call to the Hocking County sheriff. My sarcasm didn't escape him.

"They didn't plug you, right?"

He reiterated that Jenny was eighteen, and while her encounter with Billy Ray put her disappearance into question, she was free to travel. The department didn't view her absence as a crime. I asked him when I could talk with his partner, Detective Eric Rutledge, and listen to the interview tape. He said Rutledge was due back from Vegas that evening, and he'd see what he could arrange. We disconnected, and I headed back to the condo.

Morgan stood in the kitchen rubbing fillets with olive oil. Lucinda Williams was in the air asking someone to make her moan at the ceiling. I raised my hand, but she kept singing as if I weren't even there. Perhaps she didn't hear me.

"Fillets or sauce?" he asked.

"What do you got?"

"Trout."

"Go out yourself?"

"Guy I met at Fish Head. What will it be—grill or stove?"

"I'll do the sauce."

He brushed past me with the fillets on a large plate in his right hand. Salt and pepper shakers the size of bananas hung out of the pocket of his cargo shorts. In his left hand, a bowl-shaped wineglass sloshed red wine.

"Where'd you get the glasses?" I asked. Another one rested on the counter.

"Little joint at Santini Plaza," he answered without turning and padded out the door, his bare feet slapping the tiled surface. I poured a glass of wine. I put the glass down, reached into the refrigerator, and took out a beer. I swigged half in one act. I tossed down four Oreos. A handful of cashews. Devoured a chunk of Welsh cheddar. When I'm hungry, I'm random.

I put on a pot of water and turned the burner to high. On another burner, I heated olive oil in the skillet. I diced half an onion and a whole tomato and dumped them into the skillet. It registered their arrival with a nasty hiss. I added oregano, salt, pepper, tapenade, freshly squeezed lemon, and basil. The water in the pot convulsed in a boil. I gently placed a pound of royal red shrimp into the frothing surface, being careful not to splash—I had no shoes on, and I had experience in how painful it could have been. I added a sprinkle of garlic, and at exactly four and a half minutes, I took the reds out. I stripped them of their shells and legs, cut each one into three sections, and mixed them into the skillet. I had held two back and ate them. Like a dog, I nearly burned my tongue. I rinsed it with the rest of the beer.

I poured the sauce into a white ceramic bowl that had permanent scratch marks on its bottom, stuffed two bottled waters into the pockets of my shorts, snatched a loaf of bread, and started toward the door. I returned and added forks, plates, and a wad of paper towels to my collection.

Morgan and I claimed a front-row wooden cabana. The cushions were stored away for the night, and the canvas was laid down. The moon hung over Sanibel as if it was tethered to the island. As the sea drank the sun, we took in the wine and the fillets buried in the Mediterranean shrimp sauce. To our right, three cabanas down, a couple sat with their arms draped over each other. Directly in front of us, a man with a metal detector and headphones waded in the shallow waters. A late-day jogger ran north to south along the beach. I marvel at the courage and audacity of people who exercise during the hours of the day that are biblically ordained for drinking. Do they not fear divine retribution? Have they not read the Old Testament? You do *not* want to piss that guy off.

"It's a super moon," Morgan said as he tore a piece of bread from the loaf, dipped it into the sauce, and paused, as if in anticipation of the moment. "Thirty-two thousand miles closer than its farthest point out." He stuck the bread into his mouth. "It won't be this close for more than another year"—he paused to swallow—"or about fourteen moon cycles."

I followed his cue, broke off a piece, and buried it in the sauce, letting the bread get a good soak. "Thirty-two K isn't noticeable, though." My phone rang. I abandoned the bread in the dish and walked away from the cabana. It was a blocked number.

"This is Jake."

"How are you, cowboy?" Special Agent Natalie Binelli asked.

"Fine, Vassar."

I had accused her, in Escobar's kitchen, of being a blue-blood Yale FBI recruit. That didn't sit very well. "Fuck Yale. I'm from Vassar," had been her flat reply.

I asked her, "Anything on the Coleman clan?" I had given the background in my voice mail.

"Still full speed ahead, aren't we?"

"How's the family?"

"Fine."

"Kids?"

"Swell."

"We done?"

"What do you know about meth labs?" she asked.

"Illegal breed of retrievers?"

"Close. Try again."

"Just the basics. Easy businesses to set up in a garage. Thousands get busted every year."

"Therein lies the problem," Binelli said. "You need to dispose of the toxic waste. The government cut back on the funds they allocated to the states for that purpose, so local authorities don't actively search and destroy anymore. They don't want to find a lab. They have no means to dispose of the chemicals, or precursors, used to manufacture the drug."

"Does that mean even more local labs?"

"One would think. But the Mexican drug cartels are believed to have created meth super labs, even though the drug's key ingredient, pseudoephedrine, is illegal in Mexico and now restricted in the US."

"Where does the cartel get the precursors from?" Before I finished, I deemed the question inconsequential.

"China imports to Mexico; the cartel manufactures and ships to the US. Prices have fallen over the past few years, despite the Mexican government's war on the cartel. This tells us—"

"How are the Colemans involved?"

"If you don't want to know, Slick, don't ask."

The man with the headphones packed it in for the night, and the jogger ran south to north. She was likely forced to turn around, as it was high tide, and access to the last half mile of the beach was blocked, unless one was willing to get wet or pick his or her way through the mangroves. Either was an unlikely choice for a runner. At least she hadn't turned into salt.

I had moved toward the mangroves and realized I was close to where Jenny had done a number on Billy Ray Coleman.

I tucked under a branch and made my way toward my target. "What else might help me?"

"Have you talked with the local law boys in the Colemans' county?"

"They won't play with me."

"Not everyone succumbs to your unique charm."

"You did."

"You slammed me into a wall and threatened to break my wrist."

"'Slam' is a little harsh."

"Would you have?"

"What?"

"Broken my wrist, cowboy. For some reason, that's the only thing that bugs me."

"I don't know."

It was quiet except for a wave that broke on the shore. I didn't know Agent Binelli that well and was prepared for the line to go dead. I wanted to ask her again how the Colemans fit into this but decided to let her reenter at her own pace.

She started in, and I was relieved to hear her voice. "I assumed you'd irritated the locals, so I made a few calls. The Colemans are wannabes. They're suspected of teaming, or attempting to team, with organized crime in Tampa."

"Who?"

"We're not sure. But we—"

"Do you have names? Locations?"

"Neither. We think a Chicago group is trying to make inroads into Florida and have a presence in Tampa. But with the lack of funding, there's no incentive to chase them. What's the prize here?"

I expanded on what I had left in my voice mail. "A young woman's been abducted. She killed the youngest Coleman when he attempted to rape her, and now, two days later, she's AWOL. Because she's eighteen and had just skipped out of her childhood home a few days earlier, the police only have mild interest. Problem is she left her phone behind."

"Signs of struggle?"

"None."

"How long has she been missing?"

"Couple days."

That busted the pace. I knew what she was thinking. She cracked the silence. "Who's investigating?"

It was a meaningless question, designed to kick-start the conversation. "Sheriff's detectives. Guy named McGlashan and his partner Rutledge. I haven't met Rutledge, but McGlashan shoots straight and feeds me what I know. Keep looking. If you find who they—"

"Name sounds familiar."

"McGlashan played football."

"And I would know? I majored in theater, remember?"

"Ever do Virginia Woolf in the nude?"

"That's absurd."

"Touché."

She disconnected. Guess we were done conversing. I found myself entangled in the mangroves. The area where Jenny had been attacked and successfully defended herself was still roped off. There was nothing there but sand and sticks. I made my way back to Morgan and threw my saturated piece of bread on the sand. Dinner was cold.

That night, somewhere between the sheets of sleep and consciousness, I remembered I wanted to hear—or at least read the transcript of—Rutledge's interview with Jenny. I wanted to talk to Rutledge directly; I sensed McGlashan was tiring of me. Maybe Rutledge could lend some fresh insight into Jenny's state of mind.

I dreamed there was a cross with Jenny's name on it. Queen Anne's lace was crowding it out. The wild plants towered over it, dancing and taunting—like the sailboat's spinnaker flirting with the sun—and I thought it was total bullshit that Queen Anne's lace would know the difference between dancing and taunting, but it did, and it made all the difference.

CHAPTER 15

McGlashan hit me a little after eight the following morning. "Rutledge's back from Vegas."

"Hand in his resignation?"

He let out a huff. "I don't think he clears a plug nickel there. But it's not due to lack of effort."

"He roll the dice often?" I find Vegas about as attractive as being stuck in an elevator with overweight, inebriated transvestites. I speak from experience.

"Moved down from your neck of the woods little over a year ago. Since then, every opportunity he gets. He lives from one trip to another."

"You sound as if you disapprove."

"Don't give a flying crap either way. He likes hot concrete and pushy people palming titty cards."

"You've been there."

"Twice, for conventions. That was three times too many. I like to fish and got a fifty-seven Chris-Craft I'm restoring with my son. That's the far side of the moon from Vegas."

I had finished my beach run, sweated my weight, and seated myself at a table next to the sparkling waters of the resort's pool. When McGlashan had called, I was getting ready to open an e-mail from Mary Evelyn. The subject line read, "Ta-Da!"

"When can I talk to him?"

"He's not as cooperative as I am."

"Meaning?"

A man carrying a beach bag entered the pool area through the white gate and headed toward the hot tub. Two children, a boy and a girl, took turns diving to the bottom of the pool and bringing up a large rubber dog bone. The girl barked.

"You're a civilian, and the department doesn't think we should be chasing Ms. Spencer."

"What are we going to do about that?"

"We? I don't think there's really a—"

"You know"—I stood and started pacing—"that an eighteen-year-old doesn't split without shoes and her cell."

"There's only so—"

"No cell. You know—"

"I'll tell you what I know." He came in with force, and I got out of the way. "Two thousand people—about a hundred every hour—are reported missing in this country every day. Most of them are under twenty-one. That's too big to chase. The case is closed at our end. We know who killed Billy Ray. We know he killed at least one other girl. Ms. Spencer should get a sticker by her name. She's from a troubled childhood, ran once, and now she's slipped out again. And since the day she vanished, several thousand others have joined her club. You think I don't care? I do. You think I've got time? I don't."

Jenny's decision to leave home without notifying her parents—Angie and Boone—was coming back to hurt her. I wouldn't gain anything by alienating McGlashan and whipping him into a frenzy. The man in the hot tub eyed me as he took out a bottle of champagne and poured himself a glass.

I took a deep breath. "I need to listen to the interview tape."

"I'll see what I can arrange. What did you find in the timberland? This isn't a one-way street."

"Tall pines, bugs, and leftover paraphernalia from their chem lab. And this: Jenny spent a day on a boat with Zach Coleman last summer."

"The hell, Travis? You going to keep that to yourself?"

"No time, remember?"

"I can turn you off right now."

"It was a dead end," I said. "She never saw him again, and according to my source, it was her older brother, Orry, who invited Zach. Orry didn't even know him that well. But you might want to tell the Hocking County elves about it so they can—"

"You find something like that, you call me. Understand?"

I deserved his attitude. I should have notified him immediately about the encounter between Zach and Jenny. Maybe I didn't trust him, but Susan deserved a better effort than that. So did Jenny, dead or alive.

"You're right," I said quickly. "My source was certain it was only a chance meeting."

"Your source?"

"Jenny's stepfather."

He paused. "You leave him breathing?"

"Against my better judgment."

"Okay. That might be enough to put a manhunt on for the Coleman boys, but we've already looked. As far as we know, they've vanished. The sheriff up there interviewed their known associates, and none of Jenny's relatives were on that list."

I thought about Daniel's comment about Randall driving from the motel and asked, "Can you check and see if the Colemans have, or had, any property in Florida?"

"Why do you ask?"

My phone buzzed, indicating another call. "They were regular visitors to a motel on the northern end of the island, the

Buccaneer. Guy there says he thinks Randall took off to a familiar place and returned the same day. Might have met a person
named Wesley."

McGlashan came in slowly. "When did you have this conversation?"

"Yesterday."

"You keep me up to speed. Got that?"

"We're talking about someone's life."

"And I'm talking common reciprocity."

"I want to hear the tape," I told him.

"I'll see what—"

"Every minute she's gone, it's less—"

He hung up on me. Just like Binelli had.

I retrieved my voice mail. It was Applegate from MacDill
Air Force Base. He said he had nothing on the Colemans and
didn't leave any other comment. He wasn't getting involved.

Liquid salt dripped down my face. Before McGlashan had
called, I had swum hard in the Gulf for thirty minutes, emerged
from the surf like a fish testing its evolutionary legs, and run for
three miles. I'd tried to kill myself the final half mile. At the
end I was bent over, hands on my knees, staring at a coquina
shell that marked the water's farthest encroachment upon the
land. It had intense orange color at the edge, as well as rings
of lighter shades toward the middle. A set of toes in need of a
pedicure had obliterated my little buddy. I'd lifted my head,
and a lady with a floppy wide hat and John Lennon sunglasses
inquired if I was okay. I gave her toes a dry heave and told her
I was fine. I like to go to the edge every morning. It enhances
life.

I grabbed my shirt, which I'd left on the white fence when
I'd first come down from the room, and went to the pole with
faucets on it. I stuck my head and shoulders under the upper

one and let the water carry the heat away. I wiped my face with my shirt. A woman with blushed cheeks and dinner-theater red lips joined the man in the hot tub. They both held condo-stocked wine glasses high above the steamy water. The man laughed. The little girl in the pool let out a series of woofs then dove headfirst into the deep end. I wished I had something that simple to retrieve. I remembered Mary Evelyn's e-mail and sat down to read it.

Wesley. She'd solved the puzzle. I stood up.

"Hey, mister. Can you get my bone?"

The little girl gazed at me from across the pool. "My bone went in the deep end. Can you get it?"

Why not? I was at the shallow end and wondered whether I could cover the pool with a flying leap. I took a few steps back, vaulted, and stretched for the sky. I wanted to land directly over the bone, but I crashed several body lengths short. I dove for the rubber bone and brought it to the side of the pool. The girl squatted. I handed her the bone.

"You forgot to bark," she said with a trifecta of disbelief, disappointment, and hurt.

"Woof."

"Woof, woof!"

Cute little tyke.

Still wet, I took the stairs up to the condo. It felt like a walk-in cooler. I snatched a towel from Morgan's bathroom, dried off, and entered the kitchen. Morgan was making his way to the balcony with a bowl of scrambled eggs. He glanced back at me and said, "Get the toast and coffee."

Two slices poked out of the red toaster. I snatched them along with a jar of cherry jam and the pepper grinder. The coffeepot and two mugs were next, and I managed to get it all to the screen porch without losing anything overboard.

"The Colemans have a property about a half hour north of Tampa," I said while I peppered my eggs. "We eat and drive." I didn't let the grinder rest until my eggs were covered with a gray, lumpy sheet. I can*not* consume eggs without pepper on them. Eggs without pepper will never happen.

"You need to stop by and see Susan before we leave."

I had told him yesterday about my aborted encounter with her. "I don't have much to share with her," I said.

Below and out on the beach, men were finishing setting up their business for Jet Skis, kayaks, and paddleboard rentals. They had started before sunrise. It would be a tough day—thin summer crowds and a high sun. Morgan glanced at me and said, "That's not the point."

"Tell me."

"You know she's waiting—every minute, every second—for her phone to ring. She deserves more than a stopover at her bar."

Screw it. Everybody was telling me they deserved more from me. I stood and took some dishes into the kitchen. I wanted to move, as if it would help me not think about what Morgan had said. I did need to confront Susan. Sabotaging her at the bar like I had, when I knew she'd be frantically busy and the bar scum would be mentally undressing her, was pure horseshit. What was I afraid of? My commitment to Kathleen, or that Susan had higher expectations of me? Either way, avoidance was a convenient route.

I do that sometimes—take the easy way out and pretend I'm better than I am. It's an old act and one that was never very good to start with.

CHAPTER 16

Susan didn't answer the door, so I strolled around through her white gate. She sat on the end of her dock with her elbows on her knees, her body curved like a quarter moon. I felt bad for invading her time. She would never want anyone to see her like that. A quiet moment on a Sunday morning. Not such a tough girl. Not at all.

She turned when I was still a few paces from her.

"I didn't hear you," she said. She bolted up straight and picked up her coffee mug. This was a woman more comfortable with action than repose. She wore a sea-green T-shirt and khaki shorts. No jewelry. No shoes. Her eyes barely peeked out from under her bangs.

"I tried the door. I thought I'd give you a progress report."

Progress report? *Progress report?* Every time I got within the scent of this woman, my circuit board misfired.

I sat next to her. Not too close. Not too far. Her umbrella was up, but the sun paid it no attention. It penetrated the fabric as if it were a minor nuisance, nothing more than a piece of facial tissue blocking a blowtorch. I wouldn't have been the least surprised if the umbrella had burst into flames. Such a delicate balance: any closer and we'd burn, yet if it weren't for the sun's gravitational pull, we'd float away as ice crystals. The entire planet is on the razor's edge.

The sun's presence was nothing compared to Susan's.

"Well?" she asked. Her eyes flickered to me then instantly returned to the waters of her canal, as if she weren't done with whatever meditation or thoughts I'd disturbed. Or maybe she just didn't want to look at me.

I told her about my encounter with Boone and the local sheriff, and my conversations with Tuesday and her employees. She held her gaze on the water while I talked. There was little I could do to make it sound like anything other than what it was—an unsatisfactory progress report. When I finished, a juvenile brown pelican—it still showed white underneath—violently dove into the water to our left. The brown pelican, the pelican most common to the Americas and considered a large bird, is actually the smallest of its breed. When the splash came, Susan reflexively turned her head; I didn't. Our eyes locked, and this time she didn't shy away.

"I'll find her," I said.

"It's been days, Jake. Time can't be our friend. It rarely is." It rushed out fast. I wondered how afraid she was of those words. How long they'd been dammed up in her mind.

"We've got a lead on some property the Colemans own. I'm going there now."

"I appreciate what you're doing." She started to return her gaze to the water but caught herself. "I didn't know who to call, and the police see no crime in her disappearance."

"McGlashan's been helpful. I think he views her absence as being connected to her encounter with Billy Ray, but he can't devote official resources to the cause."

Susan asked, "Why?"

"Due to her age, he—"

"No…you," she said and held my eyes. If another woman on the planet had such perfectly matched hair and eyes, I hadn't met her. If another woman on the planet owned a

ROBERT LANE

Grady-White and looked like *that* in a short, black dress—I
didn't want to know. She gave a slight starboard tilt of her
head, which was unbecoming of her fast-forward style. Her
hair, untied, followed to that side. "I mean, I called you in
desperation, and now...all the time and trouble. I'll reim-
burse you for your airfare—"

"Susan."

"You don't even know her. You—"

"Susan."

"You don't even know *me*." She looked down at the water.
I'd never seen her down and sensed it was unfamiliar territory
for her as well. "We had one night, just a dinner really, and you
didn't even say good-bye, and what was—"

I put my arm around her and pulled her into me. She smelled
good. Fresh. Just out of the shower. She resisted; I insisted. I
felt her relax as her breath left her and her body melted into
mine like a chord that had finally resolved. Her soft left breast
pushed in against my chest.

Now what?

Totally lost. Out of gas and no paddle. I felt I should contribute something, so I tossed out, "I couldn't bring myself to say
good-bye. That's why you called me. That's why I came. I *will*
find Jenny." It came out with the sap of a junior-high love song,
and not a particularly good one. She pulled away. I brought her
back and kissed her high on her forehead. I released her just as
she gave me a playful shove accompanied with a smile.

"We're good?" I asked.

"Find her, Jake. She's a beautiful young woman, and you're
the only wrecking ball she's got."

"Tell me about you."

"What about me?"

"I know you've met my friend Grouper—"

Susan coiled away from me like I had a nasty cold. "I don't need you patronizing me."

"I wasn't patronizing. I—"

"The hell you weren't. Like you're the only guy who ever walked into my life?"

"I was just—"

"Here's a newsflash about your friend. He's married."

My turn to snap to attention. "Grouper?"

"Mr. Pete himself. Tied the knot in Key West, and neither one of them remembered it the next day. Even now he's lucky if he thinks about her one day a week."

"To who?"

She leaned over and graced my forehead with a kiss, and then just as quickly, she was gone, but her body wash was still there. "Figure it out yourself *after* you find Jenny."

Our eyes locked for a couple of beats. I wondered why she kissed me. I knew why she kissed me. Time to hustle. "Fair enough." I got up to leave, and when I did, Susan's left hand floated up with me, but her face remained straight out toward the water, like a sculptured figure torn in two directions. I took her small hand. She squeezed and just as quickly let up on the pressure. I let go. It's hard to believe there are things we don't want even though we crave them so very much. I left without another word.

Morgan was cross-legged in the passenger's seat when I opened the door and climbed in.

"No headphones this time?" I asked.

"Once we're off the island. I've been enjoying the ospreys. The mates are calling each other."

I waited for more, but that was it. Most people listen; Morgan enjoys. On the turn before Matanzas Bridge, I hesitated about whether to take a sharp right and see whether the Grouper tale was true. It would have to wait. My phone buzzed. I glanced at it and saw a confirmation from Garrett.

Morgan asked, "What time does he get in?" I had told him that Garrett was coming after he'd concluded as much from my end of the phone call as we'd checked out.

"Six."

"Plans for tonight?"

"Dinner downtown."

"What are Jenny's odds?"

I glanced over at him and saw I had his full attention. Morgan is fully engaged when talking with another person—a human operating at top efficiency. Despite my efforts, I largely feign interest when listening to other people. If conversation's an art, I'm the guy with crayons who struggles with stick figures. Morgan had posed a question that had assaulted my mind countless times over the past few days, and each time I'd met it at the gate and turned it away. No more.

"I don't know," I said. "My guess is she either died in the first twenty-four hours, or she's still out there. With the first scenario, we're only pursuing revenge."

"I wouldn't do that."

"You and I are different in that regard."

He changed tack. "How did you find out where the Colemans' land is?"

"Mary Evelyn came through. Not the FBI, not army intelligence at MacDill, but an Irish-Catholic secretary."

"Not even a fair match."

"No, it's not."

"How'd she figure it out?"

I glanced in my rearview mirror as a white pickup crawled up my ass. I don't like tailgaters. I don't like a person toying with my—and other's—lives. "I told all three that Randall mentioned something about Wesley. No one found any person named Wesley in the Coleman family circle."

"But our friend lives outside the box."

I chuckled at my own thought and said, "Don't they all? Mary Evelyn told me she stared at the word *Wesley* and then a map of Florida. On a whim, she ran a search and came up with Pasco County. It was outside of her initial search radius."

"Wesley Chapel," Morgan said. It was a small town off I-75 just north of Tampa.

I cut him a look as the white pickup zipped passed me on my left. "Randall Coleman bought remote acreage there about two years ago. We scout it at dawn."

He nodded and stuck in his earplugs. My thoughts charted their own course. What if Jenny was gone—dead for days? Revenge was fine with me, even though it's a postmortem act. I get it. Believe in it. Revenge is the great voice, the Magnavox of silenced victims.

CHAPTER 17

"She's all yours," I told Garrett as we walked down Beach Drive in downtown St. Pete. I had just collected him from the airport, and we were meeting Kathleen and Morgan for dinner at Mangroves. Kathleen had swung by and picked up Morgan after she'd visited Sophia.

A brunette, who appeared to have dropped serious money in her quest for Ponce de Leon's dream, had just strolled past with a dog that looked like my running shoe with a beard. She had given Garrett her undivided attention. He wore, as always, jeans and a tight black crew neck T-shirt. Garrett had alopecia totalis; apart from eyelashes and eyebrows, hair would never find his body. His ancestors were a passionate mix of French and Louisiana Creole. At six three, his bronze body—some guessed Cherokee—resembled what most people recalled a Greek god looked like in a sixth-grade textbook. They'd just never met one.

"Who?" he asked.

"Fluffy's friend."

"You squeeze Boone hard enough?"

"You think Florida makes me soft?"

He didn't reply as we sidestepped a two-man combo outside a restaurant. I nodded at the black man with the eye patch and the clarinet. He reciprocated with a tilt of his head. Morgan and I had drained several bottles listening to—*enjoying*—his Southern roots.

Garrett said, "Tell me you've got a plan."

"Even better. I *do* have a plan. If our trip's a bust, I got a couple of guys I'll park for surveillance. I won't take the chance that we drive out and they saunter in a few hours later. Anything from your man up north?" Garrett had hired a firm to keep tabs on the Colemans' property in Hocking County, seeing as how I'd failed to reach a peace treaty with the descendents of the Iroquois.

"Nothing," he said. "You're picking this up, right?"

"I am. Forward the bill to me. Keep them on it twenty-four/seven."

"Already done on both counts."

Morgan and Kathleen were at a high four-top that fronted Beach Drive, Straub Park, and the waters of Tampa Bay. Kathleen faced the concrete wall of the restaurant. I didn't know why she'd chosen that particular chair. She knew better. Garrett and Morgan did the man-hug thing. Morgan wore a buttoned-down shirt and white linen pants. Despite his proclivity for wearing baggy shorts and a T-shirt every day, Morgan always donned long pants when dining out. "A man should never be seen in a restaurant," his father had told him, "in anything other than long pants." His parents, he'd said, insisted that he and his sister dress up whenever they rode at anchor and took the tender into a port for dinner.

I'd asked him once why he felt compelled to obey his deceased father's dictum, especially while dining outside in the summer. "It's his wish," he replied, as if puzzled by my question. Morgan never referred to his parents in the past tense. It was a simple, short conversation, yet I felt that in some manner my question had let him down.

Kathleen rose to greet Garrett. She had on a tastefully body-hugging deep-brown dress and a single layer of pearls. Her hair was tied back. When I stepped in to give her a light kiss, she reciprocated with parted lips and open eyes. Lord, help me. I pulled her closer and hovered my mouth over hers. A faint smile formed on her lips, and she blew out a puff of breath that I took in.

Yabba dabba doo.

I took a seat and crossed my legs. I had the bird dog spot, overlooking the other patrons, the street, the park, and the water. "We took the liberty and ordered a bottle," Kathleen said. "You can drink tonight, can't you? Morgan said you were checking out a lead tomorrow."

"That's correct," I said. Her smile still lingered from our kiss. I stared at an age line just starting to crease her skin at the edge of her lips. It was oxygen to a fire. "It's less than an hour from here, but I don't know what we'll find."

The waiter came with a bottle of Cab, and Morgan did the honors. He proclaimed it safe for consumption, and the waiter proceeded to fill three glasses. Garrett kept to water. I uncrossed my legs. I couldn't stand it any longer; she had to know.

"Let's switch," I said to Kathleen as I stood up.

"I'm fine. Really."

"Pronto. You know the drill."

I'm not comfortable at a table with a lady unless the lady has the best seat. The situation isn't tolerable. She knew this. I wondered why she even had claimed that seat when all four were available. She rose and gave Morgan a smile. I cut him a look as he took a long sniff of his wine. Morgan smelled and chewed his wine as much as he drank it. Garrett let out a chuckle.

"Everybody having a good time?" I asked.

Morgan brought his nose out of the glass. "I never noticed your chivalrous trait. Dr. Rowe insisted you wouldn't last more than two minutes having the better seat than her."

I swatted Dr. Rowe on the ass as we traded places. "And how did I do?" I kept my attention on Morgan.

"Little under a minute," Morgan said, glancing over at Garrett. "Wouldn't you agree?"

"He's got some wires crossed."

"It's physical," Kathleen interjected. "He literally can't sit still unless I have the best view. He'll fidget like a schoolboy who's soiled his pants. It's quite entertaining to watch."

"Nice to know the company I keep is so cheaply amused."

"And appreciative of your idiosyncrasies," Morgan said.

It was dark by the time we split one serving of banana cream pie with graham cracker crust and dark chocolate crumbles on top. When the waiter placed it in the center of the table, it was the only time in my life I wished my three friends would simultaneously die—or just conveniently faint. I decided to spend the night at Kathleen's, so Garrett and Morgan took my truck back to the island.

We rode the elevator to her ninth-floor private entrance. The money was from her ex. He had died just prior to Kathleen filing; she gained millions by *not* divorcing him. He was murdered three days before he planned to turn state's witness against the Chicago mob, the "Outfit." We had reason to believe the Outfit also wanted to silence her for information they erroneously believed she possessed. She knew nothing, but they decided not to take any chances. Garrett and I made the same decision—not to take any chances. They dispatched two men to deliver a warning. We packed them limping back home, and in doing so, we may have inadvertently, and falsely, signaled that Kathleen *did* have knowledge of her deceased husband's business affairs. They doubled up and kidnapped her, but with Morgan's help, we found her before they accomplished their mission. After we left four dead bodies on a deserted state park beach, we made the decision not to look over our shoulders for the rest of our lives. Colonel Janssen located a body and facilitated the identity change. Lauren Cunningham, who had approached me at the bar at the pink hotel more than a year ago and—not that I harbor any resentments—fed me nothing but lies in an effort to run from her past, died on that Florida beach. Her headstone was above Lake Michigan. Lauren Cunningham became Kathleen Rowe.

That had been the only time Colonel Janssen had intervened in my extracurricular activities.

I told Kathleen not to fear repercussions from the mob and that she was secure with her new identity. Nonetheless, I kept a constant glance over my shoulder. She was careful not to express too much concern, although I suspected that she harbored nagging paranoia. I wished she would be more honest. She might have thought the same of me.

As we entered the dim foyer, I said, "You and Morgan got a kick out of that, didn't you?"

"We did. He put me up to the test. He was surprised he'd never noticed your chivalrous nature before but said he could see how it was so much like you."

I thought of the young girl I'd seen diving into the pool for the bone. "What kind of treat do you give a dog for doing easy tricks?"

She kicked off her shoes—I don't know how she did it that fast—and dropped several inches in height. She started to let down her blond hair. "Allow me," I said. I kissed her slowly, and our stale breaths were scented with wine. *Of the rough lips and bourbon times.*

I didn't stop with the hair. I was patient. I left the pearls on. The hand-scraped walnut floor collected our garments and served as a thin mattress. I like making love to Kathleen on a hard surface. It doesn't allow for her body to shy and shrink away from mine.

Afterward, we lay next to each other, studying her ceiling. Actually, I was thinking of how quickly and diplomatically I could escape to bed. Trust me on this as well—after a man makes love, it's lights out. She said, "I don't know how you do that."

"Do what?"

She tilted her head. "Make love like the whole world depends on it."

"I'm a soldier on leave." I tried to suppress a yawn, but it had a life of its own.

"Nice try. But"—she propped herself up on an elbow and brushed the hair away from her face—"I was hoping for some words to make my head spin."

My yawn subsided. "Words ring so hollow."

"To the contrary. They're the most powerful drug."

"Kipling?"

"Mm-hmm."

"You know," I said as I rotated on my elbow to mimic her position, "he encouraged his son to enter the Great War, and the lad was killed at eighteen. He then wrote, 'If any question why we die/Tell them, because our fathers lied.'"

"This is pillow talk?"

"We have no pillow."

"Well"—she gave a slight shake of her head—"you certainly know how to flutter a girl's heart. Tell me, do you write poetry as well?"

"Sadly, I cannot."

"A shame." She traced a finger over my chest. "And why is that?"

"I have a rare neurological disorder, typing Tourette's."

"Hmm…I can see how that might create issues."

"It does make for interesting lines."

"One can imagine."

"If any question why we die/Tell them, because our fucking fathers lied."

"Well, then"—she flipped her hair again off her face—"that certainly deepens the tone just a tad."

"It does."

"You tired?"

"Beat."

"Do me a favor?"

"Anything."

"Kiss me hard."

And to think that I was looking for an early exit.

Later, as Kathleen slept, I crept out to her patio. Her balcony in downtown St. Pete offered panoramic views of Tampa Bay. The moon illuminated the water like a low-voltage bathroom night-light. Lightning echoed around the horizon. Tampa Bay registers thousands of strikes a year, and *Tampa* is believed to be a Calusa Native American word meaning "sticks of fire." Or maybe "a place to pick up sticks." No one really knows.

Susan's words split my head as if they were fired from a drone: *her wrecking ball.*

No doubt what that meant.

I refused to believe Jenny had voluntarily left her phone. Therefore, if alive, she was in danger and existing in horror while I had pushed back my investigation so I could enjoy a glass of wine, a sampling of a banana cream pie, and vouch as to the authenticity of a hand-scraped hardwood floor.

I texted Garrett. He instantly confirmed our new departure time.

At four thirty in the morning, when you don't know whether people on the street are still up from the previous day or are in the new day, my black truck emerged around the corner. I climbed into the passenger's side. Garrett punched the gas, and we were doing thirty before I got the door shut.

"You map it?" I asked. He didn't bother to answer, nor did we speak for the first half hour. Morgan's old red spinnaker bag was in the backseat along with a pile of clothes. I changed into jeans, boots, a T-shirt, and a tight jacket with inside pockets. I strapped on a shoulder holster.

I riffled through the spinnaker bag and extracted my Boker knife and Smith & Wesson.

CHAPTER 18

Jenny

The morning birds greeted Jenny with a discordant, symphonic background that sounded like the tuning of nature's third-string piccolo section. The rooster crowed like a deranged conductor with no sense of the time signature.

She checked on her spiked bottle. Good to go. She made another notch on her wall calendar with one of the nails she'd freed from the now permanently crippled Adirondack chair. She did some sit-ups but collapsed on the mat after a dozen or so. Her muscles were fine; it was her will that was atrophying. It wisped out the cracks of the old garage like a reverse breeze. She lay on her back on the mat and stared at the bottom of the rowboat that hung over her head. A new concoction of panic and fatalism had taken up residence in her mind, and like water in her ear, she couldn't shake it out.

She'd given up playing songs in her head; that just made her mad. She'd tossed in the towel on dreaming about the sun and the beach—look what that had gotten her. She felt herself slipping and not dreaming at all, but dreading the next day, the next hour, the very moment it took it to draw another breath.

What was that poem, she thought, *that Shields—excuse me,* Dr. *Shields—creamed his pants over in English class? Something about raging against the dying of the light.* She'd had no idea what he was talking about. Not then.

"Hey, Shields"—she stood up and shouted to the black air—"you out there? 'Cause guess what? I get it, dude. I mean I get it *way* beyond what you could ever hope to lift from a page. You and your sorry English-teaching ass have *no idea* what you were talking about."

Like the smell of "forgotten," she thought, *rage against the dying of the light is a terrible thing to have to figure out on your own. And at my age? Really?*

Her body shuddered, and she thought she might cry. She wanted to cry. *Might even be good for me. Okay, girl. Let's give it a go.*

Ah, shit. I can't even cry.

She poured a bottle of water over her head. She tossed the empty bottle into the white plastic pail with the busted handle.

"I am forgotten," she said as she watched pellets of water drop from her hair onto the concrete floor. *Like dripping off a roof, and I'm the roof.* She paced a circle and said it again, "I am forgotten." Shouting now, "I am forgotten!"

Someone fumbled with the lock.

She went to the freezer, her mind like the ice within.

Take it in with strength.

Nasty right back.

CHAPTER 19

We took a cloverleaf off the interstate. A lone Mobil gas station rested at the bottom of the exit ramp and reflected dawn's timid light like in an Edward Hopper painting. A dark sedan flashed past us going in the opposite direction. I made a note to double back to the gas pumps. Maybe it had security cameras. The five-inch, folded Boker knife was in my left inside jacket pocket, the Smith & Wesson in the shoulder holster.

A few minutes later, Garrett pulled the truck under a gnarled oak with lower branches the size of offensive linemen. Spanish moss bowed from the tree and dusted the top of a split rail fence. I checked my watch—twenty-six minutes to sunrise. I estimated a five-minute trek to reach the house, which, according to public records and Google Earth, was the only structure on the eight acres except for what appeared to be a single-car garage.

We left my truck and sprinted low through a field of ancient oaks. Fifty yards out, we went to a belly crawl. I was rooting for the dark, but it was retreating as if it had an appointment on the other side of the world and was running late. I cursed myself for not starting earlier. I was only half in this game, and that was a dangerous, tenuous position to be in. I was in no man's land—figuratively and literally. We stopped about thirty paces from the house. Its paint was so flaked that a stiff breeze could prep it for another coat. It had a slanted porch and a tin roof.

"No vehicle," Garrett said as we lay in the grass before our final charge.

"I think we're playing inchworm for nothing," I said. "Hard to believe that someone would be in the middle of nowhere with no transportation, but let's not assume that. Could be something in the garage, and for all we know, they got Gatlings trained on us."

"Man's first WMD."

"And now they're viewed affectionately in museums." I kept my eyes on the house, as did Garrett.

"We're a sick species," Garrett said.

"Dr. Gatling was actually an MD," I said as I flicked a spider off my left hand. "He invented the machine gun to shrink army sizes and to reduce disease-related death in the army."

"The garbage people feed themselves. Are you done?"

"I am." I stood. "You got me?"

"Do now." He reached over his back for his M110 SASS.

I ran low at the house. A rooster crowed once, and then again, momentarily interrupting the morning argument of birds. Garrett circled to the rear of the property but still had me in his view. I jumped onto the covered porch. I took a step back, kicked in the door, and went in with my gun raised.

"Jenny!" I yelled. "Jenny Spencer."

Nothing.

I hit a light switch. A solitary lamp lying on the floor next to an overturned wicker side table flicked to life. Place was trashed. Three open doors were off to my right. Bedrooms. A kitchen in the corner. Dirty dishes. Every drawer was open. A TV with rabbit ears sat on a table with a leaf down. Garrett blew through the back door and went to the kitchen. I cleared the bedrooms. Pillows, blankets, and clothing littered the floor. The closets were inside out.

"We're late," Garrett said as he opened the refrigerator and peered inside.

"I'm checking the garage out back." I was eager to search the single outbuilding, as I still held hope that Jenny was on the property, although that light was dimming faster than dawn was brightening.

The two swinging doors to the single garage were shut, but the padlock hung open on the hardware. The doors swung out toward me, which wasn't an ideal way to enter a potentially hostile room. I unlatched the doors, and while I stood with my back to the one door, I hooked my foot around the other door and kicked it open. I spun around the corner and found my gun aimed at a grill that was missing its propane tank. No need to injure it any further. I shouldered my gun. A rowboat hovered above my head. I gave it a swing. Light. Empty. A workout mat was on the floor with sheets neatly tucked in beneath it. I recalled how neatly Jenny's bed had been made at Susan's house. My foot hit something, and I cut my eyes to the floor.

I picked up a partially frozen water bottle with two nails protruding out of its side near the bottom. One had dried blood on it. A strap was tied around the end with the cap. My guess was that it was close to seventy-five degrees in there, yet the bottle had slushy ice in it. A plastic bucket held empty water bottles, and the concrete around my feet was wet, as if someone had spilled one.

The crude weapon captured my curiosity. I couldn't ascertain the purpose of ice-ensconced nails, but it was nasty. I went around the corner and checked the outhouse. It had red shag carpet and a picture of the cast of M*A*S*H. "Good times," I said to Hot Lips on the way out. Garrett was in the garage when I returned.

"Clues?" he asked.

"Look's like someone might have slept in here." I nodded toward the workout mat. "But that's not much to go on."

I wished Morgan were along. He had an uncanny ability to sense what I couldn't. And the garage was screaming—I just couldn't hear it. Instead of staring at the objects in the room, I focused on the structure. Marks on the wall caught my attention. I peered closer at them.

"'Four, one, two, nine, one, one, one' mean anything to you?" I asked.

Garrett peered at the wall. "No." He had been examining a green-and-white Adirondack chair. Its busted arm rested on the floor. "Are those marks relatively new?"

"Appear to be." Then I saw it. "That's her number. She was here."

"Not following."

"It's deer," I said, but what I was thinking was, *She's alive.* "Four thousand one hundred twenty-nine deer and three days in the garage."

"And why is that our girl?" He ran a finger over the indentations in the wood.

"Her father, Larry Spencer, went down in a hunting accident years ago. The county's final tally that year was four thousand one hundred twenty-nine deer and one man. Mary Evelyn sent me the newspaper article, a real doozy. His death was buried and comingled with a breakdown of the harvest. So many bucks, does, button bucks, oh, and one man."

Garrett shifted his attention to me. "Bad trade. Apparently not one she's forgiven. You think the last three marks track her days in captivity?"

"That'd be my guess."

"McGlashan help us here?"

"Unlikely. Out of his jurisdiction, and the world sees her as a runaway." But like a Polaroid picture creeping into focus, my conviction was gaining higher resolution. Jenny *had* been abducted—she was alive.

I picked up the bottle with the nails and handed it to Garrett. He rotated it in his hand. "One thing I can say about her," he said. He swung the bottle by the strap twice around his head then into the wall. The nails splintered the wood.

"What's that?"

"Our girl has spunk."

I pulled into the Mobil station we'd passed on the way in and gassed up. There was a security camera behind the register. McGlashan was next; I left a voice mail asking him to view the tape from the security camera. It was a likely place for the Colemans to refuel. Garrett texted Mary Evelyn and told her Wesley Chapel was a hit.

I called PC.

I had used him and his sidekick, Boyd, for surveillance in the past. They were high-school dropouts, and PC housed an oversized IQ that made formal education a ruse. He balked at my request that he and Boyd camp out for a few days and keep an eye on the Colemans' property. Garrett eyed me. I'd told him I had plans to have the Colemans' place watched, and he obviously incorrectly assumed I'd worked out those details beforehand. I wasn't worried. I told PC to bring Savielly Tartakower's *My Best Games of Chess 1905–1954*, that I'd purchased for him. PC and I had spent sweltering hours at the end of my dock, each of us with obsessive focus on floating the other's king. We used wine corks for kings, and when he lost, I tossed his king—his cork—into the bay. He was a quick learner and soon became a worthy opponent. Tartakower was, due to his wit as much as his ability, my favorite chess player. PC relented and said Boyd could play *Angry Birds* for days. I described how to get to the vantage point Garrett and I used and told him I'd text him pictures of Randall and Zach Coleman.

The phone calls, however, only treated the symptom. I had come up empty. Even though I was doing eighty on the interstate, I was going nowhere and getting there fast. Nothing but random motion. "Never mistake motion for action," Hemingway once said. I believe he was quoting Benjamin Franklin, who'd said, "Never *confuse* motion for action." Either way, motion is no substitute for action, although for my money, Hemingway chose the better word.

My phone rang. It was McGlashan.

I said, "I think we missed her by an hour." I explained the past two hours. He couldn't offer any assistance.

"I made you a copy of the interview, if you want to hear it," he said. "I listened twice. Nothing there. Straightforward, like Rutledge said." At least it wasn't "Detective Rutledge" anymore. "Next time you're down, drop by the station and—"

"Be there in three." I pressed the pedal. "Make that two and a half. Do you need to be there?"

"No, and probably won't be. Rutledge might be, though. If not, just identify yourself."

"And the Mobil station?" I asked.

"Right. I'll see what I can do."

He disconnected. I always got that feeling that I took him to the limit—as if he was an accommodating accomplice at the start of our conversations and a reluctant participant by the end. I set the cruise to eighty-five and swung over to the left lane behind a jacked-up brown pickup truck with a Confederate flag in the back window. The driver pulled away from me.

This was Florida, not Ohio.

CHAPTER 20

Rutledge thrust out his left hand, and I extended mine. Most southpaws shake with their right, but not Rutledge. His ash-gray hair was brushed straight up off his forehead, like a male bird seeking a mate. It was trimmed around the ears, as if he'd just left the barber's chair. Some guys look like that all the time. As a general rule, I avoid those people.

"McGlashan wanted me to meet with you." He glanced at Garrett then back to me. "I've got the interview tape, but I'm afraid it won't help you much. I think that Je—Ms. Spencer just ran." His eyes were dull, as if he'd seen more than he cared for, or perhaps he never cared. "She was pretty calm the night I interviewed her, especially considering what she'd been through. It occurred to me later that, even at that moment, she might have been planning to slip out. I understand you paid a visit to the Colemans?"

We were in a square conference room. Rutledge and I sat across from each other around a maple table that no one had ever bothered to place a coaster on. Garrett stood against the wall. Outside a window, a solitary palm branch pressed against the glass as if it yearned to join us. One of the three overhead fluorescent bulbs was out. It fluttered on then off. Rutledge reached into his pocket and slid his business card across the table. It stopped just short of the edge. Another inch and he would have scored. I placed mine in the middle of the table.

I said, "I believe we just missed them."

"That's what McGlashan told me. You find anything?" He sat back in his chair and drummed the fingers of his left hand on the table. He scratched his chin with his right hand. No wedding ring.

I explained the garage, as well as the numbers on the wall and their significance. I kept the spiked ice bottle to myself.

"So you found nothing, other than you think she was there?" Rutledge asked, as if he wanted to check that box off before moving on.

"That's correct. I asked Detective McGlashan to see if we could get a visual from a gas station that's the lone fuel source at the exit."

"And we'll let you know if that leads to anything." He tilted forward and blinked hard. If he caught my respectful use of a title, which he didn't use, to preface his partner's name, he didn't let on.

"Those numbers, four thousand and whatever—"

"Four thousand one hundred twenty-nine."

"Right. You firm on that?" Still coming at me.

"No doubt."

"You think she was there?" He seemed to sense his forward momentum and backed off.

"We do."

"I'm sure"—he settled into the back of his chair—"that *Detective* McGlashan explained that Ms. Spencer has every right to slip out, but the circumstances do make her disappearance suspect."

"You think she slipped into a garage three hours away?"

Rutledge let that cook for a few seconds, his fingers dancing on the table. "I'll remind you that you're here at our invitation. Don't forget that. Scratch marks on a wall—you don't build a case on that. We have no firm proof, just suspicion on yet another missing teen. If you find her—or them—call me. We won't tolerate vigilante actions. I'm the lead, so call me first. Don't let that slip your mind."

"Loud and clear, Detective," I said in response to his rambling statement, although I was confused as to what I wasn't supposed to let slip my mind—that he was the lead or that vigilantes weren't allowed. It didn't matter; I'd say anything to keep him on our side—and then do what I damn well pleased when the time came. He slid a minicassette tape across the table.

I asked, "You don't have digital?" The light flicked again.

"We don't even have light bulbs, Mr. Travis."

"Any leads on the car?"

"Car?"

"Billy Ray's Honda."

"No."

I waited. The light flicked. The AC came on. I said, "You must have something."

"No."

I started to stay in that lane, but switched. "And the Colemans' property in Ohio?"

"Their car's gone. We assume someone told them about the raid. I doubt they'll return. Why they would break into their brother's car, though—even if it *was* them—is anyone's guess. You know the deal with funding for toxic cleanups, don't you?"

"It's been cut."

"As in virtually eliminated. These brothers are medium producers with big-time ambitions. I doubt Ms. Spencer's disappearance has anything to do with them, but it's your time you're burning. Meanwhile, we don't have the dollars to track them. That's why we're helping you help us."

I couldn't keep his signals straight. I let it go and returned to the subject of the car. "Any idea what was in the Honda that was more valuable than the Alpine GPS and speakers?"

Rutledge gave that a second and shrugged. "Probably nothing. Likely just kids, and when they started to lift the system, they got spooked. We can hypothesize—"

"Why tear apart the insides?"

"What?"

"The interior. Why trash it if the Alpine system is staring you in the face?"

"Who the hell knows? We—"

"Did the stereo system even look as if someone had gone after it?" I didn't recall McGlashan saying the stereo system looked the least bit tampered with.

He shifted his upper body over the table, his elbows on the armrest. "As I was saying before you interrupted me, we don't have the resources to hypothesize all day as to what might have occurred. You aren't here to question how we allocate our time. You want to see my calendar? I got a Viet vet at Kelly's Green that bashes his wife every night and a hit-and-run that left a German tourist with only one leg. The *Reichstag*'s all over me on that one. I got a perennial drunk who claims he passed out, and when he woke up, his wife had crammed a cucumber up his ass. Claims she'd had it with thirty years of his whining that her vegetables tasted like shit. He wants to discreetly press—"

"I realize—"

"You don't *realize* dick squat." Rutledge planted his elbows on the table and interlocked his hands in front of him like a tent. "Here's my *real* world, boys: I got a root canal at four today because Dr. Toothfuck did the wrong damn molar a month ago, and to top it off, I haven't taken a dump in three days." He pushed off the table and stood up. "We're done here."

"No one touched the stereo," Garrett said quietly. His arms were folded, and he hadn't moved since we'd entered. "And you didn't find any prints around the trunk."

Rutledge eyed him, hesitated a beat, and said, "You evidently didn't catch the drift of my previous comment." He walked out the door.

Garrett said, "He's lazy."

"We know this: no prints. Someone wiped the trunk area clean. Ripped the seats but left the stereo."

"They know something went down on that car, but it's not a crime scene. They've folded and moved on. But kids don't randomly trash a used car or take a crowbar to the trunk—"

"Then slow down and wipe the scene clean."

I pocketed the tape and Rutledge's business card; my card was still in the middle of the table. Garrett and I left the room. I didn't see Rutledge in either direction in the hall. We strolled out the front door, and the heat walloped me like a heavyweight fighter who'd been waiting for the perfect opening. The predawn hours had held hope of finding Jenny, but the day had sputtered and left me with nothing more than I'd had the previous night. Perhaps less. Hope and hard wishes have a way of becoming real, even tangible, if we don't treat them as the frivolous imposters they are. But I did have one thing.

Jenny's voice was in my pocket.

CHAPTER 21

Garrett leaned against the aqua-colored cinder block wall in Susan's office. Susan, in beige shorts and a silk gold T-shirt, sat in a black swivel chair. It had a pad on it so she would be higher. A four-by-six picture of Jenny was on a shelf to her left. The background was a hill cloaked in Midwest summer green. Jenny's home? Susan had told me she had visited there last summer, and I wondered whether that was when she'd taken the picture. I sat in the folding chair by her desk and momentarily thought it was going to collapse from my weight. A window air conditioner quietly hummed over Garrett's right shoulder.

A pink minicassette player was on her desk. We had found it at an electronics store on US 41, the Tamiami Trail. Not the nostalgic section of the road that evokes images of paradise past captured on fold-down postcards, but the congested traffic-light-regulated strip of runway-wide concrete that makes you want to leave Florida in hopes of finding Florida.

I hit the "play" button. Rutledge identified himself, as well as Jenny, the time, and place. As I heard his voice, I thought of his dull eyes and dancing hands. I like incongruity; it sparks my senses.

He asked her a series of questions about the casual run-in Jenny and Susan had with Billy Ray earlier that day on the beach. He had her recite in chronological order her actions after

Susan had departed for work and her subsequent encounter with Billy Ray. Jenny never raised her voice. She never broke.

"What did he say just prior to when he attacked you?" Rutledge asked her.

Jenny said, "Just some small talk, like, you know, 'Remember me?' I said, 'Yeah, from this afternoon.' Then he said something about Sherman."

"Sherman?"

"I asked him if it was warm like this up in Georgia—he told us earlier in the day he was from there—and he said, 'Sherman. That's his name.' Or maybe something like, 'Yeah, baby, that's his name.' He seemed pretty excited about it."

"About what?"

"Sherman."

"I don't follow," Rutledge said. "Who's Sherman?"

"I don't know."

"Did he ever mention a Sherman again?"

"No. Didn't he burn Atlanta?"

"Who?"

"Sherman."

"Oh, him. Did he really burn it, or is that just legend?"

"Pretty sure he torched it."

"Why would he talk about Sherman?"

"You're kidding, right? Why would he try to rape me?"

"All right. Let's move on. What else?"

"I told him that I was looking for turtles and that my aunt said they come to that area. He said she was hot too."

"Hot?"

"Like, you know, attractive. Then he hit his head."

"How?"

"How what?"

"How did he strike himself?"

"Slapped himself hard, like this." I heard a dull thud.

"Okay. Then what?"

"I told him my aunt was behind me. I was scared. He wasn't right. But I said it wrong. It came out weak…uncertain."

There was a pause, and then Rutledge said, "What happened next, Ms. Spencer?"

"He said, 'No, she ain't, magazine girl. I saw her drive away earlier.'"

"Magazine girl?"

"Magazine girl…whatever." She sounded ticked, and I knew why. She had picked up on the gist of the comment that had apparently eluded Rutledge. Jenny explained to Rutledge, "He said he saw her drive away. Get it? It meant he was watching. He was stalking me. I knew I was in trouble."

"Okay," Rutledge said in a conciliatory tone. "Then what?"

"He ripped off my shirt. My cheer shirt. I don't know how he did it that fast. Just yanked it over my head. Then he hit me. Hit me hard. I wasn't sure that I'd be able to hang on."

"Hang on?"

"You know, stay conscious. I started to drift, but he…he bit my breast, and I think that brought me back. I reached out, and a stick was there. I shoved it at him. Then I saw…and then…"

"Saw what?"

"Oh…nothing. I just lost track of where we were."

"Okay, then what?"

I wondered what Jenny had seen. She didn't come across as a girl who lost track of *any*thing.

There was a pause, as if Rutledge was waiting for Jenny to continue. During the time of the actual interview, it was now approximately a half hour prior to sunrise, and I heard birds in the background. It reminded me of my trip to the Ohio woods. I don't know much about birds other than rote regur-

gitation. Morgan can identify nearly every species by sound. I
know them by sight and the basics. They fly. The ones in my
'hood eat fish. One particular osprey exists just to crap on my
boat and screeches all day and half the night. And around a half
hour before sunrise, they all let loose, no matter where they are.

Rutledge coughed loudly. Birds chirped.

"I was on top of him before I knew it," Jenny said.

"How did you accomplish that?"

"I don't know *how*," she said with a tinge of irritability.
"I was just *there*. I found a stick. Listen, I didn't think of killing him—it's not like that; I just didn't want her to go down.
I pumped that stick like she was going to sink, and I wasn't
going to let that happen."

I glanced over at Susan to seek confirmation regarding Jenny's confusing reply. She shot me a quick glance, and I knew
why. I recalled her telling me of Jenny's duty to pump the boat
out and her feeling of failure—and of her desire to please her
father in her dreams. I also remembered Susan's supplication to
me. "What do you do with that?" she'd demanded.

"I'm not following," Rutledge said. "Who is 'her?'"

"My father's boat."

"A boat?"

"What about it?"

"Your father's boat was going to sink?"

"No, sir. Not on my watch."

I wondered if Jenny had put her dream to rest on the beach
that night.

Rutledge tossed her a litany of questions about her actions
immediately after she'd realized Billy Ray was dead. Jenny took
them in the same matter-of-fact voice in which she'd addressed
all his previous questions. If there was any guilt in her action, or
remorse in her decisions, it was buried too deeply to detect. She

explained how she had stumbled upon a towel she had spotted earlier and wrapped it around her before she returned to Susan's.

He inquired why she had waited so long to notify the police.

"We were talking," Jenny told him.

"Will you identify who you were talking with, please?"

"My aunt, Susan Blake."

"About what?"

"Life. Lots of things. But not about what had just happened."

"You got attacked on the beach, turned on your assailant, killed him, wrapped yourself in a beach towel, strolled back here, and then took the next few hours to repose and discuss life?"

"Washed myself off first."

"Pardon me?"

"Before I wrapped myself in the beach towel, I washed off in the Gulf. I had...stuff on me. The water was warm, not much cooler than blood. Did you know that?"

Rutledge cleared his throat. "Would you like something to drink, Ms. Spencer?"

"No. I'm fine. Do you?"

"Do I what?"

"Know that the Gulf of Mexico, at least at this time of the year, isn't much cooler than blood?

"Um...no, I missed that."

"Not by much, but I was relieved to cool down at least a little. I read somewhere that the salinity of the Gulf is approximate to the salinity of blood. Temperature, blood, and salt. Never expected to find that out for myself."

"Okay. Let's back up just a second. You returned here and talked for hours with your aunt about events unrelated to your traumatic experience. Why didn't you call the police?"

"I had more important things to discuss."

"Than an attempted rape and murder?"

"That's correct."

"With all due respect, Ms. Spencer, you're challenging my imagination."

"Eric, right?"

"Excuse me?"

"I believe you introduced yourself as Detective Eric Rutledge."

"That's correct."

"Tell me, Eric." Her voice ran decades ahead of her years and had been gaining conviction throughout the interview. "What in your male past causes you to think that you can imagine what I've been through in my life and how I should react after someone attempted to rape me and I successfully defended myself?"

Garrett let out a low whistle. I thought of the spiked water bottle and caught myself smiling.

Rutledge's voice came back in clipped military fashion. He gave the time—6:17 a.m.—and reiterated the participants' names and the location. An osprey screeched. The tape went silent.

I recalled my exchange with Officer Kevin Trimble. *"Eric, right?"* And I'd thought I was tough. I wanted to find this girl so she could teach me a few lessons.

I looked over at Susan. Her jaw was tight. I'd been too absorbed in listening to give her much attention while the tape played. "The reference to her father's boat," I said. "Is that what you mentioned? Her dream?"

Susan glanced up at me. "Even more. It was the last time in her life that things were right for her. She's just trying to get it back. That's all."

"I don't understand how that—"

"Jesus." She spat it out and bolted out of her office. I glanced up at Garrett.

"Move," he said.

I found her behind the bar, scrubbing glasses at a frantic pace. As if at that moment, as the earth spun, there was nothing more critical than the cleanliness of that stemware and the speed and proficiency with which that simple task could be accomplished. I leaned in across the bar and inquired whether there was anything on the tape that was counter to the brief version Jenny had given when Susan first had gotten home that evening. She assured me there wasn't.

"She told me what happened," she said as she finally ceased her fitful motion and dropped her hands to her hips, "but not the details she gave Rutledge."

"You need to listen again, just to—"

"Did you hear what she said?" I didn't know which part of the conversation she was referring to. Then I realized it was a question that wasn't meant to be answered by the person it was directed to, but by the one who'd asked it.

"No," I said. "What did she say?"

"Cooler than blood." A shudder went through her shoulders. She glanced down, and I imagined her staring at a sticky, black, rubber mat under her feet. "I don't know. Maybe she was in shock." She came back up. "What do you think?"

That question warranted a response. "I don't think she was in shock. I've rarely heard someone so composed and in control of her facilities." I wasn't sure I believed that, but it was what I wanted Susan to hear. I told her I'd keep her in the loop. My phone rang on my way to collect Garrett.

PC said, "The Hardy Boys are here."

"Look like the pictures I gave you?"

"Close enough."

"Any sign of a girl?"

"No."

"You sure?"

"Why ask a question if you don't believe the answer? They're cleaning up, but I don't know how long they'll stay, knowing someone—"

"Stay with them. Don't let them out of your sight." I disconnected.

I didn't bother to inform Rutledge or McGlashan. Some things are best accomplished outside of the law.

I retraced my path on I-75 north and tailgated every scumbag who got in my path. Jenny's voice took residence in my head, and I wondered what, or who, she had seen on the beach that night. She had claimed to Rutledge that she was flustered and lost track of the conversation. But then she compared Billy Ray's blood to the temperature of the Gulf of Mexico. My Polaroid picture of Jenny was going high-def.

Flustered and lost track?

No way.

CHAPTER 22

" Jake-o, man, care for a SweeTart?" Boyd asked without taking his eyes off his phone.

Garrett and I found PC and Boyd close to where I'd instructed PC to set up his observation post. It was the same place Garrett and I had started in the predawn hours on what was quickly morphing into a marathon day. PC had a T-shirt on that said, "I Love Bacon." He was a 140-pound jagged collection of bones, attitude, and enough energy to fire up a nuclear plant that supplied half of Manhattan. He wore a red sweatband that made his hair look like a mushroom cloud on the top of his head. Boyd had grown a beard since our last encounter and was halfway through a sleeve of multicolored SweeTarts.

"I'm good." I settled in next to PC. "What've you got?"

"They've been in and out, loading up the car," PC said. "But about thirty minutes ago, they went in the house and haven't emerged."

Garrett asked, "Any trips to the garage?"

"Just one," PC replied. "Didn't take anything in or out."

"Water," Boyd said without lifting his eyes off his phone.

"Water?" I asked.

"Yeah. Curly walked out with a bottle of water in his pocket. Not there when he went in."

"Okay." I glanced at Garrett. "Drive straight up? Say we're lost?"

"Let's go."

I instructed PC and Boyd to stay. Boyd brought his head out of his electronic world and said, "Roger." Garrett and I got into my truck and approached the house for the second time that day, but this time by road, not by bush. We came up the long gravel drive and past the single-car garage. Twenty feet from the back door, I killed the engine. The screen door flung open, and Randall Coleman tumbled out. His shoulders were as wide as the door, but his legs were thin, like his gym membership only included from the waist up. He had a dimple on his chin that matched a deep V between his eyes. He wore black jeans and a size-too-small T-shirt.

"Excuse me," I said as I got out of the truck. "I was looking for Franklin Dixon's place, and I heard—"

"Off my property, chum." Randall took a few steps toward the truck. "Can't you read? No trespassing."

"No."

"No, what?"

"I can't read."

I glanced at Garrett, but Garrett's eyes were locked on the house. I had Randall. I was deciding on whether to engage him in Hardy Boy trivia—Dixon was a pen name used by the numerous authors who wrote the series—when Garrett sprinted toward the house and took one leap over the three wooden steps that led to the back porch. He rocketed past Randall before Randall registered that Garrett had even moved. I covered the distance that separated Randall and me in two strides and hit him high. My momentum carried us off the porch, and I landed on top of him on the ground. The gravel embedded in his right cheek. My mouth was in his left ear. The Boone position.

"Where's Jenny? Do *not* tell me you don't know. I know you had her in the garage."

"Kiss my—"

"No, no, no," I interrupted. "You don't understand." I brought his right arm up behind his back. He winced and kicked. "Tell me what I want to know, or I'll snap your arm like a dead twig." He started to speak, but I closed the door. "I won't ask twice. Jenny Spencer. Where is she?"

"Don't know."

I raised his arm. His upper lip curled up in an involuntary spasm; his eye tightened as he grunted.

"I don't know. They took her."

"*They?* You think I'm that simple? Listen to me: breaking your arm is my appetizer. *Where is she?*"

"Okay, man. Let me breathe. We owed money, and I think they got to her. She was just gone. Key's missing from the hook, and your girlfriend wasn't—"

"She's not my girlfriend."

"I'm just sayin'—"

"Who has her?"

"Let me up so I can at least talk."

Garrett sprang out of the back door and shoved a younger man down the steps. He had bushy, curly hair and blushed, high cheekbones. Zach Coleman was a Ken doll with flesh. That made him an incongruity in his world. Not that violence and crime have a face, but they have a distinct look—an odor—and it wasn't Zach Coleman. I released the pressure on Randall's arm and grabbed the back of his T-shirt to yank him up. His shirt ripped, and his face smashed back down into the gravel before his stout arms had time to break his fall. I blew my breath out and took a step back. Zach dissolved into a ball on the ground and buried his head in his hands.

"Tell me why and how you abducted her and who you think has her."

Randall rolled over and stood up. He glanced at Garrett. "Why do you give two shits?"

"Friends of the family. Give it to us straight, and we won't call Wyatt Earp on your chemistry operation."

"Go ahead." He let out a huff. "Ain't nobody gonna come after us." He cut Garrett another look. Gauging his odds.

"Don't even think about it," I said.

Randall came back to me and took a moment.

"Just tell him." It came from Zach as he raised his head out of his hands. I was surprised at the strength of his voice. "If you don't, I will. It was wrong. I told you. I told you then that it was wrong." Zach's eyes pierced his brother.

I was going to say something but decided to let them get their thoughts in order. I saw blood on the gravel and realized it was dripping from my right elbow. Two white plastic chairs were on the concrete pad by the side of the porch. I tossed the dirtiest one to Randall and sat in the other. Randall took a seat, paused for a few seconds, and then said, "What do *we* get?"

"A life free from me."

It was Zach who told the story. They were no more than half a day behind their younger brother, Billy Ray. They raced after him as soon as they'd realized he had vanished.

"What made you think," I asked, "that he'd go straight to a motel in Florida just because he'd been there before?"

Zach answered, "He was too dumb to know or care. I doubt Billy Ray even thought of another place."

"Me and Zach," Randall cut in, "always scored in Florida. Know what I mean? Billy Ray—his battery was missing a few cells. He'd wander around the parking lot, chanting some song after we kicked him out of the room. Last spring, said he had it. Said it was time to get himself some sunshine tail. Soon as he went missing, I knew where he was going and what he was going to do."

"Okay," I said. "Then what?"

Zach explained that they drove through the night. When they didn't see Billy Ray's car at the Buccaneer, they drove down Estero Boulevard and checked other motels. They found their brother's red Honda partially hidden from the street in the public parking area McGlashan had described to me at Susan's. "We found him a little farther down the beach."

"He was all reversed," Randall added. "His insides were on the outside."

"What time was this?"

"Dunno. Early, still kind of dark."

"I found Jenny's T-shirt," Zach said. It shot out like a confession. "It had her first and last name on it. I knew her. Spent a day with her on a boat last summer. I didn't know she was in Florida."

"Why did you hightail it after Billy Ray? Skip the part where you tell me you were concerned."

"We just wanted to—" Randall started.

"The money was gone," Zach said. "We figured maybe she knew something about it."

"What money?" I took a step toward Zach, but he was looking at his brother.

Randall said, "They don't need to—"

"Two hundred eighty-four thousand dollars," Zach said.

"He had that on him?"

"Score from our largest deal," Randall said, as if now that the money was on the table, he might as well stake his claim. I turned to face him. "Takes a big kitchen to house that much dough," he continued. "Had to be in the trunk. We had a big blowup with Billy Ray night before he ditched—told him he was out of the family business. Figured he took the money to get back at us. That's why we jumped on the saddle after he left. Otherwise, we wouldn't give a flying fuck. But when we found him on the beach, his talkin' days was done. We headed back to his car, and it was locked. I needed a crowbar. By the time we got to Home Depot and back, police tape was around the car, and the trunk was open. We slowed down, like everybody else, but kept going."

Garrett asked, "Why didn't you take the lug wrench out of the trunk of your car, break the window, and release the trunk lid?" I realized I hadn't told Garrett what McGlashan had said at Susan's house—the trunk release lever inside the car was broken.

"Well, now," Randall said, "that would have been—"

"It was busted," Zach said. "Stud face here ripped it off a year ago—lost his patience with it. Only way in the trunk was with a key. Damn thing was…'bout halfway back from Home Depot, I realized I had the extra set on me. I don't know…I just wasn't thinking straight. Seeing him there like that. I mean, Billy Ray wasn't right and all, but he was still my brother."

"What time was that?" I wanted to return to the money but decided to cover the specifics first. I thought it odd that Zach referred to Billy Ray as "my brother" and not "our brother."

"Dunno. Seven thirty. Give or take."

"Someone beat you to it." I realized I'd spoken the exact line to McGlashan. It seemed that everyone connected to Jenny, like characters in a play, were a step behind to an offstage presence that no one had seen. "Someone knew the money was in the car and where the car was," I said.

"No shit, Sherlock," Randall said.

"You check his motel room?"

"Whaddya think?" Randall asked. "Zach talked some babe with a thick rope of midnight hair to let him in the room, but it didn't look like he was ever there. We was just covering the bases, though, 'cause once we saw that trunk open, we figured that was where Billy Ray had stashed the cash."

Thick rope of hair. Allison had lied to me about not recognizing Zach. She had hesitated when I'd shown her Zach's picture at Grouper's place, the Matanzas Bar and Grill. I should have picked up on that.

"Who beat you to it?" I asked.

Randall said, "Like we'd be here bullshittin' with you if we knew?"

"It wasn't all our money," Zach cut in. "We owed half of it to our partners. We were trying to break into the Tampa market, you know. We met these guys once, and they said they could use some supply. We—"

Randall cut him off. "They don't care about that."

"Pretend I do." I took a step toward Randall. "Tell me how a pair of Bobbsey Twins like you ended up with that much money."

He hesitated before he came in. "We'd done work with them before. This was our first time collecting the money, keeping the books, so to say. They supplied the material, set us up to do more quantity. We moved the product both here and up north."

"Who are 'they?'"

"A group out of Tampa. We were told they were tied-in to an operation up north, but we just dealt with the guys at our level."

"Up north?" I asked.

"Yeah. Chicago, I think."

In a dormant section of my brain, a warning light flickered on, like a soldier gently aroused from a long sleep. "I don't think any organized crime in Tampa is under a Chicago umbrella," I said. "The Trafficantes are long gone, and they had ties to New York, not Chicago. I don't think there's anything based out of Tampa."

"Yeah?" Randall held his sneer. "I'm sure they run their plans past you."

I swatted a gnat away from my face. "You think they were on to Billy Ray, and they took the—"

"No way, man. They don't know shit about him."

"You thought Jenny would lead you to the money," Garrett cut in.

Randall eyed him. "She was the last to see Billy Ray alive. We figured she even did him in. Maybe he told her about the money, and she decided to help herself, you know?"

"With a crowbar?" Garrett asked. "You think she had one in her beach bag?"

"Told you," Zach said to his brother.

"Shut the fuck up," Randall said. "For all we knew, she got someone to help her. We just wanted to question her. That's all." He sounded conciliatory. It was dawning on him that with Zach's altar-boy, confessional demeanor, he was the prime bad guy.

"How did you know where to find her?" I asked.

"Tell him, Curly," Randall bossed his younger brother.

Zach gave him a look then came back to me. "She mentioned, the one time I saw her, that she had an aunt down here. I told her we came down as well, you know, to the same area, and—"

"You pussy ass," Randall cut him off. "Just get to it. Little bro here is all country—likes Blake Shelton; ain't that so, Curly?—so when we found her T-shirt, he recalled that her aunt's last name was Blake. It wasn't too hard to find her street after that."

"How did you lure her out?" I asked Zach.

Randall came in before Zach had a chance. "That was Zach's move. He attracts chicks like flies on shit. He had her number from last year, along with the number of every other babe south of Columbus. Called her and said to come quick—said he had something to give her but was waiting on the corner for a ride he didn't want to miss. That girl ran down the street without even putting her shoes on. She trusted you, didn't she, Curly?"

"Eat shit."

"Why didn't you drive up to her house?" I asked.

"Because," Zach said, "dickhead here didn't want anybody on the street to see us. Guess that didn't work out, did it, *bro?*"

Before Randall fired off another retort and we all entered family counseling, I said, "Tell me about the money."

Randall shrugged. "Two hundred eighty-four thousand. Half was ours. The other hundred forty-four we owed our partners."

"Hundred forty-two, numb nuts," Zach said.

"Did Jenny know about the money?"

"Oh, yeah," Randall said. He put his hands behind his head and leaned back in the chair. He was top-heavy, and the chair fell over backward. He scrambled to his feet.

"You're one sorry motherfucker," his brother observed.

Randall ignored him and landed a hard stare on me. "She knew. She said Billy Ray told her that he had two hundred eighty-four big ones in the car, something like that, and—"

"She didn't know anything else about it," Zach said. "She said he mentioned something about money, but she wasn't listening."

"What's your dream, little man?" Randall asked. "Knock her up with your pygmy stick and waltz her down the aisle?"

"You can go—"

Garrett took a step forward. "Enough."

I made a note to call Rutledge and let him know Jenny might have left something out of the interview. It wouldn't be unusual, which is why multiple interviews are preferred. Often the story changes, or the witness—in this case Jenny—simply can't recall with certainty what happened or what was said. Memory, after all, is largely fiction.

"What were you birdbrains thinking?" I asked Randall. "She could finger you and Zach for kidnapping."

"She never knew we was brothers and never saw me," Randall said. "I kept a mask on. We figured she'd never press charges against Zach. Isn't that what you said, Zach? That you could charm her out of running to the cops? That she'd never do anything to put you in the big house?"

Zach brought his knees up in front of him, wrapped his arms around them, and clamped them in front. "Like she wouldn't know your voice if she heard you later? You were just too chickenshit to show your sorry face."

"That ain't chickenshit, Curly. That's being smart." Randall turned to me. "We eventually would've let her go."

"No, you wouldn't have," Garrett said.

"Well, we'll just never know, will we?" Randall shot back. I was growing impatient with the remaining Coleman brothers. Were these the best criminals we could come up with? This was our best effort? Talk about American competiveness. No wonder the Mexicans and Columbians own the drug trade.

I took two steps toward Zach, got on my knees, and stuck my face in his. "When did she disappear?"

Our eyes locked. On a good day, Mrs. Coleman might have had one son she could be proud of. "Last twenty-four hours. They called us down to Tampa yesterday to try to smooth things over. We stayed and partied a night, and when we came back, our place was trashed. We figured they searched the house for cash and then took her."

"Who has her, Zach?"

"I dunno."

"She's suffering, Zach. And you did this to her."

He whimpered.

"Oh, for Christ's sake," Randall said.

Zach blew out some air, and his shoulders settled. "You got to believe me, man. I'm not sure. Randall had told them that we had her and that she knew about the money but didn't have it. If we didn't have her, they would have come after us. But the fact that we took her reinforced to them that we didn't have the money—that we too were looking for it. You gotta realize, man, we figured they was looking at us like we double-crossed them."

"I don't get it," I interjected. "Did you give her up?"

"No. No, nothing like that," Zach said as he regained his composure and straightened his back. "Like I said, we'd told them that we had her. We wanted more time with—"

"Had they been here before?"

"Yeah. Yeah, and that's just it, man. We had some of them up here a few months ago. You know, trying to get to know who we were doing business with."

"And you think they got impatient and came after her?"

"What else? They call us down for a night and then slip up here and grab her. We figured they either thought we cut them out and took her as a cover—proof that we didn't take the cash—or she had it. Randall figured better her than us. No one believed me when I said neither Jenny or us had the money.

Then Randall told them she was a runaway to start with." He shot his brother a look. It was the first time he'd broken eye contact with me since I'd gotten on my knees. "Ain't that right, Randall?" I got up and marched over to Randall. Zach's voice came from behind me. "They said when we was done with her, they had a whole line of operations that needed homeless girls to staff. But Jenny wasn't like that. I told them she—"

"You told them she was a runaway?" I was two feet from Randall.

"Teenage bait, man. Chicks like her can—"

My punch caught him square in the jaw and stung my hand. Randall Coleman wasn't worth cracking my knuckles over. I stepped back and was preparing a high kick when he tumbled over from the force of my punch. I kicked him in the stomach. I was bringing my foot back when Garrett's hands grabbed my shoulders and jerked me back.

"I will ride a broom up your ass and pin you to the moon if any harm comes to that girl," I said, glaring down at Randall. I turned to Zach. "Tell me everything about your Tampa connection."

He gave a club address in downtown St. Pete and the physical description of two men. Randall, in an extra-inning effort to raise his standing, added a few details to Zach's story. We gave them our plan and left fifteen minutes later, after Zach reached into the back of a blue van and handed me what I wanted. We rendezvoused with PC and Boyd and told them to head home. Garrett and I settled in for our second trip back to the island that day. I was beat.

"Think the Colemans spilled it straight?" he asked.

"Zach, maybe. Wouldn't bet alongside Randall."

"Their Tampa partners got anxious and decided to grab her themselves and see what they could find out." He let it out as a declarative review.

"That might be their play. If nothing else, they get a run-away to feed into their system. Meanwhile, neither party trusts the other, and they hold Jenny in hopes that she can lead them to the money. But we've got another issue."

"Zach's call to Jenny."

"Rutledge should have known about that," I said. "He would have seen it on her cell."

"McGlashan said there was nothing of interest on it. Either Rutledge didn't bother to check, or McGlashan isn't being straight with you."

"Let's find out."

I took out Rutledge's card and hit his numbers. He picked up on the third ring. I let him know that Jenny, depending on how reliable the Colemans' information was, may have mentioned that Billy Ray had a car stuffed with cash. He cursed and quickly recovered. "She certainly never mentioned it to me," he said then accelerated his tempo. "That's why we conduct follow-up interviews. Maybe she would have mentioned it the second time around, or maybe not. She'd been through a lot that night, despite her ulterior coolness. After an experience like she had, it can be very difficult to recall exactly what transpired."

"But," I said as I gunned past a yellow Ford Explorer with a dent in the driver's door and cigarette smoke trailing out of a cracked window, "someone going for the money *would* explain why no prints were found on the car."

"Perhaps. Keep me posted."

"Zach said he called her. You found nothing on her phone?"

"Jenny's?"

"We working another case together?"

"*We* are not doing anything together," Rutledge said.

"You checked her phone, right?"

"What about it?"

"Zach Coleman said he called Jenny to lure her out of her house. His number would be on her phone under recent calls." Actually, Randall spilled that bit of information, but Zach didn't deny it.

"And we would have seen it," he shot back. "Nothing there but a dump truck load of texts, none of which have anything to do with her disappearance. Come by and look if you want to burn time, but it's clean."

"Why would Zach tell me that?"

"Hell, I don't know, Travis. Why don't you ask the meth dealer himself? If I kidnapped someone, my story would also be that I called and that they came voluntarily. Take a look at Zach Coleman's phone. You ain't going find what you're looking for."

I decided that how Zach had lured Jenny out of the house was of little meaning. Rutledge and I disconnected. Something about his reply had struck me as odd, but I couldn't recall what it was; the thought hit my mind but never took hold. I placed my phone on the center console on top of Jenny's T-shirt, which is what Zach had handed me from the back of their van. I considered turning some music on, but all I did was count crosses on the side of the road.

CHAPTER 23

I had been up since predawn, had spent eight hours yo-yoing up and down the interstate, and was eagerly anticipating a good night's sleep. Not that I have much experience in that area.

At the peak of the bridge, the pink hotel looked like it was in a snow globe as it radiated against the black Gulf. Kathleen had called and said she was at my house, since she wanted to read Maugham in the morning at the end of my dock. That girl was on a mission.

I parked in my driveway. The truck barely fit in the garage and left no room for my drop-down punching bag with the pink, smiling face. Garrett split next door to Morgan's. Before I entered, I tossed a shredded gecko into the trash that Hadley III had left for me next to my running shoes. One morning I had put my foot in a shoe only to find she had deposited a present. The half-living lizard had crawled into the toe of the shoe. I now check my shoes before I run. Minor adjustments are necessary to cohabitate with a feline hunter.

Kathleen stood in front of the Magnavox with a Bobby Darin album in her hand. I focus on vertical collections and had just completed Bobby Darin's covers. Darin—who, at age thirty-two, discovered that his parents were really his grandparents and that his sister was actually his mother—was also a chess nut. His cover of Tim Hardin's "If I Were a Carpenter" works for me every time. That neither Darin nor Hardin lived to see forty is one of those things I wish I didn't know.

It wasn't Darin's voice in the room, but Nat King Cole's.

"I'm trying to decide what to put on next," Kathleen said as a greeting. She showed me the Darin album. "Is this the latest one you bought?"

It had been a long day. I was too tired for words, and life is too short for sleep. I picked her up and carried her into the bedroom. She lobbed a few questions, but when she realized conversation wasn't on the menu, she gave into the moment. Afterward, we lay beside each other as Cole's smooth, wide voice, coupled with Johnny Mercer's classic lyrics, forever married a song with a season that Florida would never know.

We lay facing each other, our heads resting on propped elbows. Our standard postcoital position. "Tell me, stranger," she said as she ran a finger along the scar on my left shoulder, "have we met before?"

"Autumn in London. Disraeli had just been elected prime minister. Across the fields of Kensington Gardens, I saw you high on your white stallion. I—"

"No Great War poetry tonight?"

"I'm going further back."

"Do you think things were better then?"

"No doubt. I always thought"—I took her finger off my shoulder and laced her fingers with mine—"that I'd be a sucker for a hearty nineteenth-century girl. A plumb maiden who never saw a dentist, applied skin cream; who couldn't imagine daily hot showers or a life with—"

"Antibiotics," Kathleen cut in.

I brought our hands up and graced the edge of her smile with my finger. "Internet porn," I said.

"Air conditioning."

"Internet porn."

"Smartphones, and you need to move on."

"Thongs."

"That doesn't count."

"Pizza delivery."

"Oh, my God. Can we?" She broke away and pushed up on both hands.

"Whatever raises your flag." I was no longer tired, as my reserve battery had kicked in. I haven't a clue what its source is.

I grabbed two champagne flutes and filled them two-thirds of the way with Taittinger. She poured herself a soft drink. Thirty minutes later, we sat on the screen porch and opened a box of pepperoni pizza with pimento-stuffed olives that had been delivered to our door. It *is* a wonderful world.

Kathleen lit a solitary candle, and on the bay, the red channel marker blinked. She consumed her first piece without engaging customary civilized chewing techniques. "To what shall we toast?" she asked.

"To Kensington Gardens," I said, tilting my flute toward hers.

"Kensington Gardens."

I glanced up again at the red channel marker, and my mind flashed to the drops of blood from my elbow earlier that day. I wondered where Jenny was sleeping that night. I again thought of Kathleen challenging me as to why I risked *us* for causes that had been thrust upon *me*. Without risk, there is quiet desperation. Without risk, we take our songs to the ground. Like schussing down a Colorado slope, you need to relinquish control and momentarily trust your instincts. Push the envelope; trust your cape.

"You there? I said the crust is crispier this time." Kathleen interrupted my traversing thoughts, and I lost the thread.

Something about skiing with a cape, which I'd done before on Mardi Gras, but why was I thinking of Mardi Gras? Whatever. My reserve battery must have been faltering.

"Just staring at the marker." I reached for another slice. I was glad we'd opted for pepperoni. I'd been falling behind on my goal to eat more fatty foods.

"Take me there, will you?" Kathleen asked. "To Kensington. I haven't traveled nearly as much as I want." Hadley III jumped onto her lap. Kathleen stroked the back of the cat's neck, and Hadley III fired up her purr engine.

"Travel's overrated," I said. "Fatal to prejudice, bigotry, and narrow-mindedness."

"Twain?"

"It is."

"I thought he burned out on traveling later in life," Kathleen offered. "Said something about the only places he hadn't been to were heaven and hell, and he had only a passing interest in one of those."

"What a marvelous thing to say as they close the curtain."

"I suppose so. Certainly beats the tired muse about what might have been." Her chewing had slowed to a more reasonable, civil pace. "How's your search coming?"

"We came up empty today. We talked to the brothers who abducted Jenny, but someone swiped her from under their nose."

"Why?"

"She apparently told them that Billy Ray said he had two hundred eighty-four thousand dollars in his car. But she never mentioned it in her police interview, so who knows? The Colemans owe half, and we believe the party who lays claim to the other half snatched her. I have a few places—and faces—to check out tomorrow, but my forward progress has stalled like a Sherman tank in the mud."

"Twain and Sherman. Contemporaries, I believe." Kathleen pretended not to stare at the pizza box, where one lone piece awaited its fate.

I thought of Jenny's cryptic exchange with Rutledge over General William Tecumseh Sherman. He *had* burned Atlanta. Sherman was born less than a half-hour drive from Greenwood, Ohio. That might have accounted for her knowledge; maybe she'd paid attention during a sixth-grade field trip. Sherman attended a Catholic church until the outbreak of the Civil War, and then, despite his devout wife and son, supposedly never again set foot in a church. The realities of war trumped the illusions of religion. I doubt they covered that in a sixth-grade field trip.

I wanted to listen to Jenny's interview again. Maybe if I heard it repeatedly, something would come forth. I didn't really believe that, but to claim that I was stuck in the mud was to put an optimistic bent on my forward progress.

"Did you know Twain came in and left with Halley's Comet?" Kathleen asked, and shifted her weight forward. An aggressive, well-plotted move. Like I didn't know who I was up against? Like she didn't know my capabilities? I can see the board a dozen pieces ahead. I shifted my own weight to my left leg in the event the situation escalated to arms.

"I do," I said hurriedly, fully aware that every second counted. "He even predicted he would die at the comet's return, but I think he was off a day. Do not even *think* of touching that last slice."

"*Fine.*" The word exploded out, as if her lower lip sprung out from under her upper teeth. The letter 'f' never had received, or warranted, such attention, let alone such a muscular effort. She curled into the chair like a wounded animal and took a sip of Taittinger. She followed it with a gulp of sugar water. Strange bedfellows. I claimed the prize and returned to the blinking red light. I recalled my conversation with Rutledge earlier in the day. Kathleen said something about the strength of the heart versus that of death. Some mumbo jumbo about Churchill also predicting his own death, which corresponded with the date of his father's death. Day out days. Chatty Patty's contribution to my nomenclature.

"What was that?" I asked, as I consumed the last bite.

"Were you listening at all?"

"No. I really wasn't. Once I've done my reproductive act for the day, I pretty much punch the clock."

"Truer words never spoken." There was a genuine bite in her voice. I wasn't surprised; we'd been down this path before. When there was a solitary piece left in the pizza box, words flew. Feelings suffered. Bridges burned.

I closed the lid, and we hit the bed for the second time.

Later that night, when sleep dumped me like an unsatisfied lover, I left Kathleen under a sheet *and* a blanket—we had a running disagreement over the thermostat setting—and returned to the porch. I stared at the channel marker. Hadley III pounced on top of the grill and did the same. She was fond of staring at the night. I kept waiting for something to come to me, but it never did. It was just a stupid, blinking, red light. Garrett and I planned to force the action tomorrow, and the sun couldn't come up soon enough. Before I returned to bed, I cleaned the fluted glasses. I don't like days encumbered with the previous night.

CHAPTER 24

"We're not wasting any time in there," Garrett said. "You got the lead."

We were parked on Sixth Avenue North, a block from the rear of the Palladium Theatre in downtown St. Pete. We were four blocks off Beach Drive and in a transitional part of the city. The single-story building where Zach told us they'd met their contacts had barred windows so dark that I wondered why they didn't just board them. A sign said, Winking Lizard, and under that were the words Food and Liquor. A blinking three-foot neon martini glass was tilted to the left side of the sign. It labored to emit a dirty pink through years of grime. It looked original; it would have looked nice in my garage.

We stepped inside. It was like walking into night. A few hunched figures were already entrenched on their stools. It smelled like smoke. Must not have caught that law. The walls held crooked pictures of NASCAR drivers; check your football memorabilia at the door. Pairings of ceiling fans battled the heavy air. There were a few pool tables, and men with long sticks circled the flattops. All but one looked up when we came in, but their heads soon sunk back to their game with apparent disinterest. Garrett and I claimed two wood-backed stools, and I ordered a Kona Longboard. Garrett asked for iced tea. The bartender, a lumbering creature with a Shakespearean beard, said, "We don't have no ice tea." Garrett requested water. The

161

beard eyed him then casually rotated. He took down a glass from a shelf, ran it under the chrome spigot, and then dropped it in front of Garrett.

"May I please, sir, have some ice?" Garrett asked.

Here we go. At least he could have waited until I got a couple of long runs in. Our mark, as far as I could tell, was the man in the Captain Tony's T-shirt who was shooting pool. He looked as if he might match one of the descriptions Zach had given us, but it was too dark, and I wasn't going to stare. He was the only player who hadn't looked up when we'd entered. He was the only one who didn't glance up now.

"I beg your pardon?" Falstaff asked.

"I said, 'May I please, sir, have some ice?' Does that pose a problem for you?"

"Might I suggest that next time you remember to order *ice* water. That pose a problem for you, bud?" He didn't move. I took the opportunity to suck a deep draw from my bottle. Tinker Bell would never know.

"I'll remember that," Garrett said. "And you should remember to serve ice with water. While not expected in Europe, it is customary in the States, even in NASCAR country."

Falstaff kept his eyes on Garrett, reached under the bar, and came up with a fistful of ice cubes. He dropped them into the water glass. Several cubes missed and bounced off the bar's surface. I took a quick gulp from my bottle and glanced up at a security camera.

Garrett said, "See? That wasn't hard, was it? You don't have any soap, do you?"

"Soap?"

"To go with your shower."

Garrett rose leisurely with his glass in his hand. He poured the water, in a distinct circular motion, over the man's head. A few chuckles came from down the bar. One cube got hung up in his beard. Falstaff took his right fist back in a circular motion that started out on an oilrig off New Orleans in the Gulf of Mexico. It came in so slow that I had time to get in another swig before his fist entered the proximity of Garrett's airspace. Garrett dodged to his left, and the big man's fist kept going out toward Tampa Bay. With nothing to meet its force, it carried his body halfway across the bar. Garrett, with speed that humbled me every time I witnessed it, yanked the man's head, and the body followed. Falstaff went down with an audible thud. The man covered a chunk of the floor; he'd need a double plot some day.

I had seen him approach, and now the man in the Captain Tony's shirt stood over the bartender. Another man stood a pace behind him. He still held his cue stick, and it was a toss-up which was taller—the stick or him. The little fellow made up for his lack of height with muscles grossly disproportionate to his frame. He fit one of the descriptions Randall had given. "Tall as the stick, wide as the table," he'd said. Captain Tony, especially compared to the lump on the floor, was a slight man. His arms were solid ink. He wore a headband that only partially covered a white gauze bandage a few inches above his left eye. Did Jenny's club find its mark? When Falstaff struggled to his feet, Captain Tony flashed the whitest smile I'd ever seen. That confirmed these were Randall's contacts. "I'm telling you, man," Randall had tacked on to Zach's description, "absolutely supernova teeth—they just blaze."

Captain Tony said to the floor, "Let it go, Special."

"Why the hell would I—"

"He's fast and you're slow. Go catch some fresh air."

The bartender shot Garrett his best dagger eyes, mumbled something about getting back at him, and lumbered out the front door. When he opened the door, the outside light flashed in like a hydrogen bomb. As the door swung shut, the light vaporized out of the room.

"Now," Captain Tony said, "why are you cruising in here and purposely causing such a ruckus?"

Garrett sauntered around to the back of the bar. He got a glass, dropped some ice in it, and added water. He came back around, stopped in front of Captain Tony, and said, "See? Was that so hard?"

Captain Tony eyed him. "You didn't come here for water."

I drained my beer, stood, and announced, "The Coleman boys retired—failed the drug test—and we're free agents. Take us to your leader. We're here to collect our half of what you took."

Garrett and I had told the Colemans to stand down, told them we'd dive in and retrieve the half of Billy Ray's cargo that was rightfully theirs, assuming that somehow their partners had gotten the money from Billy Ray either before or after his encounter with Jenny. No one was quite sure of that, but at the moment, it was our best logical conclusion, although its position was tenuous. Maybe Billy Ray had made contact with them and had planned to give them their half and conveniently rip off his brothers. Maybe he had tipped Captain Tony off to that, and the captain and his crew had decided to grab the entire bounty. Maybe the mob really did take out Marilyn Monroe and JFK, and little green men landed in Area 51. We were full of surmises and short of facts. All we knew was that Billy Ray was dead, and the money and Jenny were missing.

"I don't know what you're referring to," Captain Tony said. "I shoot pool all day."

I replied, "It's what you do at night that interests us."

"You think barging in here and picking on Special is a way to earn my trust?"

"Special?" I said. "That's Falstaff's real name?"

"Falstaff?"

"The bartender. How do you get 'Special' from that?"

Captain Tony gave that a second then cocked his head. "His parents were riding junk for days after a Kiss concert in 1980—they only played one show in the States that year. 'Special Engagement,' they called it. Special came along nine months later."

"Unmasked Tour," I said. I didn't bother to add that it was at a different Palladium, not the one behind us, but the one in New York that NYU tore down to erect a dormitory.

"That's the one," Captain Tony said. He nodded in approval, as if we were men at war but had found a common ground. Like Christmas on the Western Front, 1915.

I turned to Garrett. "How do you feel about that? You took advantage of Special."

"Your move," Garrett said. His eyes never left the captain.

Captain Tony shrugged. "Let's go. My orders are to present you."

"You expecting us?"

"I had a call. We'll take my car."

"If it's all the same," I told him, "we'll follow in ours."

He gave a slight shrug, turned, and strolled over to a pool table. Cue Stick followed, and they started to rack the balls. I glanced at Garrett, who nodded.

"You drive a hard bargain," I said. "We'll ride with you, Tony. But I get shotgun."

Captain Tony turned to face me. "Who's Tony?"

"You. Got your name right there on your shirt in the event you forget, which is a damn good thing, as you just did."

He studied me for a few seconds then said, "You like humor, but your friend"—he nodded at Garrett—"he does not smile."

"We're all friends." I took a step closer to him. "After all, we're going to be in business together."

"That," Captain Tony said as he put on a leather jacket—it was already pushing ninety outside—"is not for me to decide. *Andiamo*. We're running late."

I wasn't surprised they'd expected us. It explained Special's hostile reaction to Garrett. Randall wasn't the type to roll that easy. But "*andiamo*" in a NASCAR joint? I wondered where Captain Tony picked up the Italian word that loosely translated to "Let's go."

I rode shotgun. As we rolled over Tampa Bay, the water was calm on my left, or north, and wind ripples scrubbed the surface on my right. I asked Cue Stick, who drove, if he had a wife and kids. I told him I would value his opinion on Florida's charter school policy. I added that if he could explain charter school funding, it would place him in the top point five percent of the nation's literate populace. He never spoke, and I replied to his silence that I respected his opinion. We exited the freeway and went through Used Car Alley.

"Certified used cars," I said. "I don't get it. Are they guaranteeing that your car isn't new? Like you don't know that?"

No one wanted to play. We passed a city bus with a sign on its side of a man tossing a smiling baby into the air. Underneath the grinning nugget was the following in block letters: EVERY BABY IS BORN TO DO SOMETHING GREAT. I'm not so sure about that. We split onto I-4 and took the first exit. We pulled behind a building on East 8th Avenue in Ybor City.

Ybor City is a slice of New Orleans dropped into Tampa. In a different century, it was a bustling Latin quarter famous for cigars, nightlife, and industry that thrived when the sun went down. That gave Ybor City dark roots. Dirty money. Lawless men. Now it houses local breweries, bars, and restaurants. It's where the past and present collide, like incoming and outgoing tides in a canal. In such places, the water boils and bubbles at the surface, literally not knowing which direction it's going. Such is Ybor City—yesterday and today, both frothing and aggressively claiming the same moment.

We shut the truck's doors, and they sounded like miniature hand grenades ripping off within nanoseconds of each other. Captain Tony said, "We're going to search you. You understand that?" His question was directed at Garrett. I was hurt; he didn't seem overly concerned with me.

Garrett said, "I'll give it to you."

Captain Tony hesitated then replied, "Slowly."

Garrett reached into his jacket pocket and handed his SIG Sauer to the captain. I handed my Smith & Wesson to the driver and said, "Here you go, little fella."

"How do we know they don't have more?" he asked Captain Tony with a scowl that looked more like a pout than a menacing signal.

"You speak," I said.

"They're fine," the captain said.

He spun, and Garrett and I followed him up a back iron staircase that hugged the wall of the brick building, its lumpy, grotesque, thick mortar frozen in place on the day it was formed. Inside the truck, it had been cool, and as we climbed, the humidity pressed down on us, as if with every step we were getting closer to sacrificing ourselves.

CHAPTER 25

"Would you gentlemen like some lunch?" the man behind the desk inquired.

"Anybody above you?" I asked.

"Excuse me?"

"I specifically indicated that we wished to see the leader. The capo."

"Yes," he chuckled. "Capo...I suppose some may view me in that manner."

We stood in a spacious room. Elegant windows stretched to the tongue-and-groove ceiling where a wood fan rotated with the speed of a tired paddle-wheeler. The planking on the floor was wider than the Mississippi in May. A small picture frame on the credenza behind the desk held a photograph of a beaming young girl with a mountain range behind her. Our host rose from his chair. He was well fed and wore light beige slacks with a short-sleeve, deep-blue silk shirt. A slim gold chain hung around his thick neck. A tightly trimmed mustache, a lighter shade than his hair but a perfect match for his sideburns, hid his upper lip. He would have made a good pitchman for a cruise line that catered to seniors. He sauntered around from the desk and extended his hand.

"Joseph Dangelo."

"Jake Travis." I shook his hand. "I've been called a lot of things, but never gentle."

That garnered a soundtrack laugh. "Likewise, Mr. Travis."
He continued to grasp my hand. "And while I fit the description, and like to believe that I possess more than the necessary
amount of desirable attributes, I sincerely doubt I've ever been
referred to as a leader, and certainly not"—he paused and finally
freed my hand—"as 'capo.' A signature, I believe, that's best
left in the minds of the romantics."

Garrett introduced himself, and we all buddied up as if we
were getting ready to smack a ball off the first tee. Garrett had
to take his hand out of his pocket to shake Dangelo's hand, and
I wondered what it was doing there in the first place. I assumed
we would be introduced to someone in the middle of the organization, but Dangelo had the trappings and persona of someone who had graduated from the middle years ago.

"Follow me, if you will," he said as he strode past us. "The
finest restaurant in Ybor is just a short walk."

Garrett and I fell in line like ducks. Two men in jeans and
loose-fitting jackets joined us outside Dangelo's office. The captain and Cue Stick had vanished, and I assumed they'd passed
our hardware to the new tag team. One of our new escorts had
a neck the size of my thigh. His sidecar had a peppered goa-
tee and wore honest-to-God wire-rimmed eyeglasses. He also
had a brain the size of my left nut. How do I know this? I
possess an uncanny ability—a gift, if you must—to make an
instant, accurate assessment of people. I'm never in doubt, and
rarely right, but that doesn't stop me from practicing my craft.
I labeled our new escorts Tweedledum and Tweedledee.

We walked two short blocks south to the Cubana Grille.
The sidewalk was grimy concrete hexagon pavers. A crew across
the street was power-washing the surface, but their efforts
would only serve to maintain the status quo, for the sidewalks,
like those in the French Quarter in New Orleans, were per-

manently embedded with the revelry of the nightlife. I got a hangover just looking at my feet.

The Cubana Grille was housed in a yellow brick building with a second-floor balcony. Flower boxes spilled green vines over a black wrought-iron rail. A music stand outside the front door displayed the menu.

It was slammed. Dangelo didn't break stride when he entered but marched past the crowded hostess stand to a vacant rear table. The Tweedle boys took a lonely table by the front door. It was the least desirable table in the restaurant. A downpour erupted as if Poseidon had dumped the oceans upon the earth. A waiter rushed out the front door and brought in the music stand. A platinum blonde—Kelly, if one was to believe the nametag—with an inch-thick line of dark roots that divided her head into two distinct halves, greeted him by name as she placed an iced tea in front of him. She had a square jaw and jittery green eyes. A black apron was wrapped tightly around her midsection like a corset. Dangelo thanked Kelly. She inquired what Garrett and I would like to drink, and we told her.

"Thank you for seeing us, Mr. Dangelo," I said.

"Please"—he gestured with his left hand—"just call me Joseph."

Now why couldn't the police in Iroquois land be like that? Do we really need criminals to teach us that we're all brothers? I responded, "And Jake to you."

"Not Jacob?" he asked with a touch of bewilderment.

"Technically yes, but I never use it."

"A pity. It's such a strong name with a rich heritage."

"You come here often?"

"When I'm in Ybor. I also maintain an office in St. Pete. It's a more convenient location for a string of businesses that we have from Sarasota to Tampa."

"And what business are those?"

"Making money. What other business is there?"

I decided not to attack on that point. "What do you recommend here?"

"I like the stacked grilled ham with double Swiss on rye with fries. But"—he methodically extracted his silverware from his napkin and placed the black cloth on his lap, an exercise he seemed to take great pleasure in—"I only indulge if I'm eating alone or with someone who isn't going to tattle to my wife."

"Your indulgence is safe with us," I assured him.

"Yes..." He let it hang out there a few beats. "I'm quite sure it is."

Kelly deposited my iced tea and Garrett's water—with ice—and took our orders. Grilled ham worked all around. I had a side seat that allowed a partial view of the room. Garrett's back was to the crowd, and I knew that grated him. I doubted he could sit like that for more than a few minutes. Exposed. Two men behind him. Most likely with guns—ours to boot. Another waiter scurried by. His ears were gauged, and gold rings the size of nickels were inserted in his lobes.

"Excuse me," Garrett said, and shoved his chair out. He went toward the back, where the restrooms were. I noted the eyes that followed him.

"When did they start doing that?" Dangelo asked.

"Hitting the head?"

"Putting holes in their ears. When did the young start drilling holes in their earlobes? I see it all the time now. I don't understand it. First they tattoo their bodies, and now this. Like they're trying to one-up each other in a perverted race to deform their bodies."

"A millennium or two ago. It's an ancient custom, even a ritual in some societies."

"You'd think we'd move on, make progress."

I leaned in a tad. "Yes, you'd think that about a lot of things, wouldn't you?"

Dangelo met my gaze. "Tell me, Jacob, what is it you believe that I can do for you?"

Every time I hear that name, I look for my John Deere, a woman with a bonnet, and my seven kids. But I wasn't going to let Dangelo get under my skin. I asked, "Why did you agree to see us?"

His eyes narrowed. "I don't normally receive a question to my own question."

"Indulge me."

He chuckled. "Very good. It's my understanding that you're representing associates of ours who are missing some funds they owe us."

"The Colemans."

"Their names aren't familiar to me."

"Naturally. But if you believe someone owes you money, don't you take a bat to their knees?"

Dangelo shook his head. "So offensive. We—"

"Save it."

He paused then continued, "We have reason to believe they're being honest with us. Again, what is it you think I can do for you?"

"They've retained us to negotiate on their behalf."

"No. I don't think so."

I let that rest for a beat then said, "Don't think what?"

"I don't think," Dangelo said as his eyes pierced mine, "that you care about the Colemans, whoever they are. I don't think they retained—your word, I believe—you to represent them."

"Why did you agree to see us?" I inquired for the second time.

Dangelo and I went mano a mano in a staring match. "Because," he said, "I'm missing a considerable amount of money, and you coincidently dropped into my world. I don't believe in coincidences."

Garrett returned, and Kelly placed our lunches in front of us. I complimented her on keeping the orders straight. She ignored me and smiled at Garrett. The rain had stopped outside, and the sun's indirect rays illuminated the room as if someone had flipped the switch. I said, "Considering your money, I don't know who took it or where it is, but I was hoping to arrange a simple quid pro quo—an exchange, in the event that I do locate your missing funds, for something I'm missing." I studied Dangelo's face. I was going to take the plunge and would have only a split second to gauge his reaction.

"I'm always receptive to lucrative business arrangements. Exactly what it is that you're missing?" He hurriedly took a bite out of his sandwich that reduced his outstanding lunch by a quarter. My guess was that he'd been anticipating lunch since 10:00 a.m.

I waited until he was deep into his chew, and then I dove in headfirst. "Jenny Spencer."

Dangelo paused a barely measurable tick of time then continued with the consumption of his bite. But I knew. And I knew that he knew that I knew. He worked his grilled ham as if he were in a contest in which the slowest person to digest his lunch won. He took a sip of his iced tea. He wiped his mouth with the napkin. "Eight Days a Week" played through the speakers. McCartney was in a car and asked the driver how he was doing. Driver said he was working eight days a week. The former Quarryman liked the phrase. Wrote a song.

Garrett rose partway, kicked around his chair, and sat back down. He now had a partial view of the table that held Dangelo's bodyguards. I was surprised he'd lasted as long as he had, but I admired his timing. Dangelo paid no attention to Garrett's offensive move and said, "I don't know who you're referring to."

"That's right, Joe. You don't do names, do you?" I buried a french fry in ketchup and stuck it in my mouth. It was salty. Next year, I'll add "Eat more salty foods" to my resolution list. His eyes tightened, and I decided to back off. I needed him more than he needed me. "I understand," I started in, "that the Colemans owe you about a hundred and forty-two thousand dollars."

"Go on."

"What I don't follow is why you'd snatch the girl if you'd recovered the money. Therefore, you don't have the money, nor do the Colemans. But neither side trusts the other and figures the other party will lie about recovering the cash for the opportunity to double their profit. Meanwhile, the last person to talk to the man who stole the money is an unfortunate young lady who's being passed around like a discarded teapot—as if holding on to her will shed light on which one of you is double-crossing the other."

Dangelo rolled his tongue inside his upper lip, and his mustache moved like a wooly worm. "Interesting theory," he said. "First off, I don't double-cross. Second"—he took his napkin across his mouth—"kidnapping is a federal offense. I have no knowledge of this girl that you're so passionate about. But if we were to go with your story, oh"—he tilted his head and brought his palms up in front of him—"to indulge each other, you're correct in one assessment."

His turn to make me squirm. I asked, "And that is?"

"If I had the money, I would have no interest in the girl."

"And you were correct in your assessment."

He smiled and said, "Please."

"I don't give a damn about the Colemans or the money." I leaned in. "If I were to locate your missing funds, do you think,

Joseph, that would make a material difference in my quest to locate a safe and healthy Ms. Spencer?"

He paused a beat then said, "Possibly."

"If neither you nor the Colemans possess the cash, who does? Who in your organization is double-crossing you?"

"Why me? Why not the Colemans?"

"One of them already did, and he's dead."

"But for entirely unrelated reasons."

"I thought you had no knowledge of the Colemans. That *is* what you stated, is it not?"

Dangelo pushed his empty plate off to the side. Outside, a truck hit a pothole, and water drenched the sidewalk. The same man who had brought in the music stand now placed it back outside. Must have been in the job description.

Dangelo relaxed back into his chair. "Technically I said their names aren't familiar. That isn't to be construed as a lack of understanding of the prominent points of the situation. Tell me, do you like history, Mr. Travis?"

"Your point?"

"This place"—he took his right arm and arched it over the table—"remembers every person who's ever walked its streets, toiled in its stuffy cigar factories, cried at its demise, and now rejoices at its rebirth. People like you and me have been conducting business for more than a century in this very room."

He stopped, and I wasn't sure where he was going or whether I was supposed to question his tenets on history. I took a sip of iced tea and let two pieces of ice slide into my mouth. I gave one an audible crack and swallowed its remains.

"Sometimes"—he went back into it—"those participants misjudge each other. Such cases oftentimes do not turn out well for one of the parties. Neither of us desires that to be our case."

"Touching," I said. "First of all, such cases often do not turn out well for *either* party. If you're harboring a kidnapped woman, you're in a puddle of trouble." Garrett made an indiscernible grunt. "And my bet is that—"

"Why your interest in this young lady?"

"Pardon me?"

"The lady. Why?"

I corrected him. "Ms. Jenny Spencer."

"Why do you give a damn about Ms. Spencer?"

"That's not what you're asking."

Dangelo's eyebrows arched. "No?"

"No." I leaned across the table and kept my voice low. "What you want to know, Joe"—I cracked the last piece of ice—"is how badly I want her. Will I disappear for a twenty? Maybe a grand, and my buddy and I take a walk? Or is there something else behind me? Something that threatens you— that jeopardizes your ability to walk in here a free man and have your spotless table waiting; to have Blondie see you at the door and drop an iced tea on the table the moment your ass hits the chair. I'll make it simple for you. My motive isn't your concern. What *is* your concern is that we won't go away until she's released. Free and healthy. If I think you have her, I'll be a thorn in your side. If I know you have her, I'll become a sword. If there's any part of this conversation you don't understand, it's in your best interest, capo, to come forth now."

Dangelo's chest rose and fell as he let his breath out. "You're a presumptuous man." I leaned back in my chair. "You assume," he continued, "that I have knowledge of this girl and that I'll work with you."

"Neither of us has a choice if we want to meet our primary objective."

He considered that for a moment, or perhaps he was thinking of his short game—I don't know. He leaned in, and I did likewise.

"Of course this has all been hypothetical," he said. "You want the lady, and I want the funds. Not my *half*—the entire amount. That's the other party's penalty, which"—he leaned back into his chair and spread his hands—"isn't a bad sentence considering how these things used to be settled and still can be. You find my money, and I'll ask around about Ms. Spencer."

I leaned back into my chair. "You're the victim of an inside job. There's no way that I—"

He came at me across the table. "You don't think we thought of that?" It was the first time he'd displayed any emotion. It could have been an act, but I didn't think so. Someone had ripped him off 142K. That's why Captain Tony had brought me directly to Dangelo. The big guys get the big problems. "It is *not* within my organization," he continued, but his voice had geared down. "You find my money, and your troubles go away."

"If you find it first?"

"I'll help you find her, wherever she may be."

"Where is she?" I leaned in fast. I was starting to feel like a damn rocking chair. Dangelo's eyes held mine. He didn't move; it was worth a try. I backed down. "I'll take that deal," I said, "with one provision. The young girl in the picture on your desk—she's your daughter?"

He rotated his head slightly to the right. "Be very careful, Jacob."

"Ms. Spencer is treated like her. No games. Do not drop her into one of your clubs or circle her with stiff dicks with no conscience."

"This talk is not necessary."

"I don't take chances."

"Nor do I." Dangelo stood up. "Find my money." He took a step and leaned over, his mouth hovering over my ear. He smelled of ham and aged Swiss cheese. "Look elsewhere, Jacob. It is not in my organization."

I stood, and Garrett did likewise. I'm sure he'd rather play Whac-a-Mole with the bodyguards' heads, pummel Uncle Joe into a confession, and hope that Jenny emerged unscathed. I preferred we try it slow and easy. No need to get another mobster on my bad side. In addition to the shootout on the beach, my actions to retrieve the Cold War letter had inadvertently put a Palm Beach Mafioso, Walter Mendis, huddled behind a legion of lawyers as he battled to avoid incarceration for human trafficking. I didn't need more organized enemies; my sleep was already becoming increasingly broken. What if these people were connected? It could lead back to Kathleen.

While I had no reason to believe Dangelo, his associates, or Walter Mendis were on the same playbill as the cast on the beach, I had no reason to believe they *weren't*.

Dangelo stalked out the door, and Tweedles followed him. They discreetly returned our weapons outside. Kelly had never presented the check. I assumed Dangelo got a monthly bill. Maybe he owned the place.

"What do you think?" I asked Garrett after Dangelo had cleared the building.

"Discarded teapot?"

"I was trying to keep things loose and friendly."

"Puddle of trouble?"

"Fine. Next time you talk, and I'll kick chairs."

"We played right into Dangelo's hand. He hired us to find the money and will compensate us with Jenny. Do you think that's really a good idea, working with a man we don't know or trust?"

"We'll find out."

CHAPTER 26

Jenny

"**O**uch? You get your big moment, take your best swing, barely nick the dude, and all you elicit is, 'Ouch?' Way to go, girl. You're just impressing the hell out of me here."

She'd taken to talking out loud. Why not? She told herself it was to make sure her vocal cords were still operational, but she knew there were other reasons as well.

When she had heard the rattle of the lock, she had planted her feet wide and held the strap of her spiked water bottle in her right hand by her hip. If she'd held it higher to start with, her angle would have been that much better. She'd grown weary of berating herself over that. When the door had opened, she'd swung up at the man with the inked arms. He danced his head like he'd played that game before and it was no biggie. One of the nails did manage to find its mark and create a stream of red, but the man had only said, "Ouch," followed by, "Let's go."

"Pathetic, girl," she said. "Pure, plain, pissy, pukey, pathetic. And now I'm sinking." She blew out her breath. "Just going down."

Jenny figured she was talking out loud as a mechanism to maintain her spirit and give a voice to hope. She wondered how many games her mind would conjure up in an attempt to shield her from reality, to keep her from sinking.

"Stay afloat. That's the key," she addressed her trepidation. *Like my daddy told me, don't fear the water.* But those words stayed in her head, for Jenny kept her father deep inside, close and tight, and was unwilling to verbalize them with the world. Even an empty one.

She'd never understood why her father had insisted that it was good for the Trojan's hull to get a good soaking. Not only a good soaking, Larry had impressed upon her, but it also was important for the boat to *remain* wet. Yet he would insist that she pump the water out once the gray floorboard had started to float.

"How," she had asked her father one day while he treated the aluminum poles that supported the canvas top, for Larry Spencer couldn't be on his boat without cleaning his boat, "can the water be good for her if too much will sink her?"

"She likes the water," Larry had replied. "It swells her boards and keeps the rest of the water out. You see, she uses water to keep water out. It's only when her boards aren't swelled, when she's not prepared for the water, that the water harms her. There's nothing to fear about a little water being in a wooden boat. It needs it. Too little and too much are what's bad."

She paced. *I've got to embrace fear*, she thought. *Let it swell in me so it can't hurt me, can't sink me. Like the boat used water to keep water out, I'll let a little fear in, just the right amount, and it'll keep the rest of it out. Don't flu shots work that way?* She wasn't sure, but she thought she'd read that someplace.

"I've got to stay wet," she said. It came out in her best Mickey Mouse voice. She could always do a mean Mickey. *Welcome to Crack-up City*, she thought. *Everybody on the planet's got a one-way ticket, and mine was punched early.*

Jenny plopped into the leather couch. Her new room was a basement, and she hated basements. This basement had brick walls and a ceiling so high that she couldn't touch it, even when she jumped. The floor was cluttered with a round table, high barstools, a glass display case, two cigarette machines, and a candy machine. The leather couch was larger than some of the trailers she'd seen people live in back in Ohio. In the corner was a toilet behind a hinged wooden door. Next to the door was a white sink the size of a small bathtub. A PVC pipe ran from it to a plastic drain cover on the floor. The floor around the drain was crusted with dirt, as the drain was a half-inch too high, and the water stagnated before reaching the top of the drain.

Jenny figured she was still in Florida. It had taken around an hour, maybe more, to get there. A city. Stop-and-go traffic near the end of the trip. A short man with fat muscles had blindfolded her. *Seriously,* she thought, *I've had enough of that for a lifetime.*

Then the questions. The man with the inked arms, and now a white bandage plastered to his forehead, had launched them. "Do you have the money? Do *they* have the money? Are you sure? What did he tell you about the money?" She had answered, "No. Not that I know of. Why ask me if you don't believe me? Already told you, and everybody who asks me— which is like half the frickin' state—that he said he had two hundred eighty-something. That's it, really. It's *all* I know."

He had stood by the candy machine. "Tell me, girl—did you really do to him what they said you did?"

"Yes. I really did. Can I ask *you* something?"

"Sure."

"How'd you get your teeth so white?"

"I brush three times a day."

"Uh-huh. Can't you let me go?"

"No."

"You mad at me for taking that swing at you?"

"No."

"Sure?"

"It was a good effort. I admire that."

"Could you do something for me?"

"What?"

"I *really* miss my shoes. Can you get me some?"

"Maybe."

"You gonna hurt me?"

A nervous no. He had shaken his head and thrown out an unconvincing laugh.

"Why not let me go? I won't tell anybody anything. I promise."

"That's not my decision."

"Even if I would talk, what would I say? I don't know you… don't even know where I am."

"That's not my decision."

"How long are you going to keep me?"

"That's not my—"

"I *promise. Please*, just let me go."

"That's not—"

"Okay. Okay. Jesus, I got it."

"You're a pretty girl."

Pretty girls can do well in life, use their prettiness. She'd said nothing but thought, *Is that even a word?*

"Question for you, pretty girl…"

She remained silent.

"You were saying something—shouting—right before I entered the garage. What was it?"

"I don't know."

"Sure you do."

"No, I don't."

He shrugged and walked up the stairs.

Forgotten.

Zach and Green Mask were clowns. Wannabes. But this guy? Calm. Composed. A quiet attitude that screamed violent indifference.

She paced in her new cage. Eight steps in one direction, eleven in the other. Not bad. *A real gymnasium,* she thought, *compared to my old digs.*

"I've got to stay wet, stay in shape." She hit the concrete, and her left hand landed on the ribbed surface of the drain. She started her push-ups but collapsed onto the floor after a failed second attempt.

Come on you, idiot! Get up! Too much water. Don't let him scare you. Pump!

But all she could do was lie on the floor. She wanted nothing more in the world than to be able to stand, but there was nothing in the world to help her do that. She lay on the floor and looked at the sharp edge of the drain. She wondered how many tears she would need to cry to form a puddle large enough to drip over the raised edge. She scratched marks into the crusted dirt. She rolled onto her back and stared at the ceiling.

"Look at what happened to me, Puddles. After all I've ever dreamed about, here I am, talking to a ceiling and a stuffed duck."

Pretty girl.

Her body shuddered.

She punched out her breath. "Come on, Jenny," she admonished herself. "You'd be an idiot not to be afraid. Deal with it, girl."

She took a long, deep breath, her lungs expanding to capacity, and let it out slowly, as if she wished to deflate all the air out of her body. She closed her eyes and found herself back in the shower, the water swirling around the drain, Boone's sorry ass walking out the door. She had lain there, in the fiberglass stall, the water growing cold, hoping for an epiphany. It didn't come. Not that day. *I can't go back*, she thought. *Back to a fetus curled up on the floor of a shower. I've got to take my stand. Have my vision. And I know what it is. I found it when I was up above the clouds.*

Jenny stood, squared her shoulders, and stared at the piss-ugly couch. *It's all so stupid*, she thought. *Stupid hope. Stupid words. Stupid life. Just say it. Say it, stupid girl. Say it and get it over with.*

"There is a place I bring all of me, and it is undoubtedly the sea."

CHAPTER 27

"Slainte," Morgan said, and raised his wineglass as the sunset charter sailboat, *Fantasea*, glided past on its return trip from the mouth of the channel. The rest of us took his cue and clanked our glasses together. We occupied the four chairs on the screen porch where we had just finished Morgan's dinner of conch chowder and grilled hog snapper with spiced lemon butter. Everything was gone except the dirty dishes. Elizabeth Woolridge Grant's voice floated out of the speakers and got lost in the salty, muggy air.

I had placed another call to Binelli and asked her to look into Joseph Dangelo. I wanted to know as much as I could about the devil I had just jumped into bed with. In my message, I told her about the missing cash. I had also called Susan and filled her in on what had transpired. She listened without comment then asked a few pointed questions about Dangelo that I couldn't answer. She was relieved, which had surprised me. "It means she's alive. I know you'll find her."

It came out with such childish innocence that I didn't dare reply.

Magic trailed *Fantasea* by two hundred feet. Passengers sat on her bow with their legs dangling over the side. A pair of dolphins surfaced, hands pointed, and voices carried over the water. *Magic* cleared the end of my dock, where my boat *Impulse* was suspended eight feet above the medium tide. She wasn't happy sitting in her lift. She was made for the sea, not to float above its surface. Grady-Whites are tough boats; they welcome angry waters and tend to sulk when left unattended and unchallenged.

What kind of woman owns a Grady-White and wears a tight black dress?

"Jake?" Kathleen asked. The sound of her voice triggered a physical response, and I glanced at her.

"Yeah?"

"What are you thinking?"

"Just watching the sailboats."

"Let's take it sometime."

"The sunset cruise?"

"Sure. I want to see what it's like, being out there and looking in at us."

"Whatever," I said. The callous word came out with more sympathy for her idea than I possessed, for I had none whatsoever.

"I'll go with you," Morgan told her.

"Thank you," Kathleen replied with a sharp edge of English propriety that was clearly aimed at me. "How are things on the front?" she asked me. She knew I was preoccupied and was willing to surrender the field to me. I wonder if I'm capable of a similar act of maturity. Sometimes it just seems beyond me.

"We're stuck in the trenches," I said. My neighbor Barbara's side door slammed shut. I told her I'd get a new pneumatic closer for her, but I kept forgetting.

Kathleen asked, "No leads today?"

"We met a man we think has Jenny," I replied. "We negotiated an agreement. We help him find the money, and he—if he has her—turns her over to us."

"He's holding her hostage?"

"Yes. That's what—"

"Such a cowardly act," Kathleen shuttered. "What kind of man would that be—a man who holds another man's daughter as a hostage?"

Damn fine question. "Some small-time crook in way over his head."

Garrett, who sat on the other side of Kathleen, looked away. She said, "This hardly seems like something that—"

"Local scum," Garrett said, keeping his eyes straight ahead at the red channel marker. On one side of the marker, the water ran thirty feet deep; on the other, the grassy sandbar was visible during low tides. I've witnessed a flotilla of boats get towed off the grass or wait for an incoming tide to rescue them. Slightly miscalculating one's position, or ignoring the pulsating light due to ignorance or vanity, creates a vastly different outcome and experience

"Jake?" Kathleen said again.

"Yeah?"

"Wherever you are, it's not here. I'm going to bed. Five-star dinner, Morgan. I'd never have the patience for your chowder recipe."

"My treat," he told her.

She rose and trailed her hand over the back of my shoulder as she slipped into my house.

"Cigar?" Morgan asked.

"Certainly," I replied. He cut a pair and passed me one. I wondered whether the smell would retrieve Kathleen. She was a sucker for a great smoke. Garrett didn't partake. Of tobacco or grapes. Or *Of Mice and Men*. I'd never seen him read a book. He read at least three newspapers a day—paper or on his tablet—but not a book.

"Small-time crook?" he asked as he waved smoke away.

"Local scum?" I retorted. I tapped my cigar on the edge of the Copacabana ashtray.

"You didn't want her to know."

"No need for her to worry. It's doubtful there's any connection."

"And if there is?" Garrett asked. "Do we want to be the last to find out?"

"I left a message with Binelli," I told him, deciding not to address his question. "Let's see what she comes up with. The feds must have something on Dangelo."

"Since when do we sit and wait for a phone call? It's a stretch to believe we cross paths with the Outfit—or its brethren—two, possibly three times, depending on Mendis, and they never finger us for burying four of their own on a deserted beach." He lowered his voice. "Even though we know Kathleen was never in possession of any damaging information about their operation, they don't know that."

That was pretty winded for Garrett. We had no reason to believe that Dangelo, Mendis, and the associates of Kathleen's deceased husband were intertwined. His assessment, however, was spot-on. You're pretty stupid if you think you can swim with the sharks without becoming their dinner.

"It's a long shot that they've tied us to their missing hit men or"—I paused and took another draw and let the smoke float out of my mouth—"that they have any plausible reason to believe Lauren Cunningham was resurrected as Kathleen Rowe." I flicked more charred tobacco leaves into the ashtray. "The question is whether we work our way up at his request or drop down in front of them. Make everyone else a day late, make them play catch-up with us."

"Whatever is best for Jenny and Kathleen," Morgan said.

I nodded. "If we don't run this, they'll run us. You saw the picture on Dangelo's desk?"

"Even better," Garrett said.

"How's that?"

"Got a picture of her on my phone."

"I didn't see that." I'd wondered why he'd had his hand in his pocket at Dangelo's office. He never does that. Too vulnerable of a position.

"That was the idea."

Garrett and I discussed our plan.

Morgan interjected, "If you threaten someone, don't you have to be prepared to fulfill the deed?"

"No." I said. "All parties understand. It's like pointing nukes at each other. It doesn't do any good if both sides launch." I answered before Garrett gave his response, which would have been vastly different than mine. Not that, in the end, we necessarily disagreed. But I still chanted mental vespers to myself that I was someone other than who I truly was.

"That's just on paper," Morgan said. "That's the rhetoric of men who sit around wooden tables and wear blue suits and talk about football games while sending young men into tropical jungles and sandlots in the name of democracy. Intellectuals who've never been at the tip of the spear. They're arrogant men, the Achilles' heel of the species."

We were all a little winded. That was a political dissertation from Morgan. He had as little interest in politics as anyone I knew. He had as much interest in other people as anyone I knew. A boat came in from the Gulf, its outboards ripping the night.

"Point well made," I said. In fact, I *had* brought too much heat when I felt Kathleen was threatened and in all likelihood *had* created much of our own problems. I tend not to dwell on such issues; denying failures makes me a happy man. "But"— I snuffed out my cigar—"you're better off playing your own game, even poorly, than engaging in someone else's."

We said our good nights, and they went out the back door and around the fence to Morgan's house. I crawled into bed with Kathleen, but I wasn't even in the same galaxy as sleep. I got up and returned to the screen porch, but that didn't work either. I dropped some ice cubes into a tumbler and floated them with Maker's Mark. I went to the end of my dock and sat with my legs over the water. A dolphin blew off to my left; I wondered if it was Nevis. If Binelli didn't call me early, I'd ring her during her morning coffee. I needed more information on Dangelo. Hadley III joined me, and we stared at the blinking red light. I thought of Garrett taking a picture of Dangelo's daughter with his phone.

I wondered whether Dangelo had a picture of Kathleen on his phone.

CHAPTER 28

I awoke in a panic when I realized the first hint of light had cracked the darkness and I was still in bed. Few things in the world disturb me more than being in bed when light comes around again. Starving children do—because I feel they should. I left Kathleen and headed to the pink hotel, which was less than a mile from my home.

I entered the pool before sunrise and swam for forty minutes. I followed that with a three-mile barefoot sprint on the beach. While running, I came across a tidal pool and attempted to clear it, like we do in our dreams when we take great leaps and almost fly. But like my attempt to cover the length of the pool to retrieve the girl's bone, I came up short and landed in two feet of water, which resulted in a slight twist in my left foot. I figured it would nag me for days. I rinsed off under the outdoor faucet on the boardwalk by the edge of the sand. At the far end of the pool, a thick man dressed in Johnny Cash black sat in a wheelchair that struggled to contain him. He had a cigar in one hand and his other hand pressed a cell phone to his ear.

I shaved in the locker room—the hotel has facilities that allow members to use it as a club—and fixed a cup of Columbian dark. I snatched a banana and a couple of newspapers and went to the second-floor balcony. I sat in a white rocking chair that overlooked the flowered tropical courtyard, the pool, and the Gulf of Mexico. The sky hung like a blue baby blanket draped over an impressionist painting. I placed the newspapers on the table to my left and tasted the first drops of coffee. I was in my office. We pick our places.

My phone rang. Binelli.

"What do you got?" I answered.

"Common courtesy, for one thing. That's more than you can muster, cowboy."

I took a bite from my banana. "What do you got, please?"

"Joseph Dangelo," she said. "From Chicago. The Mexicans are moving into the Windy City, so the Outfit is retiring south. He's been in Tampa for a little less than a year and is of mild interest to us. Tampa Bay, to fill you in, was the playground of the Santo Trafficante family, the Tampa Mafia. Typical bootleggers—they whacked a few of their own while managing to stay an indictment ahead of the feds. These guys, though, caught a slice of history when the CIA recruited them to hit Castro, and then later Santo Junior testified before a congressional committee on the assassination of JFK. You know this, don't you?"

I did. "Tell me about *now*."

"Long gone. The old New York families the Trafficantes were loosely associated with have bigger markets and bigger problems, and so do we. The trouble in the Sunshine State comes from points south. That's where we focus our resources."

"If I was smuggling drugs, I'd bring them in a U-Haul from the north."

"Jeepers, am I ever glad I called you today."

"You guys should have dialed me up years ago."

"We suspect that Dangelo runs some narcotics and attempts to get people like the Colemans to supply him product without upsetting larger organizations. He also oversees several strip joints, and we think their primary purpose is to launder the cash from the drugs. His businesses include loan-sharking, prostitution, and protection services."

"Run that last one by me again."

"Protection services. Racketeering. You pay his organization a monthly fee, and they make sure you're safe. If—"

"I know what it is."

"Then why ask?"

"People still fall for it?" Below, in the courtyard, a man sang "Happy Birthday" while he simultaneously held his phone over his head and took a panoramic view of the resort. Someone was getting a video birthday card.

"No choice. They'll break your front glass or mug you on the way to the night deposit. It's a clean business compared to drugs. They still tend to shy away from the hard-core narcotics."

"Little old-school, isn't it?" I picked up the local paper and noted the tide schedule as well as sunrise, sunset, and the moon's phase.

"The classics never go out of style."

"Anything else?"

"Dangelo's associates have ownership in three casinos in Vegas. Nothing whole, but they don't exactly put out an annual report."

"He thinks someone ripped him off a hundred forty-two grand. Half the two eighty-four that's missing."

"That would prick the hairs on his head."

I described Captain Tony, but Binelli had nothing on him. I bent my head down. A nasty spider the size of a Hummer darted out from under my rocker. I took my right foot and squished the arachnid. I wondered why I'd killed it when I'd merely flicked off the spider that was on my left hand when Garrett and I lay in the grass at the Coleman property.

"How can I get to him?" I asked.

She paused then continued. "Usual means, I assume. But that's your area. You think he has the girl?" I didn't know whether the pause was the result of our conversation or something that distracted her on the other end.

"Jenny?"

"Right. You think Dangelo has her?"

"Yes, unless he's stringing me along. Leading me to believe he does so I clean up his kitchen for him and find the missing dough. Would he risk kidnapping for that kind of cash?"

"Are you awake?"

"Withdrawn," I told her.

"Besides, it's not just the cash."

"Tell me."

"We think he was sent south to see what he can do, if he can handle his own operation and show some growth. He loses cash, he loses face. His career is done."

"Do those careers typically wind up on the wrong side of the grass?"

"Unlikely. The days of Eliot Ness are long gone."

"However…" I said, but let it go.

"The classics never go out of style," she said for the second time.

"What can you tell me about Dangelo's family life?"

Binelli didn't respond. I finished my banana and tossed it toward a seashell waste can. Below, Johnny Cash motorized across the courtyard, phone still pressed to his ear. He'd lost his cigar.

"Vassar, you still with me?"

"Why do you ask?"

"Just a question."

"Don't screw with me."

"Tell me what you know."

"Don't boss me either," she said.

I blew out my breath. If I can't screw or boss around, I'm out of things to do. Her tone reminded me of Susan admonishing me while we sat at the end of her dock.

She was silent, so I prodded, "I'm the good guy, remember?"

"That's right. But you don't play by rules."

"Nor do you, sweet pea." It came out fast and with intended sharpness.

"That was one time and—"

"We got the job done." I stood up and paced. "We worked well together. We did the right thing. That's what we're doing know." I decided not to back down or soften my tone with her. "I know Dangelo's got a daughter. Tell me about her."

For a moment, the phone was a silent instrument of hope and desire, pressed hard into my ear. "I'm not sure about any of this," she said.

"About what?"

"Don't fu—"

"I'm not. Just tell me." I tried to soften my tone.

"I don't know if I like where you're going...your course. Helping you—"

"Let's save a girl's live. Help me do that."

I gave that line less than a fifty percent chance and was upset with myself for having cut her off.

"You didn't get it from me." She was talking before I had a chance to reply.

"One more thing," I said when she had finished.

"Shoot."

"He in the same boat as Mendis?"

"Don't think so."

"One, one more."

"You're kidding."

I asked her to run the plates on the truck Garrett and I had ridden to Ybor City in.

Binelli said, "Your turn."

"At your service."

"Would you have?"

"What?"

"The wrist."

"I don't know."

She disconnected.

I picked my banana off the gray concrete balcony floor and dropped it into the can. I can never make that shot.

Garrett was on my back porch reading a newspaper when I returned. His iPad rested on the table. Kathleen was gone. She had informed me what her meeting was about—I'm thinking two, maybe three times—but of all my senses, listening is the one that shuts down on its own. I blame it on an explosion in Afghanistan that my ears, particularly my left one, never recovered from. Pulsating tinnitus. That's mixing the literal and the figurative, like no man's land, but they often go well together.

"Binelli called," I announced, and plopped down beside him. He had the overhead fan on high, and it whipped the sticky air into a frenzy. On the water, a barge carried iron beams for the new bridge. A Jet Ski skimmed around it like a gnat circling a wounded elephant.

"And?" Garrett asked.

"Theresa Ann Howell. Lives in Austin."

"What happened to 'Dangelo?' Not like the name?"

"Married, divorced, and kept the married name."

"Kids?"

"Don't know."

"We can trade her for Jenny and—"

"Hold her over Dangelo's head if he makes us for the beach scene."

"What else?" Garrett put the paper down and guzzled half a bottle of water.

I recapped my conversation with Binelli then asked, "You run this morning?" "I did. Also performed a number on that pink, smiling face." He finished the water and opened another. "You need a new one."

"Seriously?"

"Split it with my right foot."

For more than a year, I'd tried to destroy my punching bag, but all it did was smile at me. And now Mr. Greek God informed me that he'd split it? "No doubt," I said, "the canvas became weak due to my constant punishment." A great blue heron took flight and let out its ice-age cry when a snowy egret invaded its territory.

"Austin?"

"That's what the lady said."

"We've got to move on this." He flipped open his iPad and punched some keys. "A flight leaves in three hours. We can—"

"A round trip blows a day, at minimum. We know—"

"Holzman."

"He's in Austin?" I asked.

"Dallas. Can be there far quicker than us."

"That man is junk. He's an open-and-closed case on crimes against humanity."

Garrett shrugged. "Perfect qualification."

"Didn't you tell me he was nearly killed his first day back by a repeat-offender drunk in a pickup, but his girlfriend wasn't as lucky?"

"I did."

"That's not the whole story."

"Driver of the truck died six months later. A slow death."

"How do you know he's in Southfork?"

"We talk. I'll give him a call and text him the information."

"Tell him, 'Do not touch.'" An osprey flew by with a fish in its talons. The tail was still flapping, as if the fish were swimming in the air. I wondered whether Patricia Wilkinson ever lost sleep worrying whether she'd ever see her dog, Happy, being flown away. "I don't know how long she'll work with us."

"Who?"

"Binelli. She's nervous. On the edge. Could shut me out at any moment. It would be good to cultivate a reliable source in Hoover."

"Pass her a little cash," Garrett suggested. "She can work for more than one agency."

"I don't think cash enters the equation."

"Give it a try. It's like aspirin; it cures nearly everything."

He stood and walked out the screen door. I assumed he was heading to the outdoor shower. I left Binelli a voice mail. Every time I called her, I wondered whether she would even return the call. I could be detrimental to her career or introduce her to a new one. During the short time I'd spent with her while I recovered the stolen Cold War letter and shut down Raydel Escobar, I sensed within her a taste for adventure. She had volunteered to work undercover as Escobar's mistress. It was a job that had demanded certain extracurricular activities that demonstrated not only a willingness to practice backseat morality but also the desire to venture outside the tedious boredom of everyday life in exchange for the unknown. She had displayed an intuitive understanding of clandestine operations, which could make her a useful asset. She called back a minute later.

"You do like me, don't you?" I answered.

"You're becoming a major drag on my time."

"Just a quickie."

"Just a guy."

I pitched her the monetary element but kept it low-key. I didn't think it would mean much to her and might even backfire. Nonetheless, I wanted to set the hook. She said she'd think about it and disconnected. I didn't remember the last phone conversation I'd had when someone actually had said good-bye.

I relaxed back in my chair. A crab boat came by with two men in it. They were checking their traps, which were marked by single buoys. Pelicans kamikazed the surface, and a flock of roseate spoonbill glided through the summer sky as the sun's rays blazed their pink feathers. I searched for a reason to believe the Chicago Outfit knew that Garrett and I had buried four of their own on a beach. I had no reason to believe they suspected Lauren Cunningham was alive under a new name. Even if they did know, they may well have realized she never had been a threat and had moved on. Nor did I have any reason to believe Joseph Dangelo knew of any of that. Or that Walter Mendis was plotting payback. I didn't have any reason to believe my actions to find Jenny would, in some unforeseen manner, throw a spotlight on those activities. But I also knew the world was governed with far less reason than anyone suspected.

And if the stars *were* aligned against me? Fine by me. I had my Excalibur: Theresa Ann Howell. My intellect faded as my instincts gathered arms like a Hun preparing for battle. I would use her to free Jenny and cast a protective shield over Kathleen. A two for one.

I headed out for breakfast. After all, an army marches on its stomach.

CHAPTER 29

I took a counter seat at Sea Breeze, a pine-walled breakfast-and-lunch establishment that had been flipping eggs since the 1930s. The air was thick with grilled breakfast and REO Speedwagon.

"The usual, Jake?" Peggy asked.

"I was thinking of doing something different this morning," I replied as I perused the menu, which I hadn't glanced at in more than a year. "Maybe fresh fruit and a bagel with light cream cheese. Do you have any yogurt?"

She had one hand on a hip, and the other clutched a coffee pot. She snorted, spun, and stalked off.

Garrett and Morgan had taken off to buy new speaker wires for *Impulse*. I planned to stake out Dangelo's hangout in Ybor City while Garrett kept an eye on the Winking Lizard. We wanted to see who came in and out and try to pick up any sign of Jenny. I also wanted to talk to Kelly, the waitress at the Cubana Grille. She seemed well acquainted with Dangelo.

The guy to my right wore a Pier House T-shirt and was reading *The Wall Street Journal*. He pestered me with questions about the local economy. I asked him if the current banking regulations were strict enough considering that it had taken Wall Street only ten years after the repeal of Glass-Steagall to leverage their own money by thirty to one and bring the developed nations' financial systems to their knees and nearly plunge the world into an unimaginable dark age. We jostled for a while. He was a talker, and you know how I feel about that breed. He asked what I do for a living. I said I fish and plug the occasional bad guy. He laughed and said, "That's different. What do you really do?"

"I just told you."

It worked.

He pulled out a twenty, left it on the bar, and scooted out the door. He also left a strip of bacon on his plate. I ate it. I slid the *Journal* over and started reading.

"Here you go, Casanova," Peggy said a few minutes later as she dropped a plate on top of "Money and Investing." A red bowl of onions followed and blotted out a graph of the ten-year treasury.

"No yogurt this morning?" I asked.

"You ask that girl to marry you yet?" She punched it out the same way she dropped food on the counter.

"How do you—?"

"Whole beach knows. And let me tell you, you won't do any better than her. Don't blow this one, you hear me?"

"Yes, ma'am. But I'm still trying to get in touch with—"

"You're so full of it, I don't know how you squeeze through the door. You grab her and never let go. And stop scaring away the new patrons. I heard what you said to that guy."

"I was being truthful—"

"Don't be." She pivoted and vanished into the kitchen.

I dumped the sautéed onions over the eggs and crispy hash browns. I showered the plate with pepper. What a gorgeous canvas—it was almost a shame to tear into it. When I was finished, I left Peggy a buck more than usual. She'd be insulted with anything more.

I strolled out the front door, hesitated a beat, and went to an apparel store half a block toward the Gulf. I was supposed to meet Kathleen for lunch downtown. I got that part; I'd just forgotten what her plans were for the morning.

I spent the next two hours helping Morgan help me fix my boat speaker. Garrett already had departed for the Winking Lizard. We were treading water while we waited for Holzman to come through; it's not my favorite activity, but it's not sinking. When we finished, I showered outside; donned a clean, button-down, silk shirt and pressed shorts; and hopped into my truck. I found Kathleen inside Mangroves at a corner two-top that overlooked Beach Drive and the side street. I had a little more than an hour before I wanted to camp outside the Cubana Grill; I wanted to be in there in case Kelly got off work after lunch.

"Not outside?" I asked and bent down to kiss her. We exchanged a quick peck. No parted lips and open eyes. Not today.

"I hope you don't mind. It's just too hot."

"I'm good." She had taken the seat that looked outside, and I sat across from her with my back to the glass. She wore a murderous butter-yellow dress. Her jewelry, which I didn't recall seeing before, had a Western flair that complemented the dress.

A young man wearing the name "Irving" on his left chest took our food and drink orders simultaneously. I gave him my credit card with our orders. He stomped off. I wanted to be in and out as quickly as possible, but even when I'm not in a hurry, I give the card well before the check comes then review the chit when I sign the receipt. I leave a restaurant when I want to leave. I can't tolerate waiting and having someone else determine when I stand and walk. Irving departed, and I explained to Kathleen why I had to eat and run. She said that was fine; after her busy morning, she was pressed for time as well.

"How *was* your morning?" I asked. With a little luck, she'd fill me in on whatever it was she had told me she was doing that I hadn't paid attention to. We've all been there.

"Good. How was yours?" She did that occasionally—deflected questions about herself with a short answer then lobbed a question of her own. It was a ploy I constantly used as well. I figured very few people really gave a damn, so why fake it? The real test is whether they bring the question around again.

I took a sip of water that had been waiting for me. "I went to Sea Breeze for breakfast and enlightened my stool mate that I fish and don't like bad people. I got a free strip of bacon out of the deal."

"It would behoove you to be a mute sometime."

"Behoove?"

"Yes." She smiled. "You need to work on behooving."

"That word should be reserved for admonishing a ranch hand. And your morning?" I asked for the second time, because even if I was a poor listener, I gave a damn about Kathleen more than the heavens would ever know.

"It was a good seminar, but it cut short my morning reading session on your dock."

I had no idea what seminar she was even referring to, so I went with her reading comment, thankful that she'd thrown it out there. "Well, you can return to your experiment tomorrow." I took another sip of water and let an ice cube sneak into my mouth. It was the square type with a hole in the middle, which I stuck my tongue into.

"I suppose, but it might be more difficult due to what we all decided at the meeting."

Did she rope me in on purpose? I went in over my head and said, "That's good. Everybody show up?"

Kathleen gave me a sympathetic smile. "You're totally lost, aren't you?" It came out with an appropriate dose of pity.

"I just wasn't there last night. What *did* you do this morning?" That was three times now.

"What's in the box?" And twice for her. She sucked her left cheek in between her teeth. She really was a little ticked. Good thing I had the box.

I placed it on the table. "For you." I said.

Another smile. Point for me. "What's the occasion?" she asked, as she picked it up.

"Felt like it."

I heard Peggy's voice telling me not to blow it. Kathleen opened the box, and a copper-tone summer dress spilled out. She gushed that it was beautiful, that she loved the color, that it went with the jewelry she had on, that it was the right size, and how'd I know? All that stuff I barely heard. Then this: "It's the first thing you've bought me."

I started to protest; after all, certainly I'd bought her a gift before, right?

She leaned over and gave me a kiss. She reclined back in her chair. "You're a lucky fellow. Your timing couldn't have been better."

"So what *did* you do this morning?" That made four times, and despite my efforts, I was sensing a pattern here. I wasn't going to take that hill. Not today.

"Oh, no," she replied with a smile and slight shake of her head that was just enough to jiggle her earrings, "you don't skirt that easy. Tell me about what you're doing to find Jenny."

Irving dropped off our lunches. Kathleen speared a piece of salmon, and I took a Grand Canyon bite out of my cheeseburger. Breakfast seemed like eons ago. I told her we suspected Dangelo to be part of a larger group, but I left it at that. I debated telling her he was organized crime with connections in her old stomping grounds. I sensed she thought of asking more, but she remained silent. Irving asked us if there was anything else he could get for us. "We're done," I proclaimed, but he already had spun and headed to his next table. Little twit. Why even ask? Kathleen commented that one didn't see many young Irvings, which led to a litany of Irving writers. Stone. Wallace. John. She got stuck when she tried to recall the name of Garp's youngest son.

"You know, don't you?" she asked.

"Think Sidney," I said, and my mind flashed to the Laundromat.

"That's a clue?"

"It's a variation of 'Disney.'"

"Disney. Okay, I'll run with that. Goofy, Donald—"

"Think corporate."

"Fine. Walt...Walt!"

We clanked our glasses in jubilation. Irving dropped off the bill. The pen he provided had the name of a gastroenterology practice on it. Did the same group that owned the restaurant also own the medical practice? Hopefully there's a law against such an alliance.

We strode outside, and the heat socked me back to reality with an uppercut of guilt as I recalled Garp's mother. *Jenny.* Like the night of the banana cream pie, I had just enjoyed a cheeseburger and an air-conditioned brainteaser lunch with a woman who knew me yet still loved me. An unusual combination for any of us. If only briefly, my biggest concerns in life had been a waiter who hadn't sucked up to me and a pen that never should be found in a dining establishment.

I was Jenny's hope? Her wrecking ball?

I begged off walking Kathleen back to her condo, as my truck was in the opposite direction, and I had to hustle. As I cut the corner, I glanced through the window at the table where Kathleen and I had just lunched. It was neatly set for the next patrons. *Like we were never there.* Garrett called as I opened the driver's door to my truck.

"Anything?" I asked. I knew he was at the Winking Lizard.

"Not here, but I talked to Holzman."

"And?"

"Hopefully by tonight. With the time difference, my bet is after midnight our time."

"Sure it's the same girl?" I climbed into the truck.

"I texted him the photo. Positive ID."

"He knows not to touch?"

"He's not really wacko. That's—"

"No, that man flies without radar."

"On certain occasions those are the perfect people to have on your side."

"Kathleen's not to know of this." I turned the key and put the truck in drive.

"Tell me something I don't know."

I disconnected and headed to Ybor City.

The rest of the afternoon crawled by with the dull consistency of a metronome. No one entered or departed Dangelo's building. Kelly was working, but her shift must have run through the afternoon, as she never ventured outside. I ducked into cafés and consumed a gallon of iced tea. I dodged a cloudburst and sauntered into an independent corner bookstore. I wondered whether in the future, buried deep in some doctoral thesis of bygone species, independent bookstores would be listed as *Liberum editio negotium*, right next to some South American ant. I grabbed a beer at a sports bar with seven flat screen TVs all broadcasting a different event. I found a kettle corn stand and devoured half a bag.

At our luncheon, Dangelo had informed me that he pre-ferred his St. Pete office for its proximity to both points south and north. I hadn't asked him where that office was; I should have. He may or may not have told me, but that doesn't excuse my mental lapse. I doubt it was the Winking Lizard; he had too much class for that.

He finally exited at six thirty and headed straight to the Cubana Grille. I took a high stool in a coffee shop window across the street, which I'd scouted out earlier as a perfect van-tage point. He claimed the same table he had with us, but this time a white cloth dressed up its surface. The Tweedle team took up its post. I wondered whether the bookstore carried a copy of Lewis Carroll's *Alice's Adventures in Wonderland*, which is where the pair originated.

Dangelo had a dinner guest whom I didn't recognize. The man joined him shortly after Dangelo sat down. His dinner partner was a stocky man in an ill-fitting summer suit. While Dangelo was in short sleeves, his guest kept his jacket on. They dined for a little more than an hour. When they left, I snapped some pictures with my Canon as well as my cell phone. I fol-lowed Summer Suit to his idling, generic, black town car with the limousine sticker in the rear widow. A ride to and from the airport. An out-of-town visitor. I realized Binelli hadn't got-ten back to me yet on the plate on the truck Garrett and I had ridden in from the Winking Lizard to meet Dangelo. Without some formal commitment from her, I was always afraid that our last conversation would be our last conversation. I went back to my post and kept an eye on Kelly.

She left at nine twenty-five. A long day. I scampered across the street and followed her to the three-dollar lot. I wondered if she needed to pay that every day or if the restaurant cut a deal for the staff. I closed in on her just as she reached into her purse for what I assumed were her keys.

"Kelly?"

She jumped and turned; I had scared her. "Yes?" She held keys in her right hand.

"My name's Jake. I wonder if I could have just a couple of minutes with you? I'd like—"

"Are you some off-duty cop?" Her shoulders slumped. She drew the word *cop* out, and it lasted longer than the first four words combined.

"A cop? No, I just want to—"

"Listen, man"—she pitched her head off to her left—"I haven't been *near* that mama's boy since—"

"Near who?"

"Leonard. You're not here about my restraining order?"

"No. Nothing to do with that. I just got a couple of questions about someone you serve."

"Well"—she brightened up a bit and picked up the pace—"who are we talking about?"

"A regular patron of yours, Joseph Dangelo."

"You mean Mr. Dangelo?"

"Sure, doll. *Mr.* Dangelo."

"Don't get smarty on me."

"My apo—"

"Hey, I waited on you yesterday. I'm good at that—observing and remembering people I wait on." Kelly took a step forward, and her head tilted back a few inches. "You didn't bring your friend, did you?"

"No."

"Pity." She shook her head. "I'd die to have that skin tone. Talk about unfair. Well, Jason, you going to buy me that drink or not?"

"It's Jake."

"Are you or aren't you?"

We walked two blocks to a brewery. I'd never asked her if I could buy her a drink.

Kelly, over a glow-stick martini, gave me what I wanted to know about Dangelo, but first I had to sit through the Leonard chronicles. She'd gotten a little too physical with her ex-boyfriend, and he had cried to the police. "I've got a temper," she said in a voice totally at odds with her personality. "And Leonard—he's so sweet; he really is—but he can't take a punch for shit. Is that my fault? My therapist says I need to stop taking things so personally."

She swore she'd never before seen the man in the summer suit with whom Dangelo had dinner.

I asked, "Who do you think was in charge, Dangelo or the suit?"

"The kitchen was one short, and the new prep guy still doesn't know pastrami from corned beef. Marlene called in sick—there's a shocker—so I did a double again. You think I got time to notice that stuff?"

"Just asking."

"I'd say they were equals."

"Why do you say that?"

"Because I feel like it."

"Okay. What causes you to feel like that?"

"Mr. Dangelo held his own. He never needed to raise his voice, you know? Pretty hard to ruffle Mr. D. But Suit Coat? He was intense."

"How so?"

"He was like you, the day you came in. Didn't even know I was there. Hey, why'd your bronze buddy kick his chair around and face away from the table?"

"He was done eating."

"No, he wasn't."

Kelly promised not to mention to Dangelo that I'd sought her out. I promised not to mention to him that she had confided in me. Not that she had that much to spill. I wondered if my time would have been better spent trailing Dangelo, but I had cast my lot.

I escorted her back to her car. When we got there, she turned to me, flipped her head, and let her hair fall over her right eye. I said, "You never inquired why I questioned you about Dangelo."

"No, I never did, Jim."

"It's Jake." It came out with more irritation than I felt.

She smiled. "I know, *doll*," she said. "*You* need to stop taking things so personally."

She shut the door before I had the chance to serve up a retort. I'm glad she did. I had nothing to say.

I drove back to St. Pete and met Garrett at a bar on 4th Avenue South, not far from the Dali Museum. The joint looked recently remodeled, yet it was empty. Someone was losing his shirt. I nursed a beer while we compared notes. Garrett produced a photo album of the traffic in and out of the Winking Lizard. It was the usual suspects: Captain Tony, Cue Stick, and Special. I felt as if we'd spent the entire day swimming against the tide.

"Did you check the sign?" I asked.

"Two screws. Barely hanging in there. Five minutes tops."

My phone buzzed, and I took it out of my pocket. It was a text from Binelli.

owned by long sally industries
under fed investigation for
racketeering chicago
local address long sally's bar grill

"We just launched," I said.

"What'd you get?" Garrett asked as he stood and pushed his barstool in.

"Dangelo's St. Pete location and a possible umbrella name." I passed him my phone. "The plate from our ride yesterday." He handed me back the phone.

I brought up the address on my phone. "Six blocks north. You ready?"

I followed him out the door.

We drove but couldn't get within three blocks of Long Sally's Bar and Grill. We would have made better time if we had walked. I paid the cover to an enormous man in suspenders who was hunched over on a high, backless stool. He held a wad of bills in his hand like it was Monopoly money. No taxes due on those greenbacks. We advanced two feet into the room and were enveloped by a gyrating, rollicking crowd. Whatever the room's occupancy level was, they were fifty over. A band was crammed onto a small corner stage, and the trumpet player stood front and center, blowing his cheeks out. They looked like miniature pumpkins under his eyes. He nailed a few notes clean off the register. Somewhere Maynard Ferguson smiled. A girl in a purple shirt with one of its straps down by her elbow brushed up to Garrett. She shouted something about a drink. I couldn't imagine someone holding Jenny in such a populated place. Still, I'd decided to circle back in the morning. Garrett caught my eye, and I nodded. He hated crowds more than I did.

"Refunds?" I asked the man on the stool. He didn't even blink.

CHAPTER 30

I hoisted the kayak over the seawall and went to the end of my dock to join Morgan and Kathleen. I was surprised to see her there so early in the morning.

The plan was for me to hit Long Sally's at the opening bell and take a self-guided tour. Garrett was searching for other establishments under Dangelo's umbrella. We would then draft a small army and stake out every joint we could possibly tie to Dangelo. It was grunt work. But if Jenny was being held in one of his places, we would crumble the walls. If we stumbled upon Dangelo's money in the process, that would be fine. If not, *c'est la vie.* I wasn't his contract worker.

Morgan sat with his bare feet hanging over the side. Kathleen was perched next to him, sitting on her crossed legs with her head buried in a book. She wore a white sundress. No shoes. When you live on water, on an island, shoes are the first things you shed. After that, layers of other things, less physical, are shed as well, and you're left to wonder where and why you picked up the unnecessary baggage. The fabric canopy partially shadowed them, as the sun was still low in the sky.

"You motored out this morning just to get your morning dock-reading time in?" I asked her. Steam rose from their coffee cups.

"I've expanded my experiment." I leaned over and gave her a kiss. "The students will not only record where they read a particular work but also how much they attribute their immediate surroundings to the overall enjoyment."

"A little subjective," I said.

"Beautiful stuff," Morgan said. His hair wasn't tied, and the breeze lifted it off his shoulders. There was a light chop on the bay that had been just enough to challenge my kayak. He continued, "Most of my early reading was done on a moored sailboat or while I tacked azure waters. To this day, I can still see the shallow water off Nevis that we were anchored in when I finished Jones's trilogy. Speaking of, did you feed her?"

"I did, but I need larger baitfish. I'm not sure it's worth her trouble." Morgan had named the dolphins of our bay after Caribbean islands. I didn't posses his gift—or eyes—of being able to identify them from a half mile out. It came easy to him; he'd once told me that by age ten he knew more dolphins than people.

"She beat you back," Kathleen said. "Morgan fed her off the dock."

"Charming."

"Do me a favor?"

"Anything."

"Bring a chaise lounge out. The dock's a little hard."

I fetched one of the cushioned lounge chairs along with a side table that I kept on the grass. She settled in, put her head in the book, then looked up and out over the water.

"Oh my," she said. "How does one ever leave?"

"That's the point."

I left them sipping their morning drugs and strolled down the dock to look for Garrett. I glanced at the sea grass, and a stingray propelled itself just beneath the surface. I rinsed under the outdoor shower, dried, changed, and was cracking eggs on the stove's surface when Garrett came through the side door.

"Eggs?" I asked.

"Thanks."

"Toast?"

"Sure."

"Holzman?"

"Texted me at two thirty-seven this morning. Half a dozen pictures plus a shot of her condo and car. I printed them and have them in an envelope. Let's arrange a meeting with Dangelo or knock on his door. Either way, Jenny's free today."

I whipped up eggs in a bowl and added some milk and chunks of sharp cheddar along with onions and tomatoes. "I've been thinking," I said. I *had* been thinking while I'd sat in my kayak and taken in the stillness and enormity of the Gulf of Mexico.

"We function best when you don't."

"We pushed too hard last time and subsequently created our own problems, and we—"

"We never know where other paths would have led," Garrett cut in. He wasn't fond of the one I was taking now.

"Granted. But what does he do when we play our hand, and what does that cause us to do? How does that get Jenny free without repercussions, and what might those repercussions be?"

"It's not a chess game."

"Everything's a chess game."

"What's your point?"

"We hold."

"No such move in chess."

"There is now."

He didn't say anything but spread jelly on his toast. He surrendered halfway through and stuffed it into his mouth.

"We believe Jenny is alive," I said, feeling compelled to further press my case. "We don't think her life's in danger. We find her as quickly as we can without creating ancillary problems. Finding Jenny and subsequently creating issues for Kathleen isn't acceptable. To locate her, we need more manpower. We're making this harder than it is. What did you find under 'Long Sally?'"

Garrett waited a beat to adequately register his protest. "Three other clubs south of here—in Bradenton and Sarasota— and West Coast Tool and Die five minutes up the road on 22nd Avenue. All registered under 'Long Sally Industries.'"

"Fine. I've got a couple calls to make. Leave in ten?"

"Waiting for you."

I took a seat on the porch and dialed PC and McGlashan. I left a pair of voice mails. Even though Rutledge was the lead, I had a favor to ask, and I liked my chances better with McGlashan. I was fishing without bait, but I'd accidently foul-hooked my share of fish before.

A man and a woman went by, each in their own kayak— one brown, one green. The kayaks. Kathleen and I, during her yoga months, tried to kayak together, but our speeds weren't compatible. "I'm not doing that again unless you pull me," she'd finally laid down. The next morning I tied a rope, and she sat in her kayak under a white parasol and read a book while my paddle rolled the stagnant water of the canals. When we returned, Morgan darted into his house and came out with his camera. It's the only picture of Kathleen and me that hangs in his house.

PC rang back within a minute. I gave him the address of a bar in downtown St. Pete that was two blocks from the Wink-ing Lizard. I asked him and Boyd to meet us in thirty minutes. We would split up from there.

McGlashan brought up the rear. I stood, brushed a gecko off the screen door, and took his call on the patio.

He started right in. "You know Rutledge's the lead, right?"

"And when I want the official line, I'll be sure to call him."

That earned a guttural comment, followed by, "You any closer to finding her?"

"I can't get over the car, wiped clean like that. Did you or Rutledge ever question the occupants of the apartment complex across the street? You know the one I'm talking about? It would take a few minutes, at minimum, to clean a car that well. Maybe someone saw something."

"I think you're grasping at straws. The case is—"

"Did you?"

McGlashan went silent, and an osprey flew over my head. No doubt he was the same one who crapped on my boat and now he had my head in his hawk eyes. "No one did, did they? I'd app—"

"It was Rutledge's call. He didn't see any sense in it. Girl ran twice in one week. He thinks—"

"Will you?"

"Will I what?"

"Ask around. Drop in on the complex. It would save me a lot of—"

"And I owe you?"

"No shoes. No phone. You can stuff your runaway theory. The only question here is whether anybody gives a damn." I regretted it as it came out. McGlashan had been more than cooperative with me, and I certainly didn't need my loose mouth alienating him.

"My son's coming home in two days, and I got a mountain of paperwork to clear before I take some time off. I'll see if Rutledge can do it. He really should have done it in the first place."

"I appreciate it," I said. But his was a conciliatory remark and not the commitment I was looking for.

He hung up. Maybe he just didn't do good-byes. Maybe no one did anymore, and I'd just missed the memo. I went back inside the screen porch. There was a thimble-size crumb of scrambled eggs left.

"Kidding me, right?" I said to Garrett.

"Morgan's fixing more. Was that McGlashan?"

"It was. Said they may or may not question the occupants of the apartment complex across from where Billy Ray's Honda was found."

"That's worse than either a yes or a no."

"I realize—"

"Your adoptive little brothers?"

"Meeting us two blocks from the Lizard. We'll scout every one of Long Sally's operations. We'll split up. Someone in Dangelo's organization is taking care of Jenny. Feeding her. We follow them, and they lead us to her."

"Dangelo wants us to do a quid pro quo," Garrett said.

"*Your* point?"

"If he finds out that we're hitting his operations, he might change his mind. Not to mention we don't have the manpower for twenty-four-hour surveillance."

I shrugged. "We won't get spotted. If we do, we'll tell him we suspect persons that he may do business with. At the worst, it forces the action, which isn't a bad thing. He doesn't have his money—he won't renege on us. And if we find Jenny before the money, we're done." I didn't respond to his observation regarding our lack of resources for around-the-clock surveillance. I was still working on that.

Garrett started to say something but pulled back.

"What?" I asked him.

"Nothing."

I marched out the side door as Kathleen strode down the dock.

"Eggs?" Morgan's voice came from behind me.

"I'll take a plate with me," I said as Kathleen came up beside me. I was eager to get going. I paused my step and asked, "How's the grand experiment?"

"You have time?"

"Always." It was an obligatory remark. Like when someone says, "I love you," and you shoot the words right back, fearful of any hesitation between the comments.

She paused then said, "I presented my theory, and it multiplied. Oprah recommends a book, and thousands of people read it and rate it. They're far more likely to like the book than if they found the title from an online review. All types of controlled studies can emerge. The same books will garner higher reader praise if read during the summer months than in December. Where you read, my personal interest, is becoming an oddity with no money behind it. What your expectations of the book are and how they were formed are taking center stage."

"Certainly applies to more than books." I glanced past her at a sailboat.

"It does. Like those wine tests you told me about where people always rate an expensive bottle of wine better than a lesser-priced bottle, even after the contents have been switched. You don't want all this right now, do you?"

"I was—"

"I'm late for my meeting."

Meeting? Was I supposed to know about this? I said, "Catch you later."

Kathleen leaned in and up and gave me a kiss on the lips. "You have a great day—keep *your* motor going." She waltzed into the house. I had the feeling I had still missed a few chapters, but I didn't have time to go back.

CHAPTER 31

Garrett, Morgan, and I piled into my truck. Morgan drove as I wolfed down a paper plate of bland scrambled eggs. I had forgotten the pepper, which really bugged me. Morgan was appropriately donned in a shirt and bona fide shoes. He'd overheard our plans, and I was grateful for the extra set of eyes. But he didn't carry any pepper, so what the hell good was he?

We pulled into the deserted parking lot where PC and Boyd were waiting for us. We all gathered beside my truck, and I gave marching orders. I provided PC the address of West Coast Tool and Die.

"Walk in and tell them you're looking for a job," I instructed him. "Get a good look at the place."

"What *am* I looking for?"

"Basement. Interior rooms. Just give me a feel for it. Think of where someone could be held against their will."

Morgan said, "When at sea, and we wanted to hide someone, we'd put them in the hold of the ship. Some boats were designed with that in mind. I would think—"

"*That's* what we're looking for," I said. Morgan, on more than one occasion, had brought whole families to the land of the free.

"We just need a quick in and out of these places," I said, aware of my accelerating speech. "We don't need to camp out. Scout for steps either up or down. Maybe a side door that leads to the adjoining building. If that building is vacant and owned by Sally properties, it's under consideration. After today, the only property that will require constant surveillance is one that could possibly be housing her."

I turned to Garrett. I had decided to go with an alternative plan. I'd grown weary of our slow progress and ineffectual actions. That, plus the lack of pepper, had placed me in an aggressive mood. "You and Morgan take the truck south. I'll rush up the middle, put pressure on Dangelo. By nightfall, he'll know it's a new game."

"What happened to 'hold?'"

"No such move."

Garrett said, "You'll need wheels. I should have driven my rental."

"I'll requisition Kathleen's car."

"Should be no problem," Morgan said. "She has that meeting at the Vinoy that runs most of the day."

"What kind of meeting?" I asked. She would have walked to the Vinoy, as it was only a few blocks from her condo.

"Publishing study of some sort. She not tell you?"

"I might have missed that."

Garrett let out a chuckle. *Did she tell me?* I called her, but she didn't pick up. Screw it. I needed her car. PC and Boyd took off to West Coast Tool and Die. Garrett and Morgan dropped me off at Kathleen's condo garage.

I entered the code and saw her bronze two-door Lexus convertible in its assigned spot. It didn't even reflect the overhead light. I took the elevator to her unit and grabbed the fob out of the Silver Springs antique porcelain dish. What the? I'd given that to her. Bought it for her one night at an eclectic art shop a block down on Beach Drive. And she tried to tell me I'd never purchased anything for her before. I'd have to set the record straight. I left a note, sent her a text, and locked the door behind me.

Long Sally's Bar and Grill was hungover from the previous night; it didn't open until 11:00 a.m. I felt dressed up with nowhere to go. I put gas in the Lexus and ran it through one of those car washes where they dry it by hand. It was a sure sign that it would rain within twenty-four hours. I felt bad for the Native Americans all those years ago. I doubt their rain dances helped much. What they should have done was wash their horses instead. It would have guaranteed precipitation and a healthy crop of corn.

I returned to Sally's, parked a block away, and walked around the one-story building. Sun Coast Cleaners anchored one end, and a one-man insurance office, "Earl Whitney, for Your Life, Your Home, Your Family," took the north end. A sun-faded picture of a smiling Earl faced the street. For all I knew, either or both establishments were in Dangelo's hand but under a different name. It was doubtful, but what if he held two dozen properties under a dozen names? Second-guessing crept into my plan, and Morgan and Garrett hadn't even cleared the Sunshine Skyway Bridge.

I didn't see any low windows or sidewalk doors indicating a basement, nor did that surprise me. Basements in Florida are as common as skyscrapers in Montana. I went inside and had the first anything served that day. A blonde with red streaks in her hair wearing a tight black Sally's polo shirt pushed the iced tea across the clean bar. She looked as if she might have closed the joint last night. I hit the head and ducked into the kitchen. Nothing. A wide staircase anchored the middle of the first floor. I took the steps two at a time. They led to an open area with high-top tables that overlooked the first floor. In the back was a door with an office sign on it. It was locked. Dangelo's digs.

I returned to my stool. Streak asked me if I enjoyed my trip. I asked her when Dangelo came in. She said, "Whenever." We chatted for a few minutes while she wiped the bar, but nothing useful emerged. She dropped her towel and headed to the lady's room. I dropped a ten and headed to the Winking Lizard. I couldn't recall whether it had a backroom or basement. I rehearsed my lines in my head.

I circled once to get a look at the building. Thick frosted-glass windows with bars stared out at the sidewalk. The place had a basement. So much for my powers of observation and memory. I parked Kathleen's sparkling car a few spots down from a bus stop. I paused at the front door and momentarily shut my eyes to prepare them for the shock of entering the dungeon. I swung open the door and strode to the bar. I wanted to surprise Special. If he knew anything, he'd be the one to reveal it. Captain Tony might see through my ploy.

Special was behind the bar. I didn't see Captain Tony or Cue Stick. Luck was on my side. I always run well with her. Special kept his eyes on me as I approached and claimed a stool across from him.

"I met with Dangelo," I started right in. "He wants me to talk with the girl. See if I can get information from her." I'd decided that I didn't care if Dangelo knew I was pounding on his doors. It was time to squeeze the toothpaste. If Special camped out behind the bar every day, nothing would go down that he wouldn't know about. The problem, of course, with squeezing the toothpaste, is that once it's out of the tube, it's a little hard to put it back in.

"I don't know who you're talking about," Special said.

That was close, but not the confirmation I wanted. I darted my eyes around and tapped my hand on the bar. I shifted my weight. "Look," I said. "Is Tony in? You can check with him."

"His name is Eugene."

"Dangelo wants me to talk to the girl. Said to just come down here and have a few words with her." I stopped tapping with one hand and started in with the other. "Now."

Special gave that a moment.

"I got to talk to Eugene." He took a step back and withdrew a phone from his pocket. His reply indicated to me that even if he didn't know where Jenny was, he was aware that they had her.

"Give him a call," I said. I strode away as I was still talking. "I'm hitting the head." I passed two guys shooting pool and took a corner toward a narrow hall. The women's lavatory was a spacious room that included a partitioned toilet with a barn-door entry, almost like a room within a room. Newer wallpaper. Not my style, but not bad. The men's room had a bathtub to piss in and a small stall with a plunger in the corner. I left and tracked around the corner and into the kitchen. A man from south of Florida glanced up from a fryer that he was stuffing white grease into.

"Health inspector, amigo," I said.

He shrugged and returned to his task. An interior door faced back into the building. It was padlocked. A closet? I doubted it. My bet was that it led to the basement. The kitchen door swung open, and Special marched in. He ducked when he passed through the door. He held a gun in his right hand; his thick paw engulfed the butt so that the barrel appeared to come out of his fleshy fingers.

"Eugene said that Mr. Dangelo gave you no such permission," he said, the gun leveled at my chest. "And this isn't the head."

Barge through the basement door now? I'd have to take Special first. I didn't think that would be an issue, but as a rule, I don't attack a person holding a gun on me unless I believe it's absolutely necessary. It doesn't take much of a shot to screw up your day. I hesitated then said, "Sorry. I'm going back to see Mr. Dangelo right now. He can't be sending me out to talk to her without letting his minions know."

"His what?"

I ignored his question, he hadn't lowered the gun, and I didn't trust my lips, slipped out the back door, and hustled around to my—Kathleen's—car. Just as I hit the opposite curb, a city bus pulled out of the stop and left a plume of gray-black smoke that covered the Lexus like a crop duster. My phone rang; I hit the button.

"What do you got?" I asked.

"Nada," PC said. "We went in like you told us and said we were looking for a job. You should have seen this guy's face when he glanced up at Boyd popping his tarts."

"What did you see?"

"The glare of condescension reserved for those who you feel—"

"The place, man." I knew he was playing with me.

"Zippo, Jake-o. Single-story, doors open, trucks in and out. A real mercantile mart of activity. No way they're hiding anyone there."

I thanked him. He was disappointed when I told him I didn't have anything else for him at the moment. Kathleen texted me and said it was fine if I wanted to take her car. I texted her a thumbs-up symbol.

I camped out at Sally's. Dangelo exited late in the afternoon. He must have entered when I was at the Winking Lizard. I trailed him to a condo two blocks from Kathleen's, where he disappeared into an underground parking garage. He lived a football toss from her. I didn't see that coming. What if he or one of his cousins recognized her? Was he even related to the group that had gone after Kathleen after her husband's death, or was I being paranoid? I thought of my earlier comment to Garrett about not creating problems for Kathleen, and here I was stirring the pot. I told myself to relax. The chances of his being tied to her deceased husband's affairs *and* of him recognizing her were remote. But I knew I was rationalizing that fine line, the razor's edge. I parked in the shade of a building, put the top down, and reached for my phone just as it rang.

"Where are you?" I asked Garrett.

"On the bridge. You?"

"Downtown. What did you find?"

"Organized crime is stressing the 'organized' part. Nice establishments. No basements. A yellowtail sandwich at one place, and a redhead waitress at another who nearly knocked Morgan out of the game. Nothing to lead us to believe that any of the buildings and businesses we saw might be holding Jenny."

"The third?"

"Deserted. We busted in. Nothing. You?" He came at me for the second time.

I recapped my day. I told him the Winking Lizard had a basement with a locked door.

"You didn't take it?"

"No. I considered it. Had a lock on the door. Would have been messy. That, plus Special was pointing a gun at me." I'd considered not telling him that last part. He had no interest in pansy excuses.

He paused. "Tonight?"

"I'm thinking three a.m." We discussed our plan.

I decided to let Rutledge in on the play. I was also eager to see whether he had talked to any of the occupants of the apartment building across from where Billy Ray's car had been found. I wondered whether McGlashan had even passed the request on to him.

Rutledge picked up on the first ring. He said he hadn't had time to check out the apartments. At least I knew McGlashan had passed along the request and followed through on his end.

I went after Rutledge. "I think the occupants of that apartment should—"

"What's with you and this girl?" he interrupted me. "Give it up; she skipped off to another island. Tanning on some b—"

"I don't think so."

"Once they run, they always run."

"I found the man the Colemans were doing business with. I believe he has her." A black two-door with tinted windows cruised by, blaring a primitive beat.

"Who is he?"

I gave Rutledge a brief description of Dangelo and his operation. He was oddly quiet and noninterruptive.

"And this man...half the money belongs to him?"

"Correct. But he wants the whole two eighty-four. Doesn't want a bad mark for letting the dough slip through his fingers in the first place. Doubling his take earns a lot of gold stars. I think he hopes to—"

"Has he talked to her?"

"If he did, he certainly wouldn't divulge that."

"How do you know him...this Dee-angelo?"

"Dangelo. No apostrophe." Rutledge seemed more interested in Dangelo than Jenny. "The Colemans led us to him. I've got a connection at the bureau, and she identified him."

"The FBI?"

"Pardon?"

"You said you had—"

"Yeah, the FBI. And—"

"The hell you doing talking to the FBI?"

"I used my source to—"

"Who the hell *are* you?"

"A concerned citizen, *Detective* Rutledge."

"What did they have to say?"

"The FBI or Dan—"

"Either."

"Rutledge?"

"Yeah?"

"I thought the only thing you gave a shit about was launching a missile and fondling the tooth fairy."

"I—we—just need to be covered down here in case the feds get involved, you know? After all, your girl Jenny did a number on a guy, and we let her skate. Well, we didn't *let* her, but we're not exactly chasing her down. So you think you know where she is?"

"I do."

"Some warehouse or something?"

"Dive called the Winking Lizard. Few blocks off downtown St. Pete. It's open till two. We plan to reopen it around three."

"Call me either way. The Winking Lizard—that's really the name? Not the Forgetful Elephant?"

"You got it."

"Keep me posted."

"Check the apartments." But I spoke into dead airwaves.

I was suddenly tired of the whole deal. Too much time trying to get Rutledge and McGlashan to help. Too much phone tag with Binelli. Too much outsourcing. A half-ass operation at best. No more.

I called PC and said I'd changed my mind. I told him to hustle down to Fort Myers Beach. I gave him the address of the apartments across from where Billy Ray's car had been found. He said it would be close to 10:00 p.m. before he got there.

"If someone's lights are on," I said, "knock on the door. If not, knock anyway. Hit them as they emerge in the morning. It's an eight-plex. There aren't that many tenants."

"What am I looking for?"

"Anything they recall seeing in that small beach parking lot across the street *before* the police arrived...and PC?"

"Still here, man."

"Someone *was* there before the police. Walkers, joggers—engage them all. Maybe a guy two streets down sweats that road every morning, and he lumbered by at the right moment. Maybe someone's doing his neighbor's wife, and he saw something when he was sneaking out of a house, but he doesn't want to come forward. I couldn't care less. Someone saw something. Always. Find that person. Split up. Hit everyone. It's an island."

"Running up a big note, Jake-o."

I had no formal arrangement with PC. After he'd helped me secure the missing Cold War letter, I'd paid him two grand in fifties. What he split with Boyd was up to him, but I was pretty sure he cut it evenly. PC was nineteen years old and operated on an IQ, in all likelihood, well north of 140. He instinctively knew that formal education was a ruse. He saw more moves ahead than anyone I'd ever played chess with. You don't find those people on East Coast–college cafeteria-recruitment days. But that's not what drew me to him.

He was on the fringe of society and could go either way. When I tripped over him, he and Boyd had just walked out of juvenile detention for computer hacking. PC had programmed the county's 911 line so that a lady with a crisp English accent came on and congratulated the caller for being selected and said to please stay on the line and take a brief survey. Despite his

228

raw intelligence, he didn't grasp the potentially heinous conse-
quences of his crime. A few years older, and he would have been
in the slammer for years. He divulged that it hadn't been their
first trip to the juvie residence.

PC and Boyd were on the edge. The more time I spent with
them, the heavier my responsibility grew—to them and to me.
I didn't want to fail.

"Find my person," I said to his comment and hung up.

I'd been too absorbed in my conversation to see them
approach, and now it was too late. Tweedledum and Tweedledee
stood on each side of Kathleen's car. Tweedledum, the nut brain
with glasses, peeled back his jacket to reveal a revolver the size
of a miniature cannon tucked into his pants. What was he
going to do? Unload it right there on the street? I might have
overestimated his mental capacity.

"Mr. Dangelo would like to see you," he said.

"And if I refuse, what are you going to do with that thing?
Contribute to a live performance of Tchaikovsky's *1812 Overture*?"

Tweedledum took his time with that, as if it were a serious question, then announced, "I don't think so. It's a common misconception that cannons are always used. Tchaikovsky
opened Carnegie Hall in 1891 with his overture, and even
though he wrote sixteen cannons into the score, I'm pretty sure
there weren't any guns on the stage that night. Now haul your
ass out of the car."

Okay, so I'd misjudged his brain. But I'm telling you, the
guy had a dick the size of a baby carrot. I had no idea that Russian composer Pyotr Liyich Tchaikosvky, born in a different St.
Petersburg, had ever conducted at Carnegie—I would have bet
money the other way—nor did I appreciate learning it from
this clown.

"Lead the way," I said.

I raised the top on the Lexus just as it started to rain. It was a light drizzle that mixed with the dust from the city bus. As we walked away, I glanced over my shoulder and saw Kathleen's car morph into a dirtier shade of clean than it had been when I'd driven it out of her garage.

CHAPTER 32

We paraded a block south to Dangelo's condo and rode to the tenth floor. Like Kathleen's, it had its own entrance off the elevator. The Tweedle twins didn't enter the room— nor did my gun, which they confiscated at the door. I assumed they'd been instructed to make camp outside Dangelo's door. Perhaps Tweedledum had brought along his music history textbook to study.

Dangelo sat at a desk that made him look big. He didn't stir when I entered. I took a seat on a white leather couch and flipped through a magazine that told me about ten fantastic Caribbean restaurants I had to dine at before I jumped off the bus. I didn't look at the article. I did look at the pictures of tan girls in white bikinis. The classics never go out of style. I helped myself to some salted cashews in a cut-glass bowl that rested on top of a glass-topped coffee table with a coral-reef base.

"Jacob." It came out as he swiveled around in his chair so he could face me. "Have you found my missing funds?"

I finished my chew. "Working on it, Joe."

"How? By going into one of my bars and informing the staff that I instructed you to talk to this missing girl whom you think I have? Such a childish game."

"Staff?"

"Yes?"

231

"I just don't see Special as staff."

Dangelo stood. "Our arrangement, in the event that you've suffered short-term memory loss, is that you find my missing funds, *then* I do what I can to help you locate the missing girl, whom you erroneously think I possess."

"That arrangement didn't hold my interest. I find Jenny Spencer, and your money won't be far behind."

"You think?" He took a step toward me. "Then you are not thinking at all—for if that were the case, and I, as you have accused, am harboring the girl, why are we having this conversation?"

"I said, 'far behind,' not 'with her.' You didn't bring me here for this." I got up and dropped the magazine onto the glass table. "I'll keep you posted." I headed for the door.

"I did a little research." His voice came from behind me. "You served for five years, but your trail gets cold the day you left the army." I pivoted. He picked up the magazine from the coffee table and glanced at it. "I don't think I even pay for this anymore. They just keep sending it." He brought his head up. "Tell me—how does one get involved in your line of work?"

"A strange question from a man like you."

"I'm curious..." He tossed the magazine, reached into the bowl, and grabbed a handful of cashews. "What chances did my two men have if you decided not to comply with my request for a visit?"

"None."

Dangelo nodded as if I'd given him the answer he'd wanted, but it was the wrong answer for me to give. I saw it too late. Arrogance is the first step toward self-destruction.

"No," he said with a tone of resignation, "I suppose not. You know"—he popped a few cashews into his mouth—"we had an incident not far from here about a year ago. We lost four employees, and the locals expressed alarming disinterest in the situation—not, of course, that we pressed them. You understand?"

"Not a clue what you're talking about." I started to circle the room.

"Sort of like me, when you bring up your missing Ms. Spencer." Another cashew met its fate. "It did occur to us, however, that even if we had pressed our cause, the law just didn't care. As if someone had hushed up the whole scene. 'Bad for tourism,' I believe the line was."

"You can't have four dead bodies in the sand in a beach town."

"I never said they were on the beach," Dangelo said.

"I read the papers." I passed the front door and with my right hand turned the deadbolt. I kept circling. The distance between us shrank. Time and distance.

"They were good men. One of them was our best. They must have encountered someone who was highly trained, a professional, and not acting alone either."

We paused. I wasn't going to lead. At that point, I could do more harm than good—and already had. "There was a lady involved." Dangelo said it cautiously and in a different tone, as if we had entered the demonic final movement of a musical score. My neck stiffened. My hand tightened into a fist. "Tragically she died on that beach." His eyes rested on mine. A car honked. "Did you read that as well? In the papers?"

"I seem to recall something about that."

"We...how shall I put this? We possibly overreacted. We thought at one time that the deceased lady might have knowledge of certain nonpublic aspects of our business. In retrospect, she probably had no knowledge at all. Our judgment was rash, but not nearly as bombastic as our adversary's."

Dangelo waited, but I remained silent, until the silence was self-incriminating. I asked, "Why are you telling me this?"

"After your sophomoric theatrics at the Winking Lizard, I had you followed. The car you were driving—"

I was on him in two steps and slammed him into the wall. His head snapped back with a thud then bounced forward so his forehead struck mine. A half-eaten cashew flew out and landed on my shirt. I choked his throat with my right hand. His neck was fat. I wanted to rip off a chunk and stuff it in his mouth. The door behind me rattled.

"What about the car?"

Dangelo took a second to get his breath. He smelled like cashews. The last time I smelled him, it was Swiss cheese and ham. "It's double-parked, Mr. Travis." His voice was tight. I loosened my grip. "Find my money, and you were never here tonight. This conversation never took place."

I dug my fingers into his neck. *"What about the car?"*

"N-nothing." I eased up even more on the pressure. "We thought—that is, my associate thought—he might have recognized it from the around the neighborhood."

"Are you threatening me?" I was ticked that I'd been followed. I should have been more alert. Too bad for Dangelo. I swung him around and pressed his face against the window. "Because I'll drop you through this window right now. Do you understand that?" His eyes widened in the reflection of the glass. I leaned into his ear and repeated what he'd told me at the deli. "Look elsewhere, Joe. The beach scene wasn't me." I gave the lie my best conviction. I like lies. Judiciously applied, they can help your cause more than a standing army. "And," I continued, "here's the new plan: find your own goddamned money." I gave him a shove and stepped back.

"Certainly," he started and then paused to catch his breath, although he tried not to show it. "Certainly you understand that if we had our money, we would be inclined to fully—no, *permanently*—support any decision made for the benefit of tourism. Whether or not, or not, you…um—"

"Save it. I have no idea what you're talking about, and I'm not making any deal with you."

"We say such things in times of—"

"The man you had lunch with the other day—he give you the script tonight?"

"No." He regained his posture far faster than I'd thought he would. Dangelo might have been all dressed up, but he clearly had spent some of his youth on the street. "I'm not the puppet you seem to think I am, and spying on me certainly won't advance your cause. Your reaction, Jacob, was totally uncalled for. All we're—all *I'm* saying is that perhaps you can help us out. I didn't mean to imply any threat. I apologize if you took my comments in that manner."

But he knew. And he knew that I knew that he knew. Still, his earnest conciliatory tone caught me off guard. I couldn't get a read on Joseph Dangelo—perhaps, though, through no fault of my own.

Regardless, I'd blown it. It wasn't my first mistake and wouldn't be my last. He had no way of knowing my elephant gun was loaded. I didn't trust myself to say anything else—I'd already behaved foolishly. Dangelo called off the dogs, and I marched out of the room.

"Lewis Carroll would be proud of your career choice," I said to Tweedledum as he handed me my gun.

"You mean Charles Dodgson?"

Screw this guy.

CHAPTER 33

I left at 2:45 a.m. with Garrett and Morgan. I had taken Kathleen's car back to my house and sent her a text. A phone call was too much work. I thought of my comment to her about failing gloriously and decided that the first word carried so much weight that it rendered the second meaningless. Some words should never cohabitate. *Moral victory. Small hurricane. Casual sex.*

I pulled up in the alley behind the Winking Lizard. Garrett and I retrieved a four-foot piece of piling out of the back of the truck. When I'd scoped the place, I'd noticed the back door was like the pine trees at Camp Tecumseh. Beefy. It also had two commercial deadbolts. I wasn't worried about the interior door, as it appeared to be standard hardware fare with a generic padlock. Although a camera was trained on the cash register, I hadn't noticed any other security system. Like the Visigoths, the three of us rammed the waterlogged piling, and the back door splintered. Morgan stayed back with the truck as our lookout. Garrett and I crossed the kitchen toward the interior door. Halfway there, I dug in my heels. My Maglite illuminated an open door. The lock was off, and the door was splintered.

I hit the lights at the top of the stairs. As I took the stairs two at a time—far more difficult to accomplish going down that it is going up—I nearly lost my footing and resprained my left ankle. I did a quick scan with my beam. The room was empty. Garrett was beside me.

"Do you think she was even here?" I asked more to myself than to Garrett.

"Someone busted the door. There's got to be a reason for that." He swept his beam across the room. "Let's see what we can see."

Garrett and I worked the room, but it held nothing other than a hodgepodge of discarded bar equipment. There was couch large enough to owe real estate taxes. An oversize white sink was against the wall. I remembered the Colemans' garage. My Maglite swept the walls, then the floor. When I first saw it, nothing registered. The floor drain was high, and the floor had accumulated dirt that extended in a one-foot radius beyond the drain. I crouched and brought the Maglite up close.

"Here we go," I said.

Garrett got down on one knee beside me. "Four, one, two, nine," he said. "She's dropping bread crumbs."

The numbers were barely legible, and the nine could have been mistaken for a four, but we knew what it was. I didn't spot a tool; Jenny must have scrawled it with her fingernails. I crunched a piece of drain dirt between my fingers. I rose to my feet, and my left knee emitted its usual series of cracks. "Did I give her up today?"

"They've got a key, right?" Garrett ignored my question and focused on what was important. "Why would they bust down their own door? This is someone new."

"Or they lost the key, had no time to find the key, dropped the key down the storm drain—there's an unlimited number of key possibilities."

"There's no way of knowing if your actions led to his," Garrett said, coming back around to my question. "If you didn't come in, you never would have found the basement. We know Dangelo's other locations, and they—"

"We already eliminated them," I said. "He has her. We—"

"We don't know that. We're fairly certain that he's the one who snatched her from the Colemans and that he *had* her. But just as he did unto them, someone may have grabbed her from him. Your key theories are a stretch, not the most likely scenarios. You don't break into your own house. I'm hitting the front door."

He vaulted the stairs. He was right. Even if Dangelo had decided to move her, why bust up your own place? I followed him up the wooden steps but then veered off to the restrooms. Both were empty, but I noted, as I had earlier, that you could park a car in the ladies' room. Easy place to set up camp until the business locked up for the night. Garrett and I met at the bar and avoided the camera's angle.

"Unlocked," he said. "Next time, we should try walking in the front before storming the gate. I think that eliminates Dangelo's crew. It's too far a stretch to think they unlocked the front door, broke the interior door, then left without locking up."

I switched off my Maglite, and Garrett did the same with his. We were at the front of the Winking Lizard now, and even though it had dark windows, there was no need to take unnecessary chances. The barstools were upside-down on the bar, and the added floor space enlarged the room. "Someone was already in the building," I said. "The last person to leave. They busted the basement door then waltzed out the front."

"The pertinent concern isn't how, but who and—"

"And we don't have a clue. There's a third party, and we're in the cold." I was fed up with the whole failure routine. It *was* a routine. We were chasing Jenny, and I had no clue whether we were even closing the distance. "Let's get out of here before the blue flashers show up."

"No Jenny?" Morgan commented as an apparent fact when we hauled our gloomy attitude like overweight luggage into the truck. Neither Garrett nor I responded. Morgan fired up the engine, and after two lefts, we were on 275 south.

"We're further from her than when we started," I said to the window as the night rushed by. "We can't even pretend to be close to her."

"We can change that," Morgan said. "You've got the tape, right? I'd like to hear her voice. I think it'll help us."

"Why not? This night's no good for sleep."

"Let's grab three hours," Garrett said. "It'll afford us the opportunity to see tomorrow as a new day, put this one behind us. We need that more than sleep." That seemed more like my line than his. Maybe that's why I liked it.

A love song was on. I wanted to tell Morgan to turn it off, but I didn't want to hear the sound of my voice. A blur on a fat-wheel bike scorched us as if we were standing still. I thought of my confrontation with Dangelo. Did he recognize Kathleen? Had he known her late husband? Should I show her a picture of Dangelo? And then what? Ask her if her ex (ex-ex, now that he was dead) ever had him over for drinks? Maybe they fired up the grill. And what purpose would that serve? Confirm her worst fears that she would never be free, even with a new identity? That at all moments she must keep a vigilant watch?

What would I do—who would I become—to shield her from all that?

It was a lot of questions, and they came with a smorgasbord of nebulous answers. At the minimum, Dangelo was certainly suspicious, and my overreaction confirmed those suspicions. My pursuit of Jenny was slamming me back into the past; the game was jeopardizing Kathleen's safety. It was never meant to be this way—escalating into warfare. Trouble followed me with the consistency of a duck's wake on a glass pond. I always had done well, performed best, when I embraced that truth, reacted accordingly, and never shied away from an unpleasant answer. I just needed to keep reminding myself of that.

CHAPTER 34

At six fifteen, after thinking I'd never fall asleep only to wake feeling as if I could sleep forever, we gathered on my back porch. Hadley III condescendingly perched on top of the grill, her wide eyes taking in the blinking red channel marker that hadn't yet clocked out for the day. She cut me a glance and meowed. She must have eaten the year's worth of food I'd given her a few days ago.

I placed the tape recorder on the glass table next to my Tinker Bell alarm clock. I hit the "play" button, and Jenny's voice filled the dawn. Her youthful voice energized me and lightened my mood. Morgan listened with his chin in his left hand and his left elbow resting on the arm of the chair. He stared at the floor. Morgan has a theory that all the senses are related and that you can elevate one by gearing down the others. He claims that's how he located Kathleen on the deserted beach where her kidnappers had taken her. I had a theory that the pulsating red channel marker was mocking me and thought that one day I might just have to squeeze off a few rounds at the son of a bitch.

Jenny's irritation over Rutledge's hang-up with Sherman was even more obvious the second time around. I glanced at my watch. PC hadn't gotten back to me yet. I assumed he hadn't been able to talk to that many people at the apartment complex last night and hoped he had remembered to hit it early. Some people leave for their jobs by seven, or even earlier. I texted him and reminded him of that. I was upset that I hadn't explicitly given him directions as to what time to be at the apartments. I knew I was berating myself to kill time, to pretend I was moving forward as I sat and did nothing. PC immediately texted back that he was already on the site. I remembered that, to my knowledge, Jenny's photo was still tacked to the Laundromat bulletin board. That hook hadn't registered a nibble. Maybe I'd have PC take it down.

Jenny said, "Eric, right?" and Morgan nodded. A little later, Rutledge gave the time—6:17 a.m.—and names and location. The birds sang, and the tape went silent. I glanced up at the bay as a flatboat with a fishing tower cleared the end of my dock. A man rode the tower like a pelican gliding over the waves. His buddy was down below, his hand on the wheel, hair flying behind him. I spent too much time watching men in boats go by and not enough time in my own boat. When you live on the water, you're constantly a fan to someone experiencing that special day they've looked forward to.

"Can you rewind it?" Morgan asked. "To the part where he says, 'Then what?'" He had paid no attention to the boat, which was an incredible feat. Just as a man watches a woman as she leaves an elevator, it's nearly impossible, living on the bay, for a man not to glance up when a boat goes by.

"Any reason?" I asked, as I punched the rewind button. I hit "play" again and came in during the Sherman exchange. That was close enough. Morgan didn't acknowledge my question but instead shrank back into his Rodin pose.

"There," he exclaimed, and popped out of his position like a cork blowing out of a champagne bottle. "Did you hear that?" He knew my hearing was poor on my left side. Between my bad ear, creaking left knee, and now bum left ankle, if I were a boat, I'd be listing badly to the port.

"Tell us," Garrett said.

"Tape's been cut."

"How do you know?" I asked. Another boat approached from around the bend. Serious fishermen are early risers. I kept my attention on Morgan.

"The osprey. You hear them—there are two—in the middle of the conversation, but they really pick up their distinct screech, or chirp, toward the end. I clearly hear where their call is interrupted—cut. Play it again. It's right before Rutledge coughs."

I hit the end of the Sherman sequence again and listened. I couldn't detect a damn thing. The osprey does have a distinct cry that is a series of short, high-pitched blasts. Rutledge coughed. Jenny said, "I was on top of him before I knew it."

"Hear it?" Morgan asked.

"I caught it," Garrett said.

"Not me," I added.

"Plus," Morgan said as he gained steam, "I think this is a recording of a recording. I think someone recorded the playback then cut it right before Rutledge asked, 'Then what?' His cough, more like clearing his throat, was inserted later."

"What if he's right?" Garrett asked. "What if Jenny's answer to Rutledge wasn't that she was on top of him? What if she said something else first?"

"But who would splice it?" I asked. "How many people had access to the tape before we finally received our copy?"

"Again," Morgan said. I fiddled with the recorder, and for the third time, Jenny's irritated voice sparred with Rutledge over General William Tecumseh Sherman. We listened without comment until the end. Outside of Rutledge's cough, nothing seemed out of rhythm.

"You met Rutledge, right?" Morgan asked me.

"We did."

"He cough much? Loud? Like on the tape?"

I glanced at Garrett as every conversation I'd had with Detective Eric Rutledge raced through my head. Garrett's stare was waiting for me.

He knew.

"No coughs," I said. "Think Rutledge tampered with it?"

I also knew. Everyone in the world knew. Like a boat's swelling wake out on the bay rolling toward me—a motion that nothing in the heavens or the universe can halt—I knew where the conversation was going long before it got there. Part of my mind had already disengaged and was waiting onshore, bracing for the tsunami.

Garrett said, "Zach's alleged phone call to Jenny."

"Rutledge said Jenny's phone didn't show any such call," I said. "But what if it did? I never did think that was a point the Colemans would lie about. Rutledge suggested they might have physically abducted her and used the phone story as a ruse to possibly lighten charges against them, saying that she came voluntarily."

"He suggested, meaning he planted it in your mind," Garrett offered.

"Maybe Rutledge never bothered to check her phone, and he's just covering his ass for a job he didn't do. Or he's been lying all along. Jenny must have told him about the money and—"

My phone rang, and I snatched it off the table.

PC said, "Bingo, baby!"

"What've you got?" I stood, and Garrett did likewise. I put the phone on speaker and placed it back on the table next to the pink recorder.

"Guy on the second floor—I was talking to him when I sent you the text. He sets up the rental stand, you know, the paddle-boards and stuff, on this end of the beach. Early bird. He takes a cup of coffee—three cubes of sugar—on his patio every morning before he hits the sand. Said he saw a car crawl down Estero that morning. Creeping, he said. Moment later, it returned from the other direction. It pulled in, you know, into that pygmy public parking lot across from him. He said from his angle he couldn't see if another car was parked there. But this guy definitely went in; his rear end stuck out a little. No biggie, right?"

"What'd it look like?"

"I'll get there. But, like two, three minutes tops, my guy says he pulls out. He didn't think much of it. He had breakfast, hit the head, and brushed his teeth—his words; personally, I brush my teeth before I hit the head—and went to close the patio door. When he did, he saw another car crawl into the same space. It's there maybe five minutes, and then it leaves."

"This guy's in the act of closing the patio door yet hangs around for five minutes?" Garrett asked.

"Roger that. Because Sugar Boy, when the second car's in there, hears glass break and then clanking, like metal on metal. Couldn't figure out what it was, but it kept him on his patio until he was late for work. He planned to check it out, but by noon the whole beach knew. Body found, police tape around the beach scene and car."

"Police ever question him?"

"Negatory, Chess Man. He grows the holy crop in his apartment, so he didn't come forward. Been afraid of a knock on the door ever since, so he moved his horticultural activity to a friend's."

"Plates? Anything to identify either car?"

"Florida on the second vehicle. Bland model. Guy says he doesn't really know wheels. Didn't need to on the first one, though."

"Why? Did the car stand out in some manner? Give me a description."

"You're going to love it."

"Just tell me."

"Sheriff's car, Jake-o."

"Sheriff's car?"

"That's what I said."

"You sure?"

"No mistakin' bacon. Lee County white with one ugly-ass green stripe down its side."

CHAPTER 35

The wake crashed onto the shore and crushed me against the concrete seawall.

Fucking idiot. Fucking idiot. Fucking idiot. All that clutter in my head, and I can't think. Can't see. Rutledge drumming his fingers, blowing off Zach's phone call, and me not checking Zach's phone. Deflecting my question about prints on Billy Ray's car. I gave up the Winking Lizard. Rutledge—I'm willing to bet—has big IOUs in Vegas. I gave her up. I've got to be the biggest—

"JT, you there?" PC asked, interrupting my annual binge of constructive self-criticism. "I said I got the guy's cell. Said you could call him anytime."

I told him to text it to me and thanked him. He asked if I wanted him to do anything else, and I told him about Jenny's picture in the Laundromat and asked him to take it down. We disconnected. I found myself standing next to my grill. *How'd the cover get so dirty? Cat paws prints all over the place.*

"Billy Ray told Jenny about the money," I said to Garrett, although I would've preferred talking to the grill, as it was incapable of judging me. "She tells Rutledge, and he takes off looking for the car. He finds Billy Ray's car and has enough prescience to keep moving. No doubt his cruiser has a GPS in it that tracks his movements, not to mention a camera. Rutledge told Susan he lived not far from her. He goes home, gets his car, and returns."

"He wiped down the trunk," Garrett said as he eyed me from across the porch. "What time did McGlashan tell us they found Coleman's car?"

"Ten."

"Any doubts on that?"

"'Around ten the following morning' was what he told me. The scene is less than half a mile south of Billy Ray's car. If Jenny had told Rutledge there was money in the car, he easily could have broken into it, taken the stash, then sat back and let it play out."

I broke away from Garrett and out toward the water. It all seemed the same. On the flats, a fisherman tossed a cast net over the side of his boat, and the sun reflected off the splash. At the marina across the bay, a boat was being brought out from the racks to where it would be lowered into the water.

"He cut it out of the interview," Morgan explained, "but in the second interview, Jenny would mention the cash. Rutledge didn't snatch her; the Colemans did. Do you think they're working together, and Rutledge had the Colemans kidnap her?"

"No," I turned to Morgan. "I'm confident the Colemans have nothing to do with Rutledge. They would've rolled when we talked with them. Plus they're the ones who initially told us that Jenny did mention that Billy Ray had told her about the money. We just didn't connect the dots."

"Zach's call to her." Garrett added.

"You know it's on her phone. Rutledge saw it. He offered to have me look at it, knowing I wouldn't take him up." I shook my head in disgust. "Nice bluff. He outplayed me." I realized what else had bothered me during that conversation with Rutledge in the truck as we'd left the Colemans—what had flashed in my mind but I couldn't hold on to. I verbalized it as the thought hit my brain. "When I informed him that Jenny had told the Colemans that Billy Ray had spilled to her about the money, Rutledge's first reaction was to claim she never told him."

"A reflexive, defensive remark."

"He moved on quickly from there," I added as I recalled the conversation. "Tried to sound nonchalant about the whole thing."

"But in the second interview," Morgan cut in, returning to his earlier comment, "wouldn't this have come out?"

"Rutledge wasn't worried about the second interview," Garrett said and took a drink from a bottle of water. "He would have blown right through her. He'd simply deny she had mentioned it the first time around. Who'd believe a runaway eighteen-year-old girl over a detective with a tape recording to back him up? Besides, we don't know exactly what he did say to Jenny. When she disappeared, it was a gift in his lap. Who are you calling?"

"Binelli," I said as I punched my phone. "She said something earlier that I didn't pay much attention to. Something about recognizing one of the names when I'd told her McGlashan and Rutledge were the detectives in charge. I'd assumed she'd meant McGlashan, with his Super Bowl ring and all, but maybe she meant Rutledge." I left a voice mail and told her to run a check on Eric Rutledge. I didn't know why the FBI would have anything on him, but it was another line in the water.

I looked at Garrett. "Toss me that." He threw his bottle of water at me, and I finished it off. "When it was just Rutledge," I said, picking up where Garrett had left off, "he could steam-roll Jenny's assertions about the money. But once we discovered there *was* money in Billy Ray's car, meaning there were other people who could corroborate her claim, her story gained credence. Her kidnapping impedes his case. He can't say she was confused and neglected to mention it during the first interview. And we led him to that conclusion."

"You're jumping," Garrett said. "Making unsubstantiated conclusions. Maybe it was McGlashan who left the crime scene and found the car. Maybe it was a third person we don't even know."

"Rutledge is a Vegas junkie. Want to bet he doesn't owe money to nasty people?"

"He might, or he could just be an opportunist."

"Rutledge didn't interview the renters at the apartment," I added, as my mind replayed all the missed signs. "Even McGlashan questioned that and said he'd ask him to reconsider. Everybody viewed Jenny as a runaway who had run again. That gave the police a free pass. No one gave a damn, and that's not the worst of it."

I paused, but neither Garrett nor Morgan was going in. They both knew and were too considerate to incriminate me. I hanged myself. "I gave Rutledge the Winking Lizard," I said to no one, and then everything was astonishingly quiet. No boats, no birds, no waves crashing off my seawall. Even the wind died in symphony.

Hadley III whined, and Garrett said, "We use that. We focus on Rutledge, and we find Jenny."

"McGlashan indicated that Rutledge had only been with the department a short time," I said, "and based on McGlashan's comment on Vegas, and his own preference for fishing, I don't make the two out to be after-hours buddies. McGlashan said Rutledge had relocated from Tampa. Maybe he still keeps a place up—"

"I'll see what I can find," Morgan said, darting into my house. He was gone longer than I would have thought. I was about to yell at him and tell him where my iPad was when he came back to the porch with it and plopped back down on the chair. I knew what he would say before he spoke.

He said, "I fed Hadley the Third."

Okay, so I didn't know. He continued with what I'd expected. "Over four million people. Too many hits to chase them down one-on-one. Middle initial?"

"No clue," I said.

Morgan punched the pad and said, "According to the Lee County site, it's Eric W. Rutledge." He struck the tablet a few more times and said, "That cuts it down, but there's no way of knowing who uses their middle initial and who doesn't."

"I'm giving McGlashan a call. I'll bring him up to speed and see if Rutledge's missing." I picked up my phone.

"Ease off," Garrett said. He kept his eye on me as a fishing boat, *Reel Girls,* with three outboards cruised off the end of my dock. I'd not seen it before.

"Why?"

"What if McGlashan's interests aren't aligned with ours?" He paced the far end of the porch like a caged cat. "You don't know him that well. He might be a political animal, and his prime concern is to protect the department. He could end up working against us."

"I'll go with my gut. He's on our side. He won't hide behind department bureaucracy. I don't think there's any love lost between him and Rutledge." I hit McGlashan's number but got voice mail. I asked him to give me a call and said it was urgent.

Binelli called back and said she was still checking on Eric Rutledge. The name wasn't the strong hit for her that I'd hoped it would be. She professed a belief that she had at least seen it somewhere because, "They generally don't pass out a list of good people." I told her he might have Vegas debt and to cast a wide net in her search for information on him. We disconnected.

"We've got another problem," I said.

"Dangelo," Garrett responded. He ceased his motion and faced the water. "He'll think we took Jenny, maybe even finger us for the money. We need to let him know it wasn't us. Before we focus on Rutledge and Jenny"—he turned to me—"we have to talk with him."

CHAPTER 36

It was a little before one when Garrett and I spotted Joseph Dangelo as he strolled out of Long Sally's. My buddy, Baby Carrot, who knew "Lewis Carroll" was a pseudonym for Charles Dodgson, got in the driver's seat of a black SUV. I thought of pen names and heard McGlashan's voice in my head: *Goes by the name of Eric Rutledge.* At the time, I had thought it was an unusual, but not uncommon, way to give someone's name. A style of speech. But McGlashan, who hadn't called me back, was a straight shooter. He had shifted his weight after he had given Rutledge's name. Did Rutledge go by a different name?

Garrett and I had dispatched Morgan on his Harley to Dangelo's place at Ybor City, as we didn't know which location he would pop in at. I texted him and let him know we had him. As I followed a block behind Dangelo's car, I hit Binelli's number again. She picked up, which I wasn't expecting. I told her to stick with Rutledge but to open it up to different first names.

"There aren't many variations," she said. "Erik with a 'k,' but that's about it."

"Erich," I said, spelling it out for her. "But it's German, and Rutledge is English, specifically northern England."

"Right. And you think he'd be true to his genealogical roots?"

"I haven't a clue. Middle initial is 'W.' Maybe you can run with that." I switched gears. "Have you given more thought to my proposal?" I was eager to solidify her as a permanent asset. I didn't like her uncertainty, which accompanied every conversation. Her hesitancy was a weak link. This is a business where everyone has to be on board, and you need to be 100 percent right, even when you're wrong. I didn't know why Binelli was afraid to commit. Fear of job repercussions? Moral ambiguities? Maybe she was considering bidding adios to the bureau and teaching inner-city junior high. If so, she was qualified—she carried two guns every day.

She asked, "Have you answered *my* question yet?"

"Which question?" I asked, although I knew what she was referring to.

"You know."

"I don't know."

It was a lie and a double answer; it could serve as a claim that I didn't know what question she referred to, or a direct response to the question we both knew I perfectly understood. She hung up. I felt cheap, like I'd been discovered to be a fraud and let down those who mattered most. I wouldn't dodge her again; I wouldn't dodge myself again.

Dangelo's car rolled up to a valet stand for a restaurant on Beach Drive. I swung the truck into the next side street. Garrett and I decided it would be best if I flew solo. It would be less threatening.

Dangelo sat at a back table along with a goateed man. I wondered where Tweedledum's twin was, but thought two bodyguards was overkill in the first place. They watched as I approached.

"This place used to have standards," I said as I stood over them. A waitress with a shirt that wanted to pop its buttons dropped by and inquired if I would be joining them.

"Yes," Dangelo answered, "he will be." He turned to Tweedledum. "Let us have some time, Chuck."

Chuck stood, brought his face into mine—his eyebrows needed to be trimmed—held that pose for a beat, and said, "'This place used to have standards?' That old horn's the best you can blow? I had higher expectations for you." He sauntered over to the bar, and I claimed his seat. It was warm. I wanted to pick it up and break it over his head.

I turned my attention to Dangelo. "His last name wouldn't be Dodgson by chance, would it?"

"No. It's Duke. Chuck Duke." Dangelo gave me a quizzical look. "Why do you ask?"

"He go to college?"

Dangelo chuckled. It was a pleasant sound. He was a hard man not to like. "I see you've had the opportunity to talk with him. Mr. Duke carries unusual mental capacity."

"Yet he's a goon for you," I said. I thought of PC and decided to redouble my efforts to steer him away from the street life.

"He has a myriad of responsibilities within our organization," Dangelo said, "and the only person who has shown tendencies of being a goon, Jacob"—he rubbed his neck—"is, I'm afraid, you."

"How's the bar business these days?"

Dangelo landed a hard stare that would register a point in a boxing match. He brought his hand down from his neck and placed both hands evenly in front of him on the table. He said, "You took the girl. I want my money."

"I have neither."

"You took her."

"I did not."

"You know where she is."

"I do not."

"You're lying."

"I am not."

He tossed his hands up in disgust and glanced away from me and out toward the restaurant. He came back to me. I doubted it had been an inside job. I'd made Rutledge out for swiping Jenny, but I still needed to eliminate the possibility of a coup within his organization. I went in strong, as if I already knew. "It's one of your men. Someone's trying to work you and—"

"Give it up," he punched out. "Why do I have to keep *telling* you that? You took her."

"No. Why do *I* have to keep telling *you* that?"

Neither of us spoke for a moment. My phone vibrated in my pocket. Next to us, a young man in a blue suit opened a leather briefcase and spread loose documents on the table. His companion, an older man in a short-sleeve shirt, gave the pile a bored glance. He reserved his real interest for the waitress—specifically her stressed buttons.

Dangelo asked, "Who is the *third* party who *has* the girl who *leads* to my money?" The words tumbled out like a poetry reading.

The waitress placed a glass of water in front of me. They needed a new dishwasher. The glass had the faint outline of a woman's lips on it. I picked it up—lip marks away from mine—and took a sip. An ice cube slipped into my mouth. I placed the glass back on the white tablecloth and leaned back in the chair. I like sipping on ice. It gives my mouth something to do when I'm not talking.

"You know, don't you?" Dangelo asked.

"You're not privy to that at this time. I just dropped by to inform you that it wasn't me who waltzed out of the Winking Lizard last night with Jenny." I planned on playing all my cards, but not yet.

"You knew she was there—you *were* there—yet you deny taking her. What more do you require of me? Join the Flat Earth Society?"

"I don't care if you sit on a roof and wait for Jesus. I batted cleanup. Someone beat me to her. Someone, as you know, who had a front-door key or was already inside the bar."

"The back door?"

"Send me a bill." My phone buzzed my thigh again.

"It looks like you took a battering ram to it. It's not even salvageable."

"Imagine that."

"But the front door was unlocked."

"Baffles me too," I said.

He leaned in. "It wasn't locked when you were there?"

"You're a fast one." I crunched the ice and put my elbows on the table. "I think someone stayed in after closing hours. Maybe in the head. Wandered in late in the evening and hung out until the place was empty."

Dangelo's eyes glazed past me as if he, too, were deciding which cards to play and when to show them. He said, "We concur. Can you give me a description? I can see if anyone remembers such a man."

"You've got a security camera."

"We reviewed it. Unfortunately, it's focused on the cash register, not the restrooms."

I decided to go all in. Jenny, as far as I could ascertain, was alive despite having been kidnapped three times. Her luck had to be close to quitting time. "Someone owes Vegas a bundle of money," I said. "But instead of paying his debt, he decided to keep it himself. He needs to silence Jenny to bury the money trail."

"Our organization has extensive interests in Vegas—"

"I imagine so." I realized I had cut him off.

"And Mr. Duke performs a wide variety of work for us."

"So you said."

He held my gaze for a moment. "He discovered an unusual connection between the missing girl and my missing funds. It wasn't at all that obvious."

Did Dangelo or his organization know Rutledge? I could have stared at the board all day and not seen that coming.

"I believe you stated," I said, "that you don't believe in coincidences."

"Yes." The right side of his mustache curled up; I'd not seen that before with him. "It bodes well for a man if he's a good listener."

"It bodes well if we stop our prancing. Let me guess. Someone she came in contact with is an individual you extended unsecured credit to."

Dangelo settled back into his chair. "We believe that to be the case."

"Eric Rutledge," I said. He tried not to flinch, but his jaw clenched, and I hadn't seen that before either. Uncle Joe was in the cooker. "When did you make the connection?"

"He was good," Dangelo replied. "He avoided the security camera at the Winking Lizard. But Eugene, when we showed him a picture, remembered him loitering before closing time. You see"—he dismissed the waitress with a wave of his hand when she was still six feet out—"we just connected the dots this morning."

"We're on parallel tracks. How did you get here?"

Dangelo waited a beat then came in. "Mr. Duke was conducting some idle research on the girl's—Ms. Spencer's—encounter with the sheriff's office. He recognized...he uncovered the name of someone who owed us some money."

"But you accused me."

"Covering my bases, much like you."

"You had his picture?"

"Such people, who owe us a considerable sum, are known throughout the organization."

"Duke trips over the connection. You flash a picture to Eugene; he confirms that Rutledge was in the bar, but now he's gone."

"Yes, although you're eliding one item that baffles us. Why was Eric Rutledge stowed away in my bar? Why that bar, Jacob? Who led him there?"

I blew my breath out. Lying wouldn't advance my cause. "I might have slipped up a bit, Joe."

A laugh escaped him. "Forgive my humorous response, but such a lighthearted admission seems so...unbecoming of you."

I shrugged. "I'm not a virgin."

"No," he said with a chuckle, "I suppose none of us is." I'm glad he found the thing so damn amusing. "Strange, isn't it?" he wondered. "A man you trusted is now the man you chase, but here you and I sit working through our issues in a civilized manner."

"Speaking of which," I said, "Rutledge creates an unusual challenge for you. He wears a badge, and you can't go in and manhandle him the way you normally operate. You can't afford to have 'cop killer' on your résumé."

"Such talk. He reached in and took a drink of water. He placed it back on the table. "But since you opened the binder, I'll remind you that your résumé is, as I've already stated, remarkably stark. Yet you hardly seem a man of inaction."

"What's in it for me?"

"The woman you so—"

"Your turn to be careful. 'Very careful' is, I believe, how you put it." Our eyes were locked in a death grip. Dangelo nodded his head up and down; I tilted forward. "Measure your words, Joe. This ain't no dress rehearsal."

"Well..." He took a breath and sat forward. "Ms. Spencer and—"

"Keep it simple."

He let his breath out evenly and said in a measured voice, "We would have no interest in you, your associates, or your friends, past or present. Frankly, Jacob, we would be in your debt."

Dangelo was offering a peace treaty that he wouldn't delve into Kathleen's past. I had to assume at that point that he was suspicious that Kathleen was the former Lauren Cunningham whose husband had been murdered days before he was to testify against the Outfit, Dangelo's association. He also likely surmised I was responsible for the deaths of four of his men who had been sent to silence her. Furthermore, he seemed to realize that his organization, as I knew, *had* overreacted when they sent the four men after her.

"Do we have an agreement?" he asked.

"And if I'm unable to find the money or Rutledge?"

"I have great faith in you. But in that unlikely event, I'll consider the mere act of your effort to seal our agreement. How did that Native American put it? 'I will fight no more forever.'"

"A good omen."

"How so?"

"His name was Chief Joseph."

Dangelo smiled, but it seemed to take something out of him. I stood, took a step toward him, and said, "You're in debt to me now. You just don't know it." I didn't wait for a reply.

On the way out, I paused in front of Chuck Duke. "What do you think?" I asked him. "Pedophile or not?"

"Dodgson?"

I nodded.

"No doubt. He would have done well with an organization like ours."

CHAPTER 37

I hit the front door and smacked into a morning deluge. I wanted to check my phone, so I ducked into a real estate office next to the restaurant. I told the receptionist, a substantial lady with a doughnut in her hand, that I was seeking refuge from the rain. She smiled, placed her pastry on her mouse pad, and handed me a sticky card. Toni Shaffer, she said, wasn't in at the moment. Refuge seeker or not, I was a potential client.

I checked my calls and punched Binelli's number. She picked up on the second ring.

"Talk to me," I said.

"I found your man."

"And?"

"Wallace Eric Rutledge."

"No wonder he went with 'Eric.' Now tell me why's he in your database."

"We keep a file on law enforcement personnel with gambling issues. A study a year ago showed they were the most susceptible to crossing the line. His name is on the list. Declared bankruptcy twice and has jumped around. Lee County is his third stop in seven years. But his record is clean, except for one incident. Gun—"

"What was that?" I realized she was going to tell me, but I'd jumped in with my question.

"Gunned down a suspect during a drug raid. Went in himself. Some money was never recovered. There was an investigation, and he was cleared. But judging by the length of the investigation, it wasn't exactly open-and-shut."

"Did you look into it?"

"The drug raid?"

"Yeah."

"Sure, I read the seven hundred pages while soaking in the tub this morning. We're talking CliffsNotes. Got it?"

"He owes money to Dangelo."

"Come at me again."

"Just met with Uncle Joe. He claims Rutledge owes their Vegas branch."

"My, oh my, oh my. What a tiny little world we live in. The Nevada guys are above Dangelo's pay grade. The heat must be on him."

I thought of his facial twitches and wondered just what type of conversations Dangelo was having with the pay grade above him. "Any known addresses? Family? Anything else you can give me?" I asked.

"Divorced twice, no kids."

"Address?"

"No longer in your neck of the woods, although he grew up just south of you. Only parcel under his name now is in Lee County."

I was disappointed at that. I was hoping Rutledge still owned property around Tampa Bay. It would have been a convenient place to stash Jenny and the cash. No way would he use his personal residence.

"Heavy gambler?" I asked. It was a moot question. I was stalling as, in the back of my mind, I was formulating my final assault on Binelli.

"An addict. Remember, you didn't get any of this from me."

"Any record of Vegas debt?" Still stalling.

"No, not that he doesn't have Vegas debt. We just have no way of knowing that."

It was now or never. "Can I put your picture on the team website?"

"You work for a shadow agency, right? Some well-financed rogue branch?" It sounded rehearsed. She had made up her mind based on what I would say. FBI Special Agent Natalie Binelli and I were going to settle this here and now.

"At times. Certainly not on this case, which is why I've been badgering you. I get into situations where I need another source, where I need help. I can't always go to my agency, and even when I can, it's often not enough—like at Escobar's when we freed those girls."

"What's the problem?"

"The problem? The problem, Vassar, is I never know whether you're all in. I sense that any phone call could be our last, and I can't have that. I need to know."

The line was quiet, and the receptionist switched her doughnut to her other hand. She picked up a call. I pressed my phone hard against my ear.

"You know what I want," Binelli said.

"How much?"

"Oh, no, cowboy. You're not even in the right playing field, and you know it. That stupid comment just got you two strikes. One more, and I hang up."

"You need to be crystal clear."

"And so do you. The truth. Would you have?" She laid it out. "Would you have busted my wrist that night in Escobar's kitchen if I hadn't gone along with your half-brained scheme to save those girls?"

"Without hesitation."

"*Busted* my wrist to get your pissant way."

"Yes, ma'am. I didn't think you'd let me, and I'm glad you didn't. But lives were in danger. Before we closed, one man was missing his head, one had bled out on the living room floor, one was floating facedown in the bay, and Elvis had lost half his blood. That's not an uncommon scene for—"

"I'll play with you."

It took a second to register. "Understand what I'm saying?"

"Crystal," Binelli threw back at me. "I just wanted to make sure you could tell me, and yourself, the truth before joining your little Sunday school group. If I ever reach the point where it's our last conversation, I'll let you know; I'll finish whatever deal we're on then shut the door. Agreed?"

"Fair enough."

"And Jake?"

"Yeah?" I don't believe she had ever addressed me by my name.

"Those other times I asked you, and you said you didn't know?"

"Yeah?"

"Don't ever lie to me again." The line went dead.

"Okay."

I turned to thank the receptionist for offering me sanctuary. She had dropped her phone and doughnut and was staring at me. "Not *that* Elvis," I said.

The rain had stopped. I stepped onto the steamy pavement and instantly jumped back up against the building as two female joggers brushed past me. Both were drenched in sweat and rain. I held eye contact long enough with the one wearing the Rays visor to count as sex. I found Garrett leaning against my truck.

"Why the smirk?" he asked, as I climbed behind the wheel. He went around to the passenger's side.

"Binelli. We've reached terms of an agreement."

"What sealed the deal?"

"I told the truth."

He grunted, and I recounted my conversation with her.

My energy surge created by Binelli's information dissipated like a fog lifting off the water. I *thought* I had reached an agreement with Dangelo that if I found—meaning turned over to him—his money, not only would he not look into Kathleen's past, but I also might be in a position to call in a favor one day. Even if I came up empty-handed, I didn't think he was a threat to Kathleen. *I'll consider the mere act of your effort to seal our agreement.* He had nothing to gain by going after her and had already indicated his associates realized she wasn't a threat, and they, like me, had overplayed their hand. In full disclosure, they *did* end up dead, and I was whistling "Dixie," but I was willing to let minor imbalances slide.

What Dangelo didn't know was that while he had talked, my mind had flashed to Kathleen's hardwood floor. *Words ring so hallow.* I wouldn't take a chance. At the end of the road, Dangelo would understand in perfect terms why he would volunteer for a slow death before any harm ever befell Kathleen. "Do we have an agreement?" he had asked.

I hadn't answered.

And Jenny? I was getting close; I knew it. One break. One tip, and she was mine. I needed her. For herself. For Susan. To keep Kathleen's past where it belonged. To keep myself from losing.

CHAPTER 38

Jenny

She opened her eyes.
I'm a big girl.
Red crayon markings on the floor. Now black. Now red.
"Run" played from far away. Down a long hall. A forgotten
hall. A song about an imagined world. About putting yourself
in better times. A title that described her life. At first, she was
just taken with the restrained soft voice that fronted the lush
orchestra and heart-tugging strings. When she'd read what the
lyrics were intended to mean, however, she'd adopted it as her
anthem. But it was fading—the hope for a better life, creating
her own place by the sea. The belief that the emotional tug of a
song could actually shape a life. *What a crock-shit full of illusions,*
she thought. *And sooner or later, they all melt away like snowflakes
on a spring day.*
The stuff you've got to figure out on your own.
She lay on her side with her head on her hand. She heard
and felt her heartbeat through her wrist. It stopped. She passed
out. She woke. She considered, *What was the last thing I heard
when I thought my heart had stopped? Nothing. Not even the static of
an empty frequency. There you have it—the smell of forgotten and the
sound of death.*

A beach, she thought. *A place in the sun.* Was that too much to ask? Something had gone wrong on the beach. What was it? She tried to focus, but her mind was a swirl of images. She was back on her father's boat, and she smelled the wood, for old boats smelled their weight. She felt the pump handle in her tight, oily fist then saw him as he walked out of the mangroves. *But he's dead. No...no...no. Did I say it out loud? Don't even think that.* She blacked out again, and this time she surrendered to the concrete floor. She went back to her father, back to when it was good. To the last trip to Club 57, the waterfront bar. It played in her head as if someone had stuck in a DVD.

I'm a big girl.

It was the last summer, which was only the second summer, that they had shared the Trojan. It was just the two of them, and it was the time of the year that got hung up in nowhere. It was hot, but not July hot. It was as if the earth was a grill that had been turned off but still radiated heat. There was no wind, like whatever had caused the early summer gusts had packed up and gone home. Good-bye. I'm gone. The planet had stopped revolving and finally come to rest before its next big convulsion. In September, in Ohio, the earth sleeps.

Jenny had spotted a vacant picnic table on the deck that hung over the water before Larry had even docked at Club 57. After she had tied the bowline—her responsibility—she sprinted ahead of Larry to secure the prize. Like mid-September, Jenny was starting to transition. She still carried Puddles, her stuffy, but Larry noticed she was getting self-conscious about it. She had spent a week at Camp Tecumseh, and Larry figured that part of her innocence had stayed in those woods. He didn't know whether she left it or it was taken, nor was he one to dwell on such things.

Jenny took her seat at the picnic table and heard a loud smack and a grunt. She looked up and saw her father towering over a man who was sprawled on the ground next to the bright blue hostess stand that had been built into the side of a gnarly maple tree. Larry's right hand was balled into a fist, his face redder than anytime she'd ever seen, and a vein the size of the Ohio River rode his neck until it disappeared under his faded red Buckeyes 2002 championship T-shirt. Three men with bandannas around their heads and Harley T-shirts—"bikers," her daddy once had called them; some of the nicest guys you'd ever meet—sat on picnic benches with their eyes darting between Larry and their comrade, who now lay on the concrete, staring at the underside of the tree and making no effort to improve his position.

"Anyone else?" Larry asked, as he stood over the table. Fist tight. The Ohio River about to break its levee.

"Take it easy, boss," the man with long braids and wearing a Hog's Breath Harley T-shirt said. (Jenny had seen so many Key West Hog's Breath T-shirts at Club 57 that she once had asked her father if Key West was somewhere in Columbus.) "The only thing I'm gonna do is hit him myself when that stupid son of a bitch gets to his sorry-ass feet. You just need to accept our apologies. Follow me?"

Jenny saw her father shrink as if he was leaking air. His fist went back to being a hand. He blew his breath out and nodded at the man. He walked over to Jenny.

"What happened, Daddy?"

"Nothing for you to be concerned with." He took the bench across from her, waited a beat as if figuring something out in his head, and then said, "Let's switch sides, Jen."

"Why?"

"So you'll have the better view."

"I thought you just did that for Mom."

"Well...it's time I did it for you. You're a big girl now." And they did switch sides, and Jenny looked out over the lake and sandbar and tossed french fries to the grateful ducks and carp below.

You're a big girl now. You're a big girl now.

I'm a big girl now.

She sat up and brushed her hair away from her face. There was red crayon in her hair. *How odd*, she thought. She felt the crayon. Crusty, not a waxy substance at all. Blood.

Last night burst free in her memory.

Detective Eric Rutledge had busted down the door, descended the steps, and proclaimed he was there to rescue her. Her spirit had ignited in relief, but before she had the chance to thank him, he clipped her temple with the stock of his Browning shotgun. Jenny had stumbled to her knees.

She had gotten up.

"What the hell?" Rutledge said, and struck her again. She went down for the count.

Now she had to get up again. She didn't know if she could. If she even wanted to. Why bother? *Why him? He's a cop*, she thought. Jenny tried to find reason for what had happened last night, but neither the energy nor the curiosity was there. She rolled over on her back and blew her breath out at the rafters. She wanted to go home. In her head now, *Please, God. I'll do anything.*

Oh, that's just super swell, she thought. *Stupid-promises-to-God time. Not yet. This floorboard might be floating—*

"But this boat's not going down." Her voice startled her.

She stood and took a moment to make sure that position would hold. *Oh, yeah*, she remembered as she glanced at the floor, *I don't have any shoes.* "Never thought that would be an issue," she said. Her voice sounded strange. *Wonder how long I was out?* She surveyed her surroundings. "Wonderful, a barn." She took stock: one wheelbarrow with a flat tire, an assortment of garden tools, empty plastic trash cans, paint cans on a shelf with dried paint coating their sides, and a red Toro lawn mower. No food. No place to sleep.

No plans to keep me alive.

Her head throbbed with every downbeat of her heart. She felt like one of the paint cans; part of her was outside her and no good anymore. She considered the cans. Could she swing one? Whack the next person through the door with it? The spiked water bottle certainly hadn't made the cut. She lifted a paint can and saw it half hidden by other cans.

A hatchet.

At the sight of it, all of Jenny's frustrations, all of her dreams, all of her battered hope, all of Jenny turned to anger. Her world seemed so much simpler now that everything was boiled down to one emotion. She picked up the hatchet by its rubber handle. "What do we have here?" she said, her voice low and outside of her. She took a swipe at the air. "The big gun, baby, and the next bozo through that door gets the welcome package."

Just like my daddy laid that man down at Club 57.

CHAPTER 39

It was evening, and I sat at the end of my dock with my buddy Mark. First name "Maker's." We go back a bit.

I wasn't going to run out this time and had brought the bottle along with a bottle of water. I have a theory that if you drink water while drinking booze, you'll be able to drink twice as much alcohol. If you know or believe otherwise, kindly keep it to yourself. I fished my phone out of my pocket and brought up the picture of Jenny. I took a quick glance and put it away. I'd had her at the Lizard. I'd given her up at the Lizard.

Her blood was on me now.

I poured some amber gold into my tumbler. I had just finished a few shots and was looking forward to a solitude binge. Hadley III, fascinated with the baitfish that skimmed the surface, hung her head over the side. I gave her a shove, and she went in with a frantic scream, paws outstretched. Easy now—it was just a fleeting thought. Even though I'd told them Binelli couldn't find an alternative address for Rutledge, Morgan and Garrett were inside, still trying to get a hit on his whereabouts, advancing the cause of finding Jenny, and generally doing constructive things with their lives. Good for them.

McGlashan finally had returned my call and confirmed that Rutledge was AWOL. His car was gone and wasn't at the airport. His house was clean. He said he'd immediately pass on any new information. He had checked the records of Rutledge's cruiser and said Rutledge had spent a little more than a minute at Billy Ray's car after he had interviewed Jenny. We agreed it was nothing he couldn't have handled if it ever came back to him. If it were me, I'd blow off any questions or accusations by stating I'd heard a rattle under the car and gotten out to check it: "Billy Ray's car was right next to me? No kidding. Nope, never saw it." There isn't much in this world that you can't bullshit your way into or out of. Take it from me; I know.

Kathleen sat down next to me. I don't know where she came from. She was just there. Plop. Like magic. Her bare feet dangled over the edge of the composite decking. We sat in silence, and no boats went by. The premonitory red channel marker was doing that blinking thing.

"I just want you to know," she said, "if the only thing you wanted out of our relationship was my car, it would be worth it. I'd do it again."

I didn't respond. Can't a guy drink alone?

"But you've got to bring it back clean. No excuses for the way it looks."

Nothing.

"I made chocolate cupcakes with cream cheese frosting."

I took a sip of bourbon.

"Oh, and I saw Elvis," she said. "He had a 'War on Drugs' T-shirt on and was having drinks with Nixon and Frost on the front porch of the Vinoy."

I glanced at her. Her hair was pulled back, and the moon illuminated her face. Hadley III had already found her lap. At that moment, I wanted nothing more than to pick her up—the woman, not the fur ball—and walk out of life. Instead, I asked, "How did you get here?"

"Nice to see you too. I called Morgan." She picked up the bottle of bourbon. "You dropped me for this floozy?"

"She understands me." I went to take it from her, but she pulled it away. Hadley III jumped off her lap.

"In case you forgot, sailor, you're on deck."

"You do know I drowned my last three girlfriends."

"*Finally*—I could never understand that swim test."

"How'd your thingamabob go today?"

"Hmm..." She put the cap back on the bottle. So sad. "It was a fine thingamabob. Kind of you to inquire."

"I don't have a clue what—"

Her finger lightly graced my lips. "Where's Jenny? She's not in that bottle. That would be Jeannie, and she's not real."

"Gone."

"Gone?"

"As in 'with the wind.'"

"That's Tuesday, I believe."

I remembered that Susan had called twice, and I had let both go to voice mail.

"Do you know who has her?" Kathleen asked.

"I think so, but we don't know where. She's been passed around, and I can't see how her current captor has any use for her. Her luck, as it was, has run out."

"And you're sitting here sparring with me and supporting the hard liquor industry?"

I shrugged then gave her an abbreviated version of the past twenty-four hours. I left out my conversation with Dangelo regarding his suspicion of her true identity and my nebulous understanding with him to trade the money for his silence.

"We hit the wall," I concluded. "We can't find him."

"What about Susan?" she asked.

"What about her?"

"Have you kept her informed?"

"No. I've been avoiding calling her because I don't want to be the bearer of bad news."

"My, such courage. Can't your friend Jack here help prep you?"

"It's Mark."

She stole a glance at the liquor bottle. "So it is. The devil has a twin. Susan deserves—"

"I know."

"—to know."

A baitfish jumped. It leapt out of its element, propelled by fear and the evolutionary instinct to survive. It didn't think; it acted.

"Call her," Kathleen said, and placed her hand on my shoulder. She stood up with my liquid savior in her hand and strolled down the dock, allowing me to call Susan in privacy. I could use a few ounces of her common sense. Couple more ounces from that bottle wouldn't be bad either.

I called Susan and informed her that I thought Rutledge had Jenny. I told her that I believed he had stolen the money and that the Colemans' abduction of her was unrelated to Rutledge, but it had forced Rutledge to cover his tracks. She was reserved during the conversation and showed little emotion, let alone disbelief or anger that Rutledge was to blame. I realized that time had been chipping away at her, eroding her hope and attacking her dreams like a virus.

"He needs to silence her," she said. It came out as neither a question nor a statement.

"I didn't say—"

"You said you can't find him."

"That's correct. We're—"

"Did you check his sister's house?"

"His sister?"

"Remember? I told you he flirted with me and said he used to take care of his sister, but she'd died recently."

"Who never married," I said as I recalled Susan telling me that Rutledge had hit on her. I stood and started jogging the hundred feet down the dock to my house. Morgan and Kathleen were on the screen porch. I didn't see Garrett.

"Tell me more," I said to the phone pressed hard against my ear.

"That's about it. Can you find his sister's house? Do you think he'd take her there?"

I stopped at my back screen door. "I don't know, but we'll look."

I hung up. I didn't trust myself to say anything else to Susan. I didn't want her to get her hopes up. So far, I hadn't done a damn thing for her except let her down. I recalled Binelli telling me Rutledge "grew up just south of you." It took Morgan less than five minutes to find the address of a Margaret Rutledge, who had passed away five months ago. The property was still in her name. It was in Manatee County, twenty minutes south of here. He asked if I wanted him to check for other female Rutledges who had died south of us in the previous six months; I replied that we'd go with the odds. I told Kathleen not to wait up, and she rolled her eyes and shook her head. She claimed a lounge chair on the porch, tugged her legs underneath her, put the side table light on low, and picked up a book.

I changed into boots, jeans, and a tight jacket with inside pockets. Garrett was in the garage, hooking up a new Ringside punching bag. I wasn't aware he'd gotten one. I gave him the new intelligence. He unlocked the steel cabinet and got out his SASS and the red spinnaker bag. It held a medical kit, currency, passports, sat phones, and a dessert tray of guns and knifes. Garrett, Morgan, and I piled into my truck.

"My bet is that at least the money is there," Garrett said. He was in the backseat with the spinnaker bag. "Been there all along. Rutledge wouldn't keep it at his house. Too much risk."

"She's there," Morgan said.

"We don't know," I started in, "but we might as—"

"He's confused," Morgan said, "doing something he's never done. He'll take her to a place he's familiar with. Not for long—he'll know that's dangerous—but long enough to regroup his thoughts, and then he'll act quickly." I didn't answer. He held strong convictions based on a different sphere, one I didn't fully acknowledge. I gave Morgan a glance. But it wasn't his face or ponytail—or flowered shirt or moon talisman around his neck—that caught my attention. He wore tightly laced tennis shoes.

CHAPTER 40

"Success," Winston Churchill noted, "consists of going from failure to failure without loss of enthusiasm." Maybe we were just chasing down another failure, but that wouldn't dent our enthusiasm.

I swung onto 275 south, and the interstate widened where a Maginot Line of tollbooths guarded the Sunshine Skyway Bridge. I clocked sixty-two on the truck's digital display through the tollbooth's SunPass lane—that was a personal best. Felt pretty good about that. We rode the bridge high into the night like a rocket trying to break earth's gravitational pull. If some unfortunate man with a six-shooter, a badge, and a pension happened to be in my path, he'd have to catch me. I'd been a step behind at every turn, and if that were to be the case again, it wouldn't be due to lack of focus. Fifteen minutes later, I took the Route 19 exit, followed by two lefts and a fork to the right that my copilot ordered. I pulled the truck off the side of the road about a hundred yards shy of our target. We were in flat-bush Florida country—the stuff that never makes a postcard despite occupying a substantial portion of the state.

Binelli called.

"What?"

"More news on Rutledge," she said. Garrett passed me my Boker knife, and I wiggled my body higher in the seat, twisted, and put it the pocket of my jeans.

"What?" I hit her again.

"Catch you at a bad moment?" Her tone held no guise of sincerity.

"I'm camped outside Rutledge's sister's house. I don't have—"

"You're where?"

"Rutledge's sister. I—"

"Listen to me. We found out that when Rutledge goes to Vegas—"

"We've been over this," I interrupted her. I wanted to get on the ground and approach the house. "He owes money to Dangelo's group. Remember, Dangelo told me. I told you—"

"*Listen,* you arrogant pinhead. You don't know what you're walking into. Rutledge worked for Dangelo. You listening now?"

"Go." I put the phone on speaker.

"Remember I told you that last year Rutledge was cleared of a shooting death in a drug raid that he went into solo? Turns out the man he plugged was trying to move into Joseph Dangelo's turf."

"I thought you stuck with CliffsNotes."

"Yeah, well, I got curious about how tiny your world had suddenly gotten, and it's a good thing for you, because I was able to requisition bank records. I found the missing money from that drug raid."

She paused as if she expected me to interrupt. "And?" I asked.

"The money was wired into his sister's account," Binelli said, picking up the speed, as if she'd just been given the green flag, "two weeks after the raid."

"Coincidence." Soon as I said it, I knew I'd wasted four syllables.

"Doubtful. Rutledge spent his Vegas time almost exclusively at casinos Dangelo's group has interest in. He lobbied hard to be on the drug case. Wasn't his to start with. Besides, it was twenty-five grand even. You know if we pulled tax records, we wouldn't see it declared."

I thought back to my conversation with Dangelo. A smooth talker, he had stumbled with his words when describing when Chuck Duke had made the connection: *"He recognized...He uncovered the name of someone who owed us some money."* Like Hemingway's nuanced improvement over Twain's quote, *recognizing* a name shows more familiarity than *uncovering* a name. I didn't think much of it at the time, but looking back, I doubt someone in Chuck Duke's capacity, even considering his mental prowess, would keep tabs on every Vegas debt holder. Dangelo had told me Rutledge owed them money, but he'd withheld the information that Rutledge had performed a hit for him. I understood why, but Dangelo still had engaged in less than full disclosure that day in the restaurant. I was ticked with myself for assuming he had shown me all his cards. When he had said Rutledge owed him money, I should have known there was more. On the other end, I had Rutledge pretending he couldn't pronounce Dangelo's name. *Dee-angelo.* Both had outplayed me.

But no one tosses my cork into the water.

"Okay," I snapped back. "Dangelo's association gets to know Rutledge by his gambling debt to them. Maybe they keep closer tabs on him; it's good to have a man with a badge be indebted to you. They see opportunity when they need someone eliminated, someone who's moving in on them, and they give the job to Rutledge. Pass him some cash, maybe even forgive a debt in the process."

"No way of knowing if he was in debt to them at the time," Binelli said, "but it's a safe bet and meaningless for our discussion. What I don't understand is why Dangelo didn't see this earlier."

"Dangelo told me they'd just connected the dots themselves that Rutledge was the guy who had interviewed Jenny. What was given to us wasn't so easy for them to figure out." Garrett got out of the truck but kept his door open so he could listen. I was trying to wrap my mind around the implication of Binelli's information. "My guess," I continued, "is that Dangelo needs to find Rutledge before I find Rutledge. Rutledge could roll and sing to negotiate a lighter sentence *if* he gets caught. Dangelo would like him dead. Probably like Rutledge dead more than recovering the money."

"You're dialed in now. You've got two sets of enemies."

"Maybe not."

"How so?" she asked.

"We've been passing the ceremonial pipe around here. Dangelo's interests are aligned with mine." I was beginning to see my enemies, and outside of Rutledge, I didn't think Dangelo's boys—assuming Eric Rutledge never saw another sunrise—were in that club. Jenny, unfortunately, held no interest to either of the conflicting parties.

Binelli's voice brought me back. "Your curtain's up."

"I owe you."

"Always."

I stepped out of the truck. "This place is either empty, or we've got a crowd," Garrett said. "If we found this house, Dangelo can too. We want Jenny alive; he wants Rutledge dead."

Garrett and I were on the same page. I replied, "That's the winning combination tonight." We discussed our plan and headed into the darkness. I didn't bother to tell Morgan to stay with the truck. He never had listened to me in the past, and something in his past made him—and based on what I'd witnessed when he'd helped us rescue Kathleen on the beach—uncannily comfortable with guns in the night.

CHAPTER 41

A two-story house. Lights on. A car parked out front. Margaret Rutledge, dead as she was, was throwing a party. I should have asked McGlashan what kind of wheels Rutledge drove. A small barn with another car parked tightly across its doors was off to my right. To keep someone inside? I claimed the barn, and Garrett took the house. Morgan was the floater, going where the noise and action drew him. Our phones were on vibrate and group text.

I sprinted through the high grass. I was still a hundred feet out from the barn when gunfire erupted from the house. I hit the ground, and my injured left ankle twisted awkwardly in a hole. Garrett's SIG Sauer retorted. I rose into a low crouch position.

"Raise your hands, Alice," Chuck Duke said, "and do it slowly."

God in heaven, I did not like that man.

How the hell did he get the drop on me? Where was Morgan? He couldn't have been more than fifty yards behind me unless he'd taken off in the direction of the gunfire. I got up. My ankle throbbed. I wanted to work out the kinks but didn't take the chance. I pivoted and stared into the barrels of a double-barrel shotgun.

"Dodgson, good to see you."

"It's unfortunate that you're here," he said, keeping his four eyes on my two.

281

"Certainly is for you. What do you say? Drop the hardware and settle this like honorable gentlemen?"

"Don't think so."

"Chicken."

"Move." He flipped his gun toward the barn. I glanced at the building and noticed that the two wide, sagging doors met in an uneven line. The car, a two-door, was parked lengthwise in front of the doors. If the doors swung out, they weren't going anywhere. The car was positioned to block direct access in or out of the barn. Was Jenny in there?

"You first," I instructed.

He replied with another jerk of his gun. I took a few steps.

I've had guns at my back before—this wasn't totally unfamiliar territory for me—and I've always vowed never to let it happen again. It does, and the only thing I can figure is that it must be a consequence of my lifestyle choice. Would he shoot? Doubtful. He certainly had heard the gunfire and knew I wasn't alone. But then again, I originally thought he possessed a brain the size of my left nut, so what did I know? Who'd ever have thought my left nut was that smart?

Besides, we were on the same side, and I think he knew that.

I stopped and turned. "Joe didn't make the trip with you, did he?"

He waved his gun as if it were a magic wand and would control my movements.

Dangelo's words came back to me. *"Your résumé is, as I've already stated, remarkably stark. Yet you hardly seem a man of inaction."* Had he foreseen this? I went with it.

"You have a dilemma here," I said. "Rutledge owes you money, and you used him in the past to silence a competitor. If you go after him—a man with a badge—the feds will swarm you. If you let him live, he'll cut a deal and expose you to save his ass. You need to silence him, but you can't be in the same hemisphere when it happens. You need me."

"I'm listening."

"Maybe you don't want that gun pointed at me."

From behind me, a blast of fire illuminated the dark and reflected in Chuck Duke's glasses. Just as the pelican had dove off Susan's dock and made an unexpected splash that she'd instinctively reacted to, Chuck Duke's eyes left mine and darted to the leaping flames that caught the periphery of my vision. I didn't care if Fat Boy had gone off—my eyes were glued to the double-barrel shotgun.

I know I should have done what was in the best interest of Jenny, especially considering that Chuck Duke had just indicated willingness to negotiate, but my instincts shuttered my brain and possessed my body like that baitfish jumping for its life. That's what I tell myself. Truth is, I'd wanted to slap the arrogant prick ever since he'd gotten the jump on me when I was in Kathleen's car.

I lunged my body at his midsection and grabbed the gun. He fell backward, and we both held a firm grip on the shotgun. He had both hands on it and eventually would have won that battle, as I had only my left hand on the barrels. That, however, wasn't the battle I was fighting. I fiddled with my right hand for my Boker knife. I extended the blade and pressed it against the edge of his neck. Chuck Duke dropped his shotgun.

"Easy, pal," he said. "We were on the verge of a merger here. We both know that." I shot a glance at the garage. The flames leapt from the rear of the structure.

Jenny.

What a perfect way to get rid of her. Morgan's words came back to me. "*Regroup his thoughts, and then he'll act quickly.*" I didn't have time for Chuck Duke and was debating my options when Morgan emerged from the dark. He said, far too quietly, "Jenny's in there."

I looked at Chuck Duke. "Is she?"

"Just pulled in a little before you."

"Can you watch him?" I stood and kept my eyes on Chuck Duke. He hadn't answered my question, but I didn't think he was playing games.

"Go." Morgan drew a gun. I wasn't aware that he was packing. Chuck Duke rose to his feet. He brushed the dirt off his clothing and dutifully straightened his eyeglasses. I took off.

"Hey, Alice."

I spun around. Chuck Duke probably could take Morgan, gun or no gun, and I felt conflicted leaving my friend in such a predicament.

"What?"

"Do the job for both of us."

I sprinted toward the flames. The house was off to my left, no more than a hundred feet. Where was Garrett? Were his shots I heard aimed at Rutledge or Chuck Duke's counterpart? I hoped Chuck Duke had a method to communicate our agreement to his partner. I should have cleared that with him.

If Jenny were in the barn, the smoke would get her before the flames. The car blocking the barn door came into focus. Ford Fairlane. Decent shape. *Named after Henry Ford's estate, Fair Lane, in Michigan. Stopped production in 1970. Focus, man. Focus.*

He stepped out from the far corner of the barn when I was less than twenty feet away. The fire's light illuminated the barrel of his revolver. I slowed, but I didn't stop.

"That's far enough," Wallace Eric Rutledge said. Blood stained his shirt from what appeared to be a stomach wound.

His hair was perfectly groomed. It seemed so odd, and I wondered why I even noticed.

"What now, Rutledge?" I kept walking. "You going to shoot me, four others, burn the girl, and walk away?"

"Not a bad idea." His voice was resigned. It was over, and he knew it. The only question was how he went out. I threw away the bargain playbook. I kept walking.

Rutledge brought his gun up higher. "I *said,* 'That's far enough.'"

I stopped. Where was Garrett? "What did you do? Grab the money then cut the tape? But when the Colemans took her and the search started, it led us to her claim that there *was* money in Billy Ray's car. Led us to the job you did for Dangelo, the man you owed money to. You thought this would work out for you?"

"Never planned much beyond taking the money, but it evolved into something like that. Your buddy McGlashan was asking too many questions, wanted to talk to the apartment residents, take a look at her phone. I couldn't take that chance."

"And Dangelo? You did a job for him once?"

"Damn straight. But who the hell would've thought he'd have any interest in some runaway slut, let alone the fact that the money would be his? Unfuckinbelieveable. Even then, I had a chance. But when you told me you were talking to him and knew where the girl was, and you'd discovered the connection between Dangelo and the Colemans, then I knew it was all busted."

"Why not come clean? Tell Dangelo you didn't know it was his and keep the Colemans' half for being honest?"

"Yeah." He waved his gun up and down. "That would have been nice. Unfortunately, I'm behind far more than I stole. Greed doesn't generate the best decisions."

I had more questions, but only one that mattered. "Where is she?" Rutledge smirked and gave a slight shake of his head. I marched straight into him. "Is she in there?"

"Tits up, baby." He took a step even closer, a mistake on his part. "Burning in hell, just like you."

I doubled over and threw myself at his knees, but I was no match for the reflex of his finger. His gun went off simultaneously with another blast before I made contact with him. My lower-right abdomen felt the graze of a bullet. I hit the ground. I jumped up just in time to see Rutledge go down, his shirt a lava flow of blood. Garrett stood thirty paces to my left, his SASS still aimed at the last vertical space Wallace Eric Rutledge ever would occupy. The flames now consumed half the barn. My body recoiled instinctively from the heat.

Burning in hell. And I was burning time with Rutledge.

I raced toward the vertical line where the two doors met. The weakest link. An arrow pierced my right side every time my right foot found the ground, and my left ankle threatened to buckle with every step. I was still a good distance out when the flames roared at me in defiance, and the left side of the building vanished into an inferno. My mind flashed to my flying leap in the swimming pool to retrieve the girl's bone and my effort to clear the tidal pool while running. I had failed in each attempt. We're so big in our dreams, so small in our lives. Yet I was all Jenny had. Her wrecking ball.

Are you watching me now?

I don't know how far away I was when I launched. All I know is that I had the sense to launch with my good ankle. I flew feet-first over the car with my body parallel to the ground. I struck the doors above the lock. They shattered. I landed on my left shoulder on the concrete. A piercing bolt of pain electrified my neck and back.

I got to my feet, but collapsed with my hands on my knees. Hell roared at me as if it were defending its homeland. I coughed. Too much smoke. Fresh blood on the floor. Mine? Another wave of heat as the Devil brought up the reserves. I couldn't focus. Coughing, but not me. I straightened. Raised my head. She came at me from out of the smoke. An apparition of death, an angel of hell. Not the girl in the picture. Matted hair. Angry eyes. Tears? A hatchet. She held it high. She screamed. She swung. I jerked my head to the right.

I was three shots of bourbon too slow.

CHAPTER 42

*E*very baby is born to do something great.

"Hand me the tube of TAO," Morgan said.

Run until I nearly die. Did I do it? I never knew if I was running from death or toward death. You know it's out there waiting for you, so you run as fast as you can, using death as fuel. It enhances life and sweetens the days. It's with you every step, every breath, coaching you into its arms. Maybe they're the same, this life and death. Maybe it's our language that has deceived us. Misled *is the better word. Who else picked a better word? She's not that bad. Death. Rather pleasant really. Must be my day out. That's what I get for fooling around on the razor's edge.*

"Now the gauze pad."

Don't put me on a gurney, whatever you do. If I touch Kathleen's hand, I'll die. Morgan knows. He knows that. Why was that girl barking when I flew?

"How bad?" Garrett asked.

I need a map back to Kentucky. Then my head will stop killing me. That's the deal—get me a map. No, wait, there was more—three components: life, home, family...no, no, no.

"Flesh and a lot of it," Morgan replied, "but I should be able to stem the bleeding. Pulse is fine. Breathing normal."

Garrett asked, "You see him fly?"

Do they know I hear them?

"I didn't have much of an angle," Morgan said. "Plus, I was keeping tabs on the big man. You sure it was okay letting them go?"

Tuesday...Grouper married Tuesday. He was surprised she let me meet her employees at his place, thinks about her one day a week. Sheeeiit, I'd think about that girl every day if she was mine. Her freckled chest. Little drops of chocolate I could taste. Bruising days. Rough lips. Bourbon times. Someone took my bourbon.

"More than okay," Garrett said. "We'll get a lot of goodwill letting those two drive off with the cash and our blessings."

Who buys a certified used car? I just don't get it. Am I the only smart one in the world? Can't they hear me? God almighty, my whole left side is burning...burning in hell. Who said that?

"You okay?" Morgan asked Garrett. "I ran as fast as I could, but you were already out with both bodies. I could barely stand the heat when I helped you. You've got to have some burns."

Told Barbara I'd put a new closer on her door, but I haven't done it. What a shit neighbor I am. Just total shit.

"Give him some of that ammonium carbonate," Garrett said.

A cat. A Laundromat. Hadley? Pauline—no, Pamela? Why do I care? Sidney! Great, a cat named Sidney.

"Wait just a sec," Morgan said.

No, no, not Sidney...Disney. Like I give a crap about Disney. That's not right. Walt? It's his brother...Garp! We're making progress here. Hey, anyone paying attention?

"That's it," Garrett said. "We'll make sure to clean it and change the bandage within a couple of hours. We don't want an infection."

Since when did he ever sound so concerned? Mr. Perfect. No alcohol ever touches this temple, baby. Hey, Garrett, want a cigar?

Garrett said, "Go on. Give him that whiff. He's been out long enough."

Garp's mother...Jenny. Yeah, I get it now. There's some serious Jenny shit going down here. I want her. Not just for her, but for Larry. Brother Larry—he served. Father Larry. I promised him at his grave. I stood on Iroquois land and promised him. The hell...I don't even know this girl. Jenny...on some beach. Who else was there, Jenny? Who else was on that beach with you?

"Jenny," I said. "Jenny. Kathleen."

Morgan and Garrett hovered over me as I lay flat on my back. My head hurt as if...No, wait, someone *had* taken a hatchet to it.

Jenny.

That mad little wacko.

"Welcome back to the zoo," Morgan said.

"I take it I'm the animal that just got mauled?" The Big Dipper was to the left of Morgan's head. It was pretty. I like the Big Dipper. Do you like the Dig Dipper? I wondered if the little dude was up there as well.

"We all get our turn," he said.

I turned my head to Garrett and tried to get in the game. "We secure here?" Like I was in any shape to contribute if he said we still had problems.

"Dangelo's men left with a suitcase of money and smiles on their faces. I gave one a leg wound, but they shrugged it off. Ms. Spencer, somewhat distraught over nearly killing her rescuer, is remarkably calm and relaxing in the back of your air-conditioned truck, and—"

"No, I'm not."

She kneeled beside me. I tilted my head and gazed into her eyes. She smelled like smoke. Her hair looked like molded sea oats. A Telfa dressing pad was on her forehead. Her face was covered with dirt, as if she'd applied makeup for a B horror movie. I risked my life for that?

"Not what?" I asked. "Distraught over nearly cutting my head off or not being in the truck?" I was impressed at my verbal agility considering my delicate mental state.

"In the truck, silly."

"Not over slicing my head?"

"I feel—"

"Sixty-five Trojan, right?" I asked, and I don't know why I said it other than I was still drifting out of the fog. Susan had told me about the boat when we'd stood in Jenny's bedroom. She'd said Jenny felt she had let her father down because she couldn't work the hand pump very well with teak oil on her hands. My mind clung to that, and I don't know why.

"You know about that?"

"I do." I nodded. *Sweet Lord, that hurt. Not doing that again.*

She gave a slight shake of her head. "He named the boat after me. Can you believe that? I didn't even know that till Boone got it out of storage last summer. The transom was covered with a tarp, and when he took it off, there it was. *The Jenny S.*"

I didn't know what to say. I thought she was going to say something more, but instead she just cracked a dismissive smile. Half my pain went away, and I don't give a crap what anyone thinks—her smile did that.

"I am *so* sorry I swung at you," she said.

"You look bad." *Great Zeus, did I say that?*

"Really?" She smiled again, and my left ankle stopped aching. I could make a lot of money bottling this girl's smile. "Your friends told me you're a bit of a hotshot...said you nearly flew into that barn. Well, I've got news for you, hotshot." She brushed my hair off my forehead with her right hand. As my hair separated from dried blood, I felt it offer resistance then break away like a Band-Aid being peeled off my head.

"What's that?"

"You should get a picture of yourself."

"Good thing you don't have your phone."

"Yeah, that's been a major inconvenience."

I shifted my gaze to Garrett and asked, "Dangelo's men?"

"Like I said, left whistling. The guy you pulled a knife on?"

"Yeah."

"Said, 'Tell Alice we're friends and to have a good life.' Any idea why, 'Alice?'"

I didn't have the energy. "No."

Morgan interjected, "Let's go."

"Wait," I said.

"What?"

"Call PC." I wanted to say more, but I was fading.

Morgan said, "It can wait."

"No. Make sure the picture's down."

Garrett asked, "Picture?"

"I told him. Take the picture down."

"Sure. I'll give him a—"

"I'm serious. Tell him to—"

"We got it."

"That's enough," Morgan cut in.

Jenny helped me to my feet. I looked over my shoulder and saw what was left of the barn glowing in a pile of red coals. "How long was I gone?" I asked no one in particular.

"Long enough," Morgan replied. "Garrett leapt into the fire like water coming out of a hose and brought you both out. By the time I got there, he and Jenny were on either side of you."

I took a second to confirm my balance before I ventured a step. I blew my breath out and looked down. There was less pain that way, with my head down. I kept that position and said, "Little big, aren't they?"

"They feel *so* good," Jenny gushed. "I hope you don't mind. Morgan said you carried extras in your truck. Why do you do that? Carry extra shoes?"

I managed to raise my head and found Jenny's eyes. "You never know when you're going to meet a woman who really appreciates a man's shoes."

CHAPTER 43

"Any bleeding today?" Kathleen asked.

"I can swim. I can run. I swim and I run. And nothing leaks out of me."

"I see. The only lasting effect is that Dr. Seuss has taken over your speech pattern."

We sat on the screen porch. The stiff sea breeze that had kicked up during the night—a common summer pattern that's the result of air heating up over land—showed little sign of relenting. Whitecaps bristled the surface of the bay. Usually by midafternoon, the anger would dissipate. I leaned over and gave Kathleen a quick kiss. I started to pull away, changed my mind, cupped her head in my hand, and kissed her again. She wore a low-cut beige top with a thin gold chain around her neck. There wasn't an inch of that neck that I wasn't intimate with. My rehabilitation had served as an excellent excuse to spend long hours in bed with her. I should let Jenny wield a hatchet at me more often.

"You're fine, right?" she asked.

"Not if you keep bugging me."

Jenny's rescue was the first litmus test, and I passed. Kathleen *wasn't* upset that I'd launched myself into a fireball for a person I didn't know. However, one can never be certain of such things, for no matter how you conduct your life, or how well you know your counterparty, there's always a song you take to the grave, one no one ever hears.

"When are they due?" she asked.

"Hold that thought for a second." I started for my phone but changed direction and ended up at the Magnavox. I put on Bennett's 1965 theme album, *Songs for the Jet Set*. Music and machine reunited. I went to the kitchen, popped a bottle of Taittinger, and took it to the porch along with two champagne flutes. A sleek red sailboat with a tan Bimini top skimmed the choppy waters no more than a hundred feet off the end of my dock. Its spinnaker billowed toward the blue sky, pulling the boat behind it. Two couples sat in the cockpit, and a woman laughed. It was a fine sound. Behind me, Tony Bennett declared what it would be like if he ruled the world.

"Oh, my," Kathleen, said as I handed her a bubbling glass. "We're starting early."

"And going late."

"Aren't you supposed to avoid alcohol when you're on your meds?"

"Don't think so."

"Pretty sure you are. They all say the same thing—'Take with eight ounces of water and avoid alcohol.'"

"No kidding." I took a healthy sip of champagne. "I thought it was, 'Drink eight ounces of alcohol with each pill. Three pills a day, and...' Well, you can do the math."

"I can see how you would misinterpret that." She took a short sip, as if testing the waters, then reconsidered and went for more. "Susan and Jenny?"

"Around six," I said. "You have time to set a personal best, sleep it off, and do it again. A real doubleheader."

"Um...I think I'll pass. Aren't Garrett and Morgan due about the same time?"

"Little earlier. Not exactly sure."

"Say that again."

"What?"

"The part where you're not exactly sure."

"Must be those pills."

Hadley III jumped through the cat door I'd installed for her. She had a gecko in her mouth and dropped it at the base of my chair. It wasn't dead, although I wished it was.

"I actually like the little guys," Kathleen said, looking at the butchered lizard, whose left side was doing considerably better than its right. "Too bad she hunts and kills them all the time."

"She can't help it. It's in her genes."

"Yes, isn't it?" She smiled, held my gaze, and then took a relaxed sip without breaking eye contact. I wondered which song of hers I would never know. I picked up the creature, opened the door, and tossed it into my untrimmed hibiscus bush.

I fixed a light breakfast. Lack of exercise was having a disastrous effect on my goal of eating fatty foods. It was a dangerous thing to experience soft mornings, as I was starting to appreciate their appeal as well as question why I insisted on ringing death's doorbell every morning. I wanted—needed—to resume my morning workouts. If one is to stay committed, it's best not to question one's routines, for only obsession, which allows no compromising incisions, forges true commitment.

After we ate, Kathleen drove off in her newly waxed Lexus. She planned to return before Garrett and Morgan arrived. They were kitesurfing at the tip of East Beach at Fort De Soto Park. They'd taken off early, thrilled with the unwavering breeze. I reclaimed my seat, took a sip of the Taittinger, and recalled the phone conversation I had had yesterday with Susan.

Jenny had gained admission to several state universities. She had applied months ago. Susan planned to pick up the considerable first year out-of-state tab not covered by scholarships that Jenny had been awarded. Susan informed me that she'd been stashing away college money for her ever since they'd first met years ago. According to Susan, Jenny showed no sign of PTSD. To the contrary, Susan indicated, she tackled each day with a vengeance, as if she were making up for lost time. Like the rejuvenation you feel when a fierce cold is finally gone. She started each day with a barefoot stroll on the beach. That was followed with long hours at Susan's bars, although Susan said she had cut her own hours to spend more time with Jenny. I wondered whether Susan had been working Herculean hours to fill a hole in her life. Once, while strolling the beach, they'd found themselves where Billy Ray Colman had attacked Jenny.

"What was her reaction?" I had asked Susan during our phone conversation.

"None," she replied. "But when we started to leave, she wandered over to some mangrove that surrounded the area. She pointed toward a thicket of them and said, 'That's where he came from.'"

"*Who* came from?" I had asked. "Was someone else there that night?" I had first considered that possibility when sitting in Susan's house and hearing McGlashan describe the scene: "*Mulched him over three square yards.*" Jenny had reinforced that possibility during her interview with Rutledge when she claimed she lost track of her thoughts.

"No...not really," Susan cut off my thoughts.

"But you just—"

She shook her head. "Nothing like that. Maybe she can tell you."

I decided not to press her, but I was convinced that someone else had shown up or something else had happened on the beach that night. I remembered Jenny's voice on the tape as we'd listened in Susan's office: *"Then I saw...and then."* Rutledge: *"Saw what?"* Jenny: *"Oh...nothing. I just lost track of where we were."* I didn't buy it then and wasn't paying for it now, especially after Susan's remarks. What did Jenny see? I made a mental note to ask her if the opportunity arose. I made another note to ensure that the opportunity *did* arise.

I killed some time puttering around in the garage. The neon martini sign from the Winking Lizard looked nice on the wall. In the corner, by the water heater, stood a four-foot-tall wood carving of a hawk perched on a log. It had arrived by UPS yesterday from the man outside of Greenwood. I wasn't sure where the flying carnivore eventually would end up, but for now he was fine.

I oiled my rods then headed to the end of the dock to wash down the interior of *Impulse* and give her a light wax. I'd neglected her for too long. Her rear drain was cluttered with seeds left from bird droppings. The osprey had taken advantage of my preoccupation and settled in permanently on my hard-top. His life was about to change big time. I cranked up my boat's stereo. It felt good to work, to get some rhythm back in my life, but I was soon out of time. I had a meeting to attend. I showered and put on a silk short-sleeve shirt. It had a stain on it, so I changed into another one that had a smaller stain.

I drove to the pink hotel.

CHAPTER 44

The pink Moorish hotel was built in the 1920s by an Irishman from Virginia, named after a character in a play from a French dramatist that was turned into an English opera, and is set in a city named for its Russian counterpart.

I still have no idea what all that means.

I hadn't been spending my usual time there. It was like coming home to a crowded place where you know virtually no one, yet that anonymity renders it so comfortable, so familiar, so reassuring.

Sheri had a beer and a glass of water on the bar before I settled into a high bar chair that faced the Gulf. I tossed my ball cap onto the white chair next to me to reserve it for my guest. I took the envelope out of my shirt pocket and placed it on the bar.

Sheri inquired, "Walk into a telephone pole?"

"Banged my head pretty good," I replied, and drained half the beer. A headband that PC had given me partially covered a white gauze pad.

"But I should see the pole, right?"

"Yeah..." I came up for air. "I taught it a real lesson."

She moved on, correctly accessing my nonconfessional mood. The pools on both sides of me clattered with the staccato voices of children that mixed incongruously with the music floating out of hidden speakers. I thought of the young girl in

Fort Myers Beach who had barked before diving for her bone. I don't think much about little people. They rarely enter my circumference. But something about that little girl's barking, her diving to the bottom. What a little ball of energy. A real spitfire. *"Hey, mister. Can you get my bone?"*

I didn't need that in my head.

I shifted my gaze to the left. A few seats farther toward the Gulf sat a young girl, maybe ten. Or eight. Or twelve. How do you know? Four years doesn't mean much in your thirties, but eight to twelve is a fifty percent jump. Her father ordered a beer and a drink "with an umbrella in it" for his daughter. She was absorbed in passionately coloring a place-mat and never raised her head. *What's with the father-daughter sightings? Usually it's the flesh parade. Are they always here, or am I just seeing them for the first time?* I glanced toward a man who was berating the woman next to him—I assumed she was his wife—with an endless barrage of sports talk as he kept his eyes riveted to the TV screen. She sat erect and fanned herself with the plastic bar menu. She wore a stylish cover-up over her swimsuit. Her eyes wandered, but not far. Her drink was half gone, and her free hand rested on the bar. I felt like telling weeble brain that his wife didn't give two shits about what was happening on the screen.

Joseph Dangelo picked up my cap and placed it on the counter. "I like your office," he said.

"I didn't say it was my office." I kept my eyes on the weeble. Who thinks a woman wants to come to a beach bar on the Gulf of Mexico and watch TV? I turned my attention to Dangelo. "I said it was where I conduct my business." He wore a soft, white, short-sleeve shirt and deep-beige slacks. Neither had a wrinkle nor, as far as I could tell, a stain. "Buy you a drink?"

"I'll take what you're having."

I caught Sheri's eye and held up two fingers. I needed a second round. I turned back to Dangelo. "How's business, Joe?"

"I doubled my money on my last deal."

"You withheld vital information from me."

He looked away then came back to me. He started slow, like he was processing each word. "Wallace—that's how we knew him—Rutledge might have engaged in...creative means of paying off his debt. Certainly you understand that the nature of such things is not to be discussed. I divulged with you, at our last meeting at the restaurant, what I could. I'm sure by now you've reached the same conclusion."

My instinct was to contend his statement, but he was correct, so I let it go. "I hope the doubling of your profit, coupled with the convenient exit of a potentially embarrassing associate, solidified your leadership position."

He nodded. "I'm quite the hero, although as I told you, I'm rarely referenced as a leader. I think of myself more as a facilitator."

"I understand Chuck Duke's buddy has a slight limp."

I was glad he was a hero in his own house; I wanted Joseph Dangelo to wield untouchable power. Sheri placed a beer in front of each of us. Dangelo touched it curiously. Guess he wasn't one to drink from plastic. "No grudges," he told me. "I assure you, if anything, we are in your debt. We owe *you*."

"No one owes anyone anything. That would imply that we'll see each other again, and that's not going to happen."

He took a sip of his beer, paused, and took another one. He turned back to me. "As I said, we may have overreacted regarding what a certain woman—a deceased woman—might have known." He let that hang, but I didn't grab it, so he continued. "We are more than even, Jacob. You had a chance to take things in a different direction that night at Rutledge's sister's house.

You—and I certainly don't want to come off even close to condescending here—chose wisely. You and Mr. Duke performed flawlessly."

"Nor do I desire to condescend, but had I not been in such a benevolent mood, you'd be missing two hundred eighty-four grand and placing a want ad for two new associates."

Dangelo tilted his head away from me and shook it side to side in disapproval, as if he'd finally given up. His hand flipped off his beer as if it were an involuntary act then settled back around it. "Do you always slip so...effortlessly into violence? Is there no middle ground for you?"

I thought of Hadley III gifting dead chameleons to me. She was a cat. She had no choice. No excuses.

"This *is* my middle ground." I said it because it was an easy thing to say, and as a general rule, I tackle the big issues tomorrow. I cut a look to my right and saw a little girl wrapped in a white towel. As she walked, it swept the paver bricks behind her like a royal robe. Her father trailed her, holding sand toys in his hand. Bright red and yellow. What did they do today? Give a discount to father-daughter combos?

"Any particular reason you wanted to see me?" Dangelo asked. His eyes dropped down to the envelope I'd placed on the bar then back to me.

Inside the envelope were pictures of Theresa Ann Howell, his daughter. My Excalibur. The original plan was to trade Dangelo's daughter for Jenny. It didn't work that way. No surprise. I've never known an original plan that went the distance. I wonder why we even bother. Then Dangelo had hinted—he'd never expressively stated as much, but my foolish reaction that night in his condo was all he needed—that he knew Kathleen's prior identity. Plan B: if anything happened to Kathleen, he'd never see the young woman in the picture again. A simple plan. A clean plan. An everybody-acts-in-his-best-interest plan.

The classics never go out of style.

But I couldn't find any reason Dangelo, or his organization, should feel threatened by Kathleen, and more important, I found no evidence that they seriously believed she was a threat. Or *had* been a threat. It was a fabrication, and it was over. Both sides knew it. Dangelo had told me as much when we'd last met at the restaurant. *Fight no more forever.* But I'd rather have blackmail over a man like Dangelo than his word.

I placed my hand on the envelope.

"I asked you a question, Jacob."

Something else had been gnawing inside me. I realized my zealousness for saving Jenny had been fueled by more than my desire to help Susan, protect Kathleen, and rescue a girl I didn't know—as if all that were not enough. A week of pills and booze had stripped me of several layers and found the hard wood underneath.

I'd done it for a man I never knew. Whose gravesite I'd visited on a hot summer day in Ohio, before I'd camped out and the temperature and the sun had fallen in harmony. Before the bugs ate me, the birds woke me, and the water froze me. A man whose grave held the same insignia I'd worn for five years. A man in my foxhole. At his gravesite, I'd made a promise to a man that I would represent him. I would stand in for him. I would fight his most important battle. When I was airborne and about to crash the barn door with my feet, I wanted to save Larry Spencer's daughter.

How does a man feel about his daughter? I haven't a clue. I don't know if I ever will. I hope I did right.

"Jacob?"

"*Hey, mister. Can you get my bone?*" She wore a yellow bathing suit with pink straps. Her face was wet. Drops of water beaded on her skin like rain on a freshly waxed car hood. A pencil-dot mole was on her right cheek, as if God had placed an inspection tag on her when she'd rolled off the assembly line. Approved by God. It don't get any better than that, baby. What does a man do to protect that? What kind of beast threatens that?

Kathleen's voice now in my head. "*What kind of man would that be—a man who holds another man's daughter as a hostage?*"

"Mr. Travis?"

I'd put the questions off for too long, pretending they were in a different language, one I didn't know. But now they cloaked me, and I needed to shake them off like a dog throwing off water.

By protecting Kathleen, would I become someone, some-*thing*, she could never love? Did I need to sacrifice my love to save her life? No. No, that's not it. Not my love for her, but her love for me. Does it work like that? Can you turn your heart, or someone else's, off? Let me know how that works out.

Think.

I was at a crossroads, yet my mind was dormant. I needed it to fire up and to bring forth with clarity those answers that I sought. I didn't want the heat from my blood to control my thoughts. I sought to be calm. Be cool. Cooler than blood.

I picked up the envelope from the bar and placed it in my shirt pocket. I looked at Dangelo and found his eyes waiting for me.

"Joseph?"

"Yes?"

"Care for some hummus and pita bread?"

"You're not going to share that envelope with me?"

"No."

"But you have an envelope."

"I do."

"May I ask?"

"Monthly bar bill."

Joseph Dangelo's eyes drifted to my shirt pocket then came back to me. "Okay," he said in a nonchalant voice. "Let us break some bread."

CHAPTER 45

Kathleen, Susan, and Jenny—in that order—sat at the end of my dock.

Kathleen and Susan. What was I thinking? Maybe you're *not* supposed to wash pain-killers down with booze.

I had just returned from the hotel. Before I joined them, I placed the envelope with the pictures of Theresa Ann Howell in my fireproof safe and retrieved a box from the closet. As I started down my dock, I heard laughter. Probably laughing at me. On my dock.

"Does it still hurt?" Jenny asked when I took a seat next to her. "I am *so* sorry." She wore a bandage high on her forehead that blended with her skin tone. Rutledge's gun had left a nasty mark.

Morgan told me that on the trip home from Rutledge's—I have no memory of it—she held my head in her lap and gushed apologies. She had since called every day to check in on me.

"Not at all," I said. "And you?" I felt ten years older than I did seven days ago, but I wasn't going to lay that on her.

"Never better. The doctor doesn't think it'll scar."

I glanced at Kathleen. "Everyone make introductions?" She wore the new dress I had bought for her.

"Oh, yes," she said. "We figured it all out."

Those words covered a lot of ground.

She smiled and looked at Susan, who turned to me and added, "We managed just fine without you. We were discussing the trip

to the hospital the night you found Jenny. Jenny said they reban-
daged her head then had her on humidified oxygen for a while,
due to her coughing. Kathleen said you didn't want to go—"

"But I," Kathleen interjected, "had insisted. Not only to
stop the bleeding, but also I wanted a brain scan—they called
it a neuroimage—of your head. Morgan told me you sang 'Old
Kentucky Home' on the ride back."

"And I," Susan took over, "said, 'How did that go?' And
Kathleen said—"

"It was negative," Kathleen cut in.

*What's with the tag team? Have these women known each other
for years?*

"In fact," she continued, "the nurse offered to give me my
money back. Said there was nothing up there to scan."

They all laughed. Again. At me. On *my* dock.

Susan calmed down and said, "Jenny was telling Kathleen
that she was almost out of the barn herself. She'd been swinging away at the door with the hatchet before you flew in."

I glanced at Jenny. "My head aches for nothing?"

"I thought you said it didn't hurt." She sounded more
pained than I felt.

I held her hazel eyes for a moment. Her hair was straight
and long. The last time I'd seen it, I'd registered it as molded
sea oats. She wore a pair of Top-Siders. No one else wore shoes.

I said, "Been meaning to ask you something."

"I think I know. The hatchet? Why I took a swing at you?"

"Just curious."

"I had no choice. I'd been kidnapped three times, and I
knew...I knew my time was running out. I found that hatchet
and decided the next guy through the door got it. When the
fire broke out, I went to work on the door right around the lock
area that you broke through. But I was losing. I—"

She hung her head toward the water, but brought it right back up. To our right and out a distance, a dolphin broke the surface and tossed a fish out in front of itself. The dolphin came up several yards away and tossed the fish again. They do that sometimes—play ball with dinner. Jenny paid no attention, or maybe she didn't see it.

"It's the only part that gives me nightmares," she continued. "The smoke—you just can't believe the smoke. And it was a hatchet. Just a lousy hatchet." She turned to me. "You came in high and scared me. How'd you do that? Come in six feet off the ground?"

"I jumped."

"I don't know what it was, but that wasn't a jump. Then you fell, just collapsed, and when you got back up, I went after you. I am *so* sorry. I was in panic mode."

"Don't worry. I'm glad you only nicked me."

"Trust me," she said, shaking her head, "it wasn't due to lack of effort. I went straight for you. I couldn't believe how fast you reacted. I thought you were dazed, disorientated, but you practically jerked your head clean off your shoulders. Then Garrett was there and dragged us both out, and I have *no* idea how he managed that."

I *had* jerked my head with amazing speed. Did the bourbon actually help me? Something to consider.

Susan asked me, "Do you remember much from afterward?"

I'd avoided looking at her, much like the day I'd walked into her house to meet McGlashan. I'm good at that—not looking at Susan Blake. I looked now. She wore long gold earrings, and as she tilted her head to see around Jenny, the left one swung out over the water. She looked younger than the last time I'd seen her. Her hair was different; it was shorter, and I wanted to tell her that it looked nice, but instead I said,

"Bits and pieces." But what I was thinking was, *What type of woman owns a Grady-White and wears a tight black dress?* I would never really know, but I knew my thoughts weren't done with me. That's the thing about our thoughts and questions—we think they're part of us, but they aren't. They have their own life, their own schedule. They can, and will, strike at any moment, on any subject, with brutal and naked honesty.

"We're having dinner with them, Garrett and Morgan, right?" Jenny asked. "I haven't had the chance to thank them again."

"They're kitesurfing. Due back any time." I handed her the box. "For you."

She gave me a quizzical look. "For me?"

"For you."

It wasn't wrapped. She popped the top and pulled out her cheer T-shirt. I was surprised it wasn't ripped. Billy Ray must have jerked it clean off her body.

"Oh, my gosh," Jenny gushed. Did I screw up? Maybe it was the last thing she ever wanted to see. For a delicate few seconds, no one spoke, and then Jenny turned to me and said, "Thank you. You can't believe how hard I worked for this—and to keep it." She shook her head, and her fingers caressed the garment. She neatly folded the T-shirt, placed it gently back in the box, and rested her hands on it.

"Help me in the kitchen?" Kathleen said to Susan. Kathleen and kitchen—the only familiarity they shared was the first letter.

"Thought you'd never ask." The two BFFs departed. I was surprised they didn't hold hands and skip.

Jenny and I sat for a silent minute. What was she thinking? I had my opportunity. I wanted to know; I deserved to know.

"Been meaning to ask you something else," I said, echoing my earlier comment.

Jenny glanced at me. "Yes."

"That night on the beach? I heard the cut tape of your conversation with Rutledge. You don't have to—I mean, if you're uncomfortable, I certainly understand. If you don't mind, I just wonder if you could give me the whole story." It came out pretty damn awkward, but I was wary of leading her where she didn't want to go.

"You think I left something out?"

"Maybe." I thought of point-blank asking Jenny if someone else was there that night, but I didn't want to scare her off. Was she protecting someone? Did someone else kill Billy Ray Coleman?

She nodded as in approval, waited a second, then said, "I don't mind. I already told Susan."

I wasn't sure if "I don't mind" was something that carried utmost sincerity when prefaced with a pause, so I gave her an exit. "I can just get it from Sus—"

"No, silly." A gust of wind tousled her hair, and she brushed it off her face, although by the time her hand had gotten there, the wind had already corrected the mess it had made. "I thought I was a goner...I'd pretty much shut down. You know about my father's boat, right? The Trojan? You mentioned it in your delirious stage."

"I do."

"I used to pump it out with a busted hand pump in the cuddy. It was a slim shaft with no handle that fit perfectly in my hands. But it was difficult, since my hands were always slippery with teak oil. My dad..." She shook her head, and I caught a brief smile. "He couldn't set foot in that boat without cleaning it."

The more I learned about Larry Spencer, the more I lamented that our time didn't cross.

"Anyway…" She brought her legs up under her and sat Indian style. "My hands were greasy—Billy Ray was smeared with lotion, which didn't surprise me. His skin was fire red. My hand reached out, although for the life of me, I don't remember sending that signal. I felt a mangrove branch. I wrapped my greasy hand around it. It felt exactly like that old pump in the cuddy of the boat. I jabbed it into Billy Ray's stomach. But then everything sort of froze. He started to reach for it—no way was my single plunge going to save me, and…I didn't know what to do."

So far, her story was what she had given Rutledge. Perhaps my suspicion that she had omitted something was unfounded. She cut her eyes out to the water as a girl on a Jet Ski skimmed the bay's surface. She straightened her back and focused her gaze directly at me.

"My father walked out of the mangroves like he'd never left me. He said, 'Pump, Jenny. Pump.' And that's exactly what I did." Her eyes were sure. If she expected me to question her story, she gave no hint. "I didn't let him down," she said, batting at her hair again. "I'm not that old, but some things in life you're lucky to get a second chance at, and I wasn't going to let him down. I pumped like the boat was sinking. I pumped because they put his death in the same article they put the deer harvest in. I pumped because I got crap for a mom, and I pumped because I wanted to kill Boone. I pumped"—she let her breath out as if she'd been holding it—"because I wanted to make him proud, and I thought it might be the last time I ever…I ever saw…"

Jenny's eyes welled up, but she didn't look away from me. If I'm ever in a fight and I get to pick sides, I'm picking this girl first. Her body gave a light shudder. She blew her breath out, and her shoulders settled down. Her eyes returned to the water. "I don't think I let him down, all those years ago when I couldn't pump very well. Heck…" She gave a slight shrug. "I was barely twelve. I know this, though." She turned to me. "He sure as hell didn't let me down. When I needed him, my father was there."

Her words on the tape now made sense. No way was she going to tell Rutledge that her daddy had popped out of the mangroves and talked to her. Who knows what tricks the mind plays? Who's to say what's real and what isn't? Perhaps natural laws themselves bow to the challenge of a father's love of his daughter.

"Pump, Jenny. Pump," I said.

"That I did," she replied with a dismissive smile that was unbecoming of her. "I found myself on top of Billy Ray, that mangrove stick riding up and down, with his insides clinging to it like the thick motor my daddy used to drain out of the Trojan in the fall."

"Well, there's a pretty sight."

She looked right at me, hesitated, then said, "How'd I do?"

Who did she see right then?

I heard Susan's words as we stood in Jenny's bedroom and she described Jenny's father. *"He was a lot like you."* I cut my thoughts short to address her question in a timely manner, as I didn't want too much emptiness between her question and my answer. "You did fine. Just fine." I felt as if I should put my arm around her and give her a good hug. I didn't, and that haunts me to this day. Maybe if you can't decide who you are, you're nobody at all.

We joined the others, as Garrett and Morgan had returned. I started to introduce Susan to them, but it wasn't necessary. Garrett and I migrated to the seawall away from the others.

"I talked to McGlashan," I said, knowing McGlashan wasn't Garrett's prime interest but putting it off as much as I could.

"And?"

"Surprised, but not really. He said, looking back, he should have picked up signs that Rutledge wasn't going by the book in looking into Jenny's disappearance. The fact that she had left Ohio without telling her mother had clouded his judgment."

"You ever find out what Super Bowl team McGlashan played for?"

"He didn't. A friend did. Died of cancer and left the ring to him. McGlashan loved the game, but a birth defect left him with a gimpy shoulder. He was a water boy and spent his youth feeling sorry for himself. He wears the ring in memory of his buddy and to remind himself of how lucky he is."

"You meet Dangelo?"

"At the hotel."

"And?" he asked for the second time. Garrett held little interest in the peripheral.

"The pictures are in my safe."

He waited for more, and when I didn't offer it, he came back with, "Didn't show them to him, did you?"

"No."

He looked out toward the bay, where a towboat cautiously approached a small cruiser on the sandbar. "That's your call."

"It's my call."

We stood in silence for a few seconds. He turned, looked me in the eye, and headed to the side of the house. I assumed he'd shower off the salt with better success than he would have in accepting my decision not to show Dangelo pictures of his daughter, Theresa Ann Howell, emerging from work, drinking cocktails with friends, and buying a bouquet of brilliant flowers at the farmers' market in Republic Square Park. That was to have been accompanied with my promise that bodily harm would befall her with a nod from my head if anything happened to Kathleen. To absolve him from the temptation to initiate action against Kathleen—and then to fake innocence by creating distance between himself and such action—I had planned to implicitly state that I couldn't care less whether he was remotely responsible. It was a simple plan to protect Kathleen, and like I said, I always operate best when I possess clear goals.

Second-guessing and indecisiveness mounted their inevitable counterattacks. They swarmed my mind like invigorated adversaries. Was Dangelo being straight with me? I already knew that, at best, he'd been disingenuous when we'd discussed his knowledge of Rutledge at the restaurant. Why would I trust a man who belonged to an organization the FBI could easily trace to dozens of murders? I should've shown him the pictures of his daughter, let him know I have nuclear capabilities. Instead, I acted in what I thought was an intelligent and rational manner.

Hey, Jake, I thought, *guess what goes with cooler than blood? What? Dumber than shit!*

Kathleen voice, like a guardian angel warring evil spirits, switched on in my head: *"What kind of man would that be?"* Now mine: *Would I feel the least bit of remorse holding another man's daughter as a hostage to accomplish my goals? What type of woman owns a Grady and...* To hell with questions I can't beat back but am too chickenshit to answer. Are we more than one person? Can we love more than one? That question cuts two ways. Double hell with it. The greatest illusion of all is that every question has an answer.

"Jake?"

I should've played my card. But I've still got it, and I know—

"Jake?"

Garrett was ticked, and he was right. *Did I let my memory of an encounter with a barking little girl influence such a decision? Good God. But I can play it anytime. Maybe tomorrow morning. That's what I'll do. Tomorrow morning I'll—*

"Hey."

I turned. Kathleen was in front of me. We stood on the lawn a foot from the seawall. The others had gone into the house. Her hair was down. It was the color of the late stage of a sunrise, when the orange and red are gone and the sky and clouds are a vibrant yellow, just before the blazing ball brightens the sky and extinguishes all color. "You look...pensive," she said. "It fits you poorly."

I gave a slight shrug. "You know"—I put my arms around her waist—"I've been slightly preoccupied the past few days. I don't know what you've been doing, where you've been, or—"

"I like you that way."

"What way?"

"Preoccupied," she said. "Gives me freedom for my preoccupations."

"You look wonderful in that dress."

"Thank you. I—"

"I bought you a dish."

"Okay...jumping around a bit, aren't we? What dish?"

"The Silver Springs porcelain dish."

"Ah...I see." She gave a slight nod and a smile. "You're right. I keep the car fob in it, don't I? Well, we both forgot— otherwise you would have vigorously defended yourself after my statement that this was the first item you ever bought me. That's what we get for running around in circles that only occasionally interlope. Let's touch the brake, shall we? Take me reading in the morning."

"Reading?"

"In the kayaks. Remember?"

"Tomorrow?"

"Are we just doing questions? If you're busy, that's—"

"No, no. I'm not busy at all tomorrow morning." I kissed her forehead. "It'll be my pleasure. And sometime…"

"Yes?"

"We'll take the sunset cruise. See what it's like from the other side."

Kathleen brought her right hand up to my left cheek and held it there. "I know we will." She said it with the absence of a smile, which seemed strange, for Kathleen smiled at everything.

We turned to go inside, but not before I caught a glimpse of the red channel marker, its pulsating reflection on the darkening water streaking toward me in a jagged, attacking line. It was always blinking, warning us of the fine line between a good day on the water and a bad day, between the safety of the deep and the dangers of the shallow, between who we want to be and who we become after we slide off the razor's edge and our answers shatter the calm, mirrored waters of our illusions.

38914062R00199

Made in the USA
Charleston, SC
19 February 2015